THE PARTY

TOMI UNGERER

Editor: Gary Groth • Design: Ungerer and Allan-Spencer
Associate Publisher: Eric Reynolds • Publisher: Gary Groth

Fantagraphics Books, Inc.
7563 Lake City Way NE
Seattle, WA 98115

ISBN: 978-1-68396-372-1 • Library of Congress Control Number: 2020935011 • First Fantagraphics Books edition: 2020
Printed in the Republic of Korea

The party.
by Tomi Ungerer

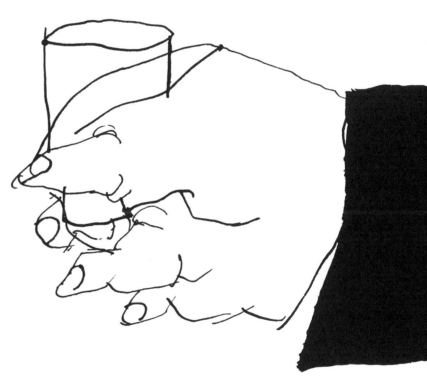

FANTAGRAPHICS BOOKS • SEATTLE

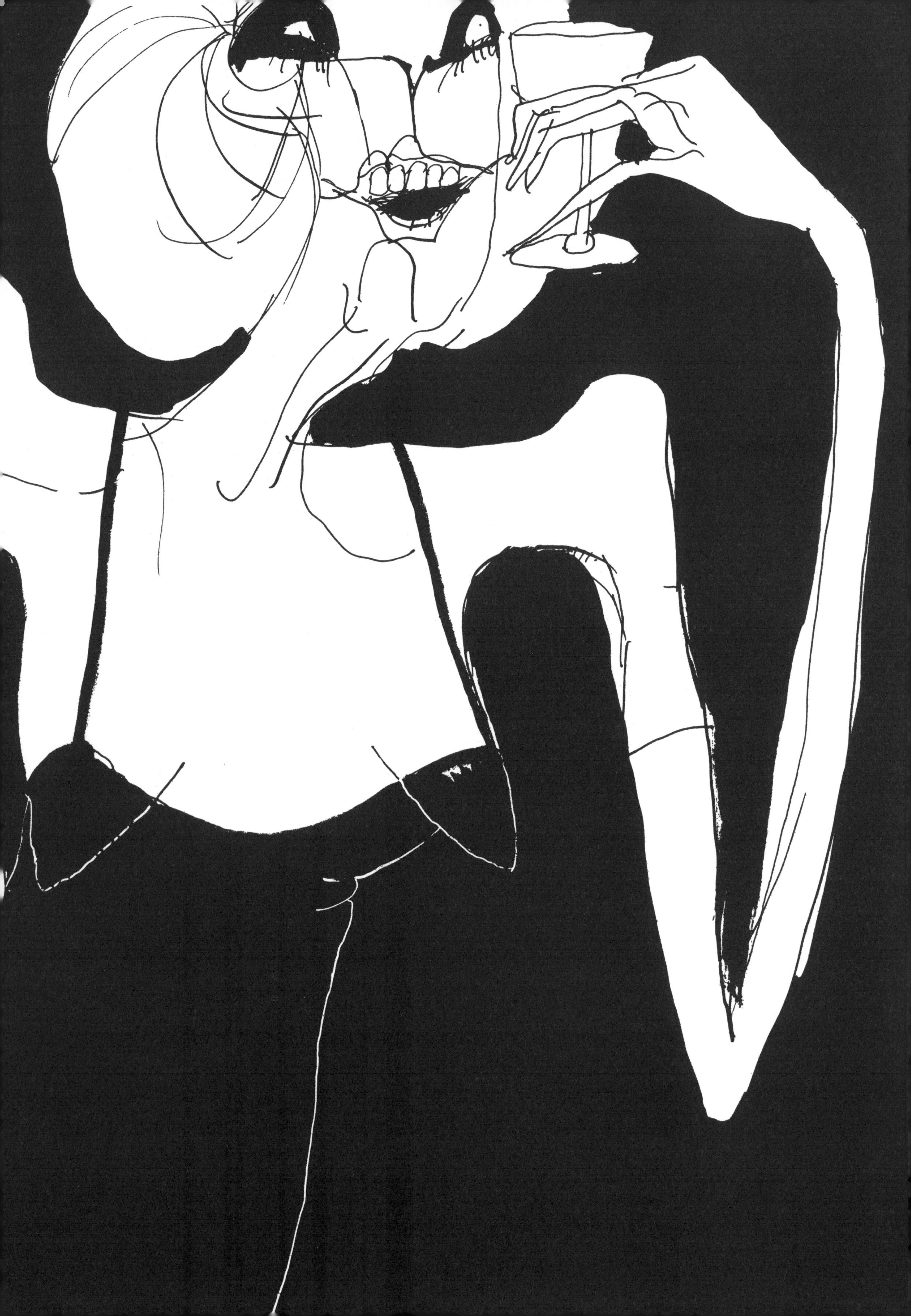

FOREWORD

MR FISH

There's no reality without absurdity.
—*Tomi Ungerer*

I'VE ALWAYS FELT that using words to expound upon the genius of Tomi Ungerer is like relying on a math equation to elucidate the poetry of a sunset. It's demeaning. Indeed, while one might be able to list the most outstanding features of any one of his drawings, the sumptuousness and humor and shear musicality of Ungerer's wit, satire, and remarkable draftsmanship is best experienced in blatant demonstration, not description, the same way that a pie is only delicious when consumed, making the recitation of its ingredients superfluous and, ultimately, pointless. That said, naming the deleterious social constructs and craven attitudes that would have the most imperious among us characterize artistic free expression, particularly the sort most critical of imperiousness, as being antithetical to good manners and civic propriety might help explain why the very phenomenon of Ungerer's success in a world largely inhospitable to truth and beauty is worthy of not just celebration but emulation, as well.

When Tomi Ungerer published *The Party* in 1966, which was the same year that Hunter S. Thompson published *Hell's Angels: A Strange and Terrible Saga* and Susan Sontag published *Against Interpretation and Other Essays* and Bob Dylan's *Blonde on Blonde* was creeping like a tarantula over our most precious and expensive china and The Beatles' *Revolver* was being held, muzzle first, against our collective chest and commanding us to hand over our low expectations of what popular music was capable of when left to the enchanted stewardship of four English wizards, the whole of the Western world was undergoing a seismic cultural shift largely inspired by a massive youth population born during the late 1940s. These were young adults who, when they were children and being raised by a generation that, due to a kind of follow-the-leader negligence and a nearly catastrophic devotion to rich and powerful people, had come close to ending all life on the planet, were encouraged to not only have dreams for a better future but also to expect them to come true. This was a generation that specifically *didn't* want what their parents had had, namely a society prone to self-destruction because it was too polite to say FUCK YOU! to those who needed to hear it most and Ungerer, as one of the many revered spokespeople for this generation, was always more than willing to say FUCK YOU! to anybody who needed to hear it — which explains his infamous 1966 publication and the complaints by the proprietous chaperones of so-called good taste at the time that his adult-themed books were immature and the work of somebody who needed to grow up.

What did this *really* mean? And what does this *continue* to mean?

Dr. Seuss, otherwise known as the Henry Ford of mass-market moralism and easily the most famous tolerance guru ever to emerge wet and yowling from a zizzer-yuzz-flunnel, once said, "Adults are just obsolete children and the hell with them." In consideration of such indirect yet pointed praise for the most starry-eyed and inquisitive among us, is it any wonder that Ungerer began his career in 1957 as a writer and illustrator who became instantly famous for talking directly and, given his mindboggling prolificacy, incessantly to children? Of course, these were children who instinctively recognized the extraordinary power and purpose of the artist's wild imagination, not because it provided a juvenile respite from a real world that required — *demanded,* even! — a much more serious and grownup form of interaction, but rather because they correctly saw the whole of our collective human experience as an enormously freewheeling exercise in pretending and sought fellowship with the most creative and life-affirming iterations available to them. And why not? Why would any of us want to settle for the bleak and demeaning imaginations of Richard Nixon, Bishop Sheen, and *The Warren Report* when, during Ungerer's reign as the Pablo Picasso of picture books, we had access to *The Mellops Go Flying, The Three Robbers, Otto,* and *Moon Man*? Indeed, this has always been the wisdom of children, this preference for joy and wonder over defeatism, and, in the case of acquiescing to defeatism over joy and wonder, it has always been the pointless curse of adults; or, I should say, *some* adults, thankfully.

So how does this curse of defeatism even work, particularly when an active embrace of joy and wonder exists as a viable alternative to cynicism?

Well, if it's true that any conclusion about the world comes to us at the moment when we get tired of thinking, the question we need to ask ourselves is this: *what makes us tired?* Well, pretense makes us tired. Confusion and forced adherence to bullshit framed as an absolute truth makes us tired. Challenging the validity of untested demands on our behavior while remaining obedient to regimented and unrelenting laws and customs rendered in contempt of our natural instinct to be autonomous makes us *very* tired. Compulsory disenfranchisement from phony class prefabs and any number of contrived social rituals invented to make all but the most privileged among us unmoored by wanting and crippled by doubts about our own self-worth will paralyze us with exhaustion!

Of course, given the fact that these confinements do not occur naturally and have most definitely been curated and maintained by human beings, maybe the better question would be: *who makes us tired? Who* confounds us with behavior that we cannot or do not wish to emulate? *Who* insists that the only way to enjoy peace of mind is to celebrate America as a flashing and magnificent orgy of surrender and compromise? *Who* insists that we cleave to a brutally unfair hierarchical system that relegates the majority of our population to the crowded lower decks of the income pyramid for the sake of perpetuating capricious pomp and flatulent circumstance? The answer, of course, is those who wish to control our fate by asserting their own. The answer, of course, is rich people; rich people and their fucking apologists and enablers.

Thusly, *The Party* unravels its condemnation of New York elites — although its ridicule is by no means confined to high society and must include anyone who willfully misconstrues the upper echelons of the aristocracy as being uniquely important or in any way respectable and beyond reproach — like a meticulous and titillating striptease that doesn't stop with the skin. *The Party* is a book that has the effect of entering the reader's bloodstream like a slow-release psychotropic drug, one that gradually morphs the egomaniacal characters into ridiculous partygoing ghouls and vulgar buffoons, the escalating distortions parodying a high that, rather than warping one's perception of the world actually brings it into a tighter focus, perhaps even a hyper one. Like all of Ungerer's work, we are shown what is typically rendered invisible by the naked eye alone and shown the naked souls of monsters that the dominant culture typically insists we revere as our esteemed heroes and leaders. In that way, it is the opposite of a guided hallucination into absurdity and more an empowering awakening that shakes off the delirium of the groupthink anesthetic that's kept us ignorant of the mercilessly classist society in which we live and shows us the bizarre and outlandish insanity that is the actual and wholly unfortunate truth.

———

And, of course, the truth, when released like a sticky web from Ungerer's pen, will always have the effect of ensnaring and terrifying us with a crude sensuality that is impossible to look away from. That said, the book you now hold in your hand has the unique ability, like all great satire, to disrupt your confidence and to explode your comprehension of life itself, so that when you gather the shrapnel from your blown mind and endeavor to reassemble your understanding of things – like what makes the so-called beautiful people *beautiful* and why you may be blessed to be wretched by comparison — you'll be forced to reconsider the soundness of your brain's former architecture and to make whatever corrections are necessary to minimize the potential of future detonations.

(Pause to listen for the lighting of this book's fuse.)

✳ ✳ ✳

Mr. Fish is also sometimes known as Dwayne Booth. His uncompromising comics and cartoons have appeared in *Harper's*, *The Nation*, *The Village Voice*, *Truthdig*, *The Atlantic*, and the *L.A. Times*. *The Miami Herald* called him "a courageous truthteller, brilliantly illustrating the world's insanity." His most recent book from Fantagraphics is *Nobody Left*. He lives in Philadelphia, Pennsylvania.

———

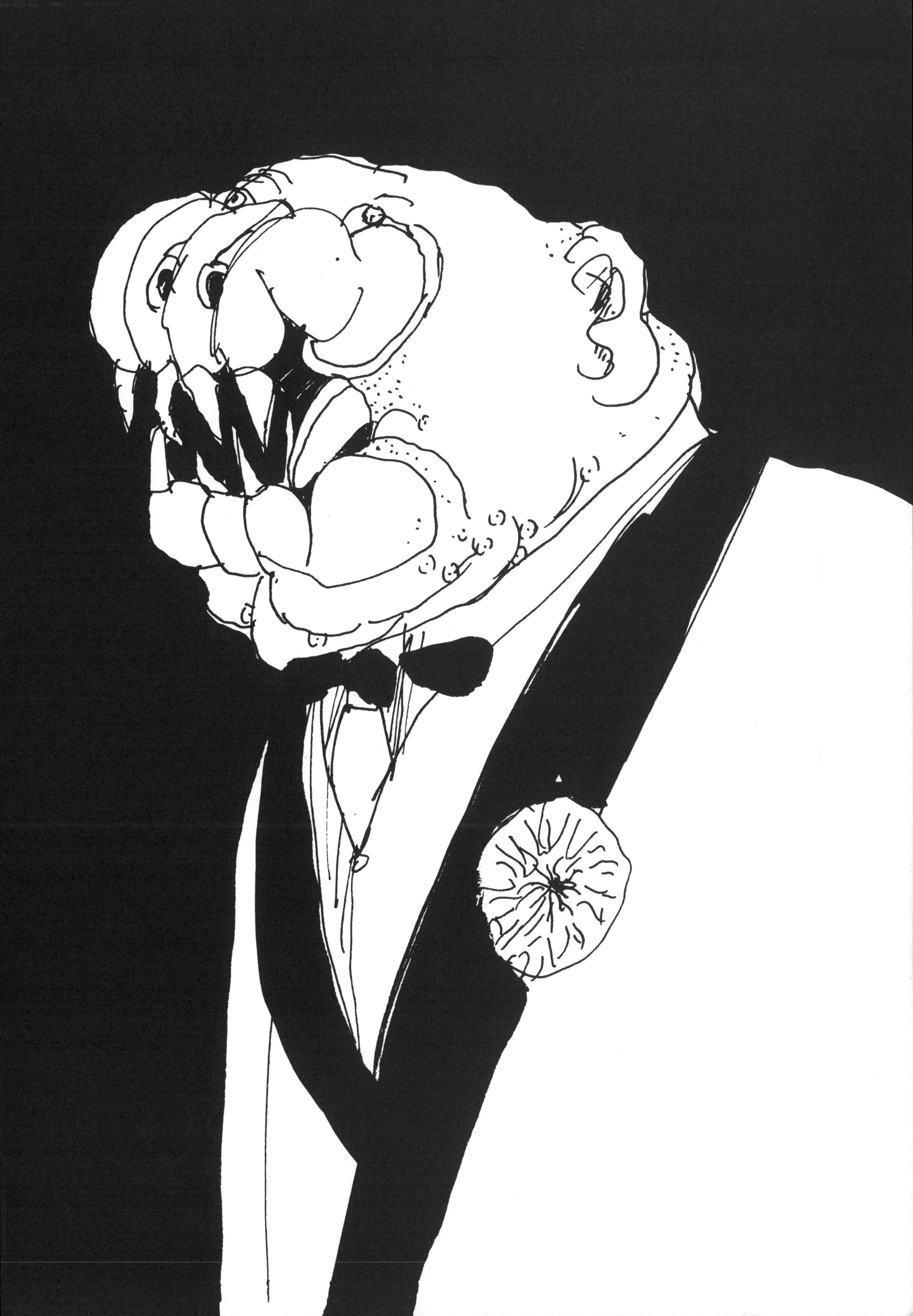

Any resemblance to persons living or dead in the Hampton's area and elsewhere is purely coincidental. The characters in this sketchbook are fictitious

There were so many people present and so much to see that it was impossible to mention them all, who came to enjoy a most, most wonderfull party.

The party was given by Mrs. Julia Van Flooze summer resident of East Hampton L.I.. Known for her charity works, she gave the party to celebrate the return of Senator Leonard Rockfester from a fact finding trip in the Orient.

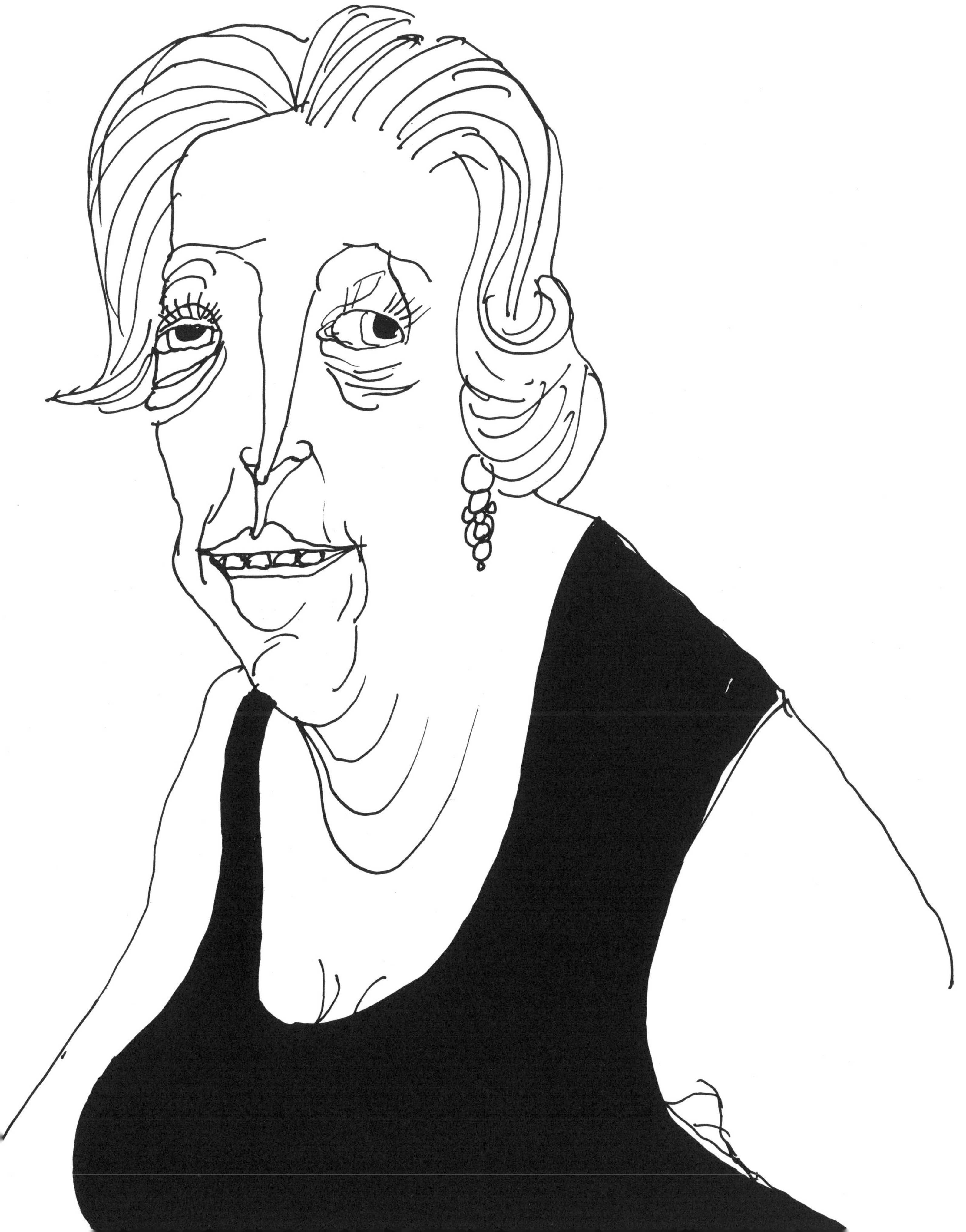

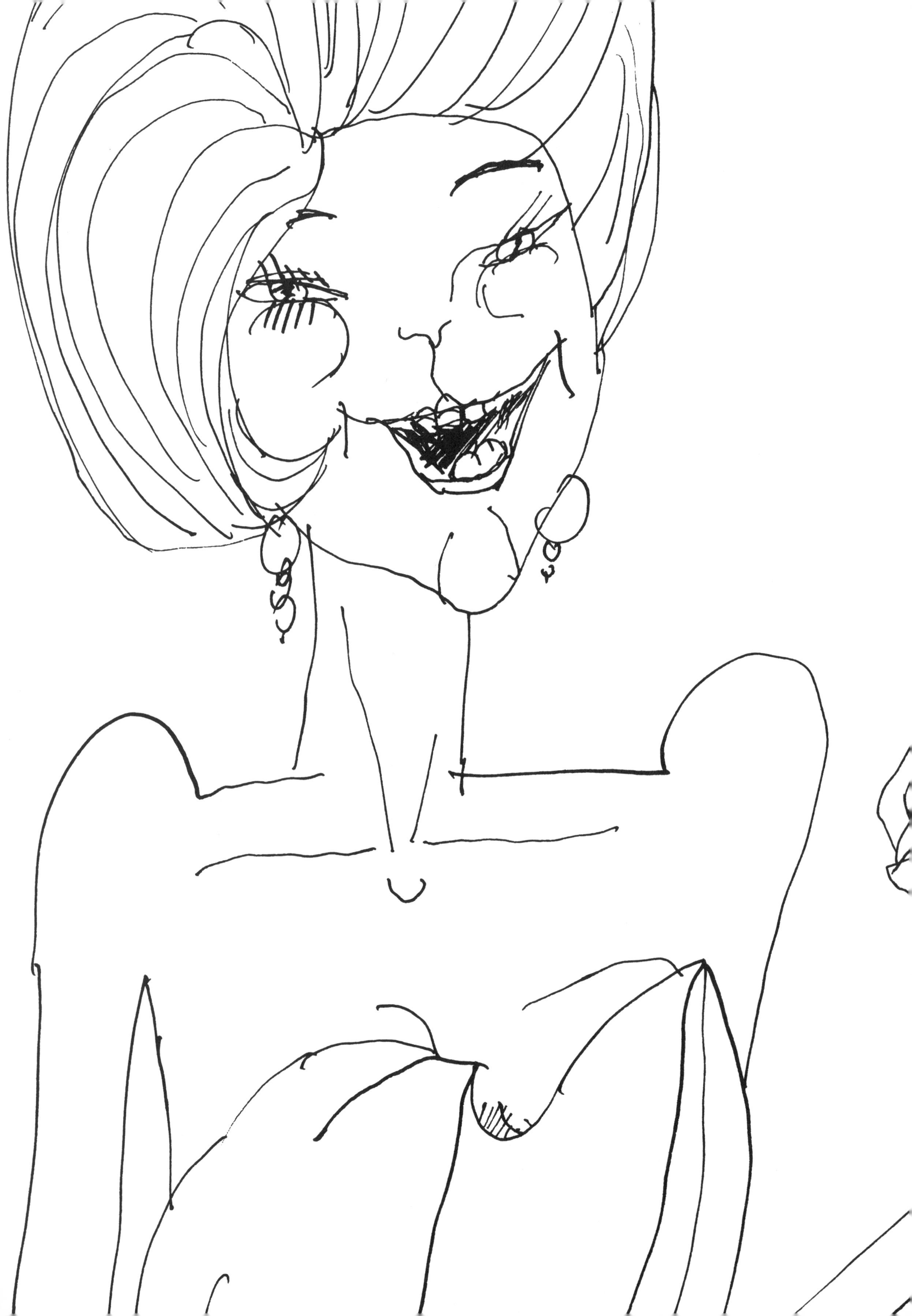

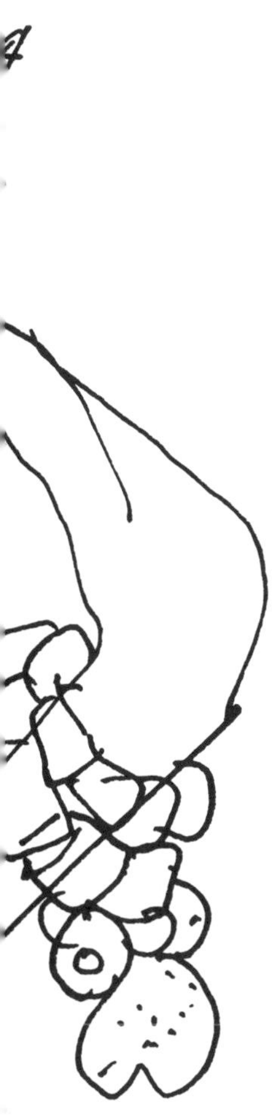

Her Stepdaughter Mrs. Celia Crotch from Charleston and N.Y. welcoming their guests with radiating grace.

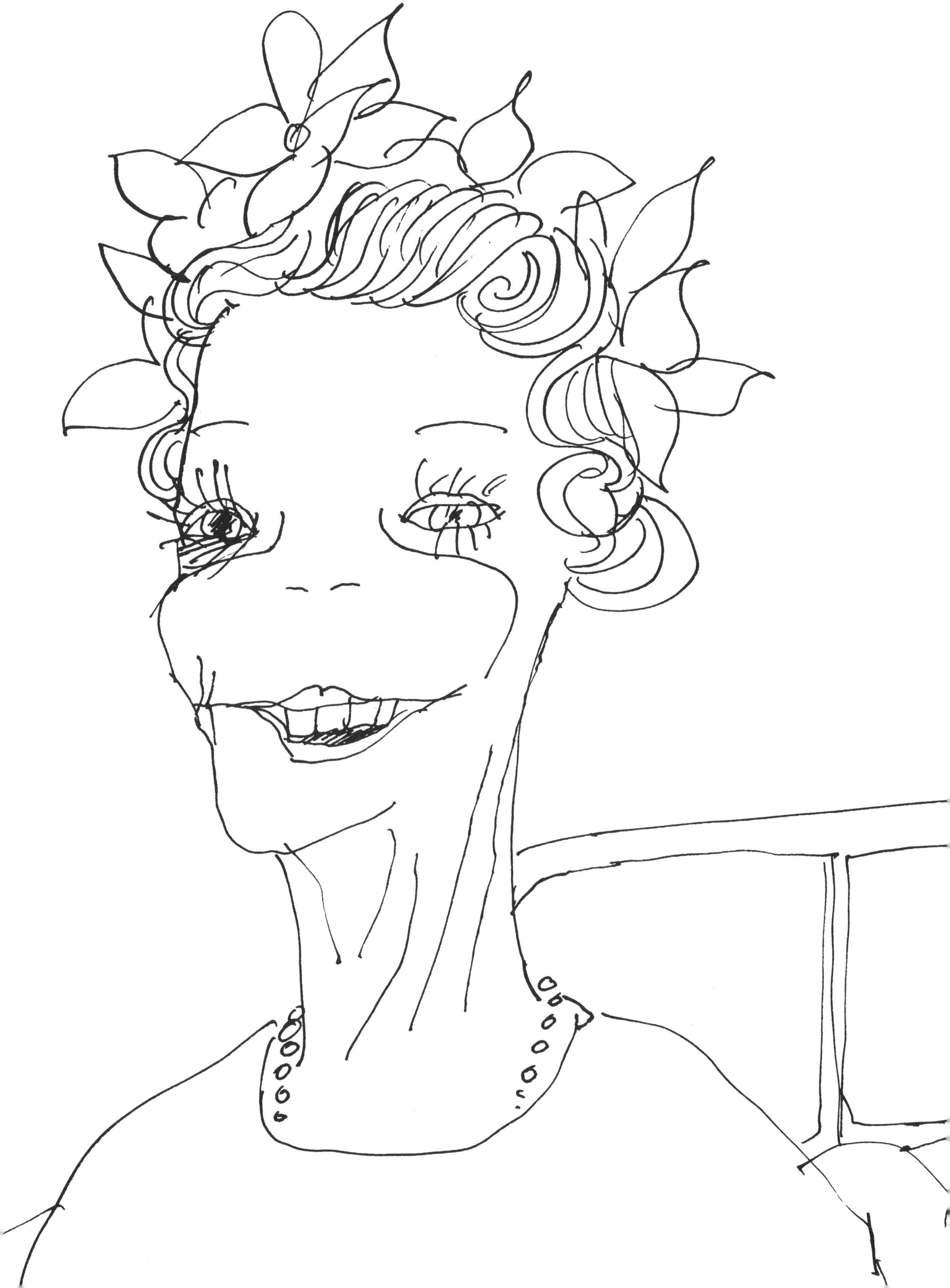

Mrs Jane Snot-Marrow from Newport R.I
was among the early arrivals....

Followed by Major Lewis Rumpstick and his wife Ann née Ficks. Maj: Rumpstick now retired devotes much of his time in Fundraising for the Alien Cripple Foundation.

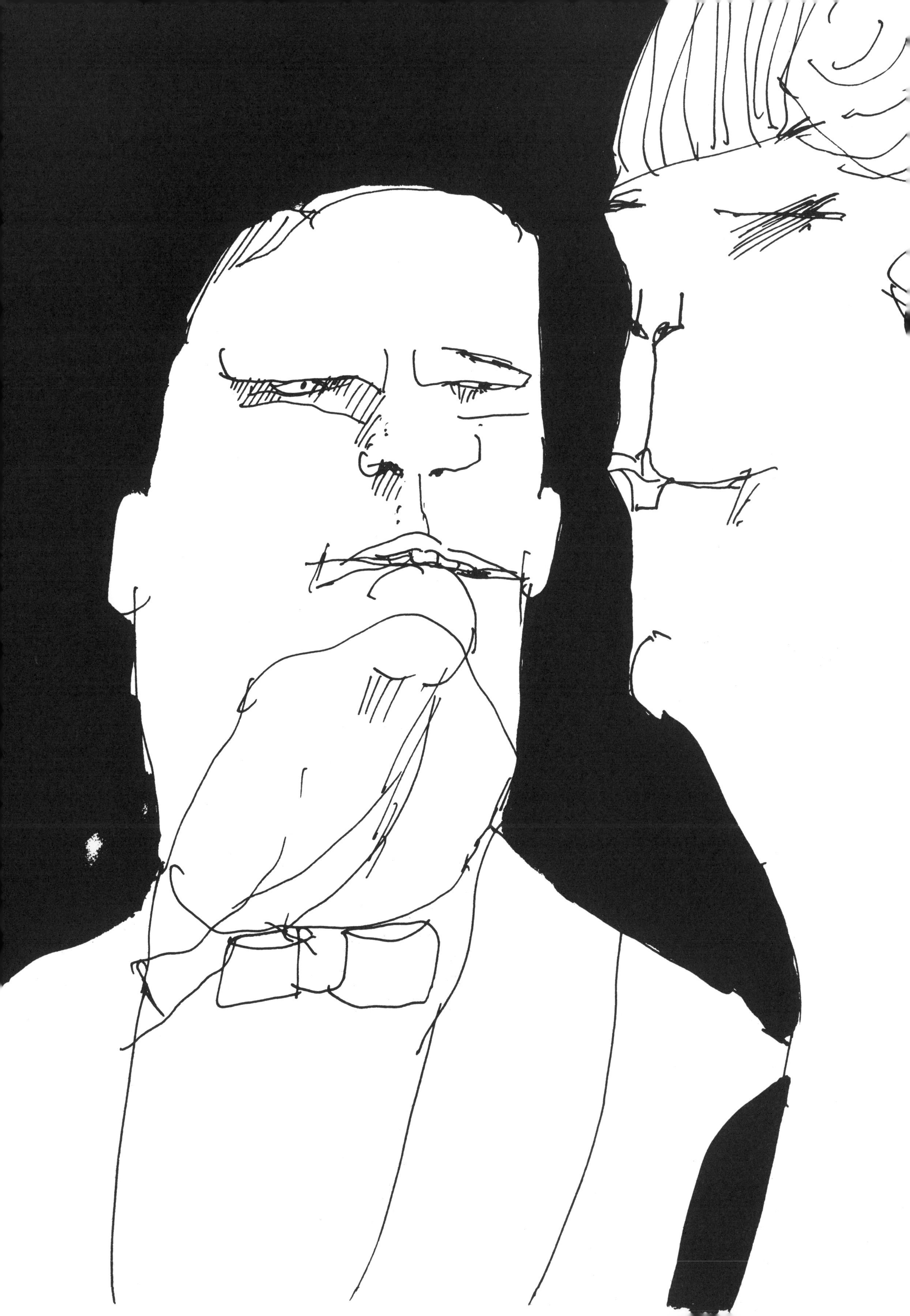

From Boston Mr. John Strutt junior

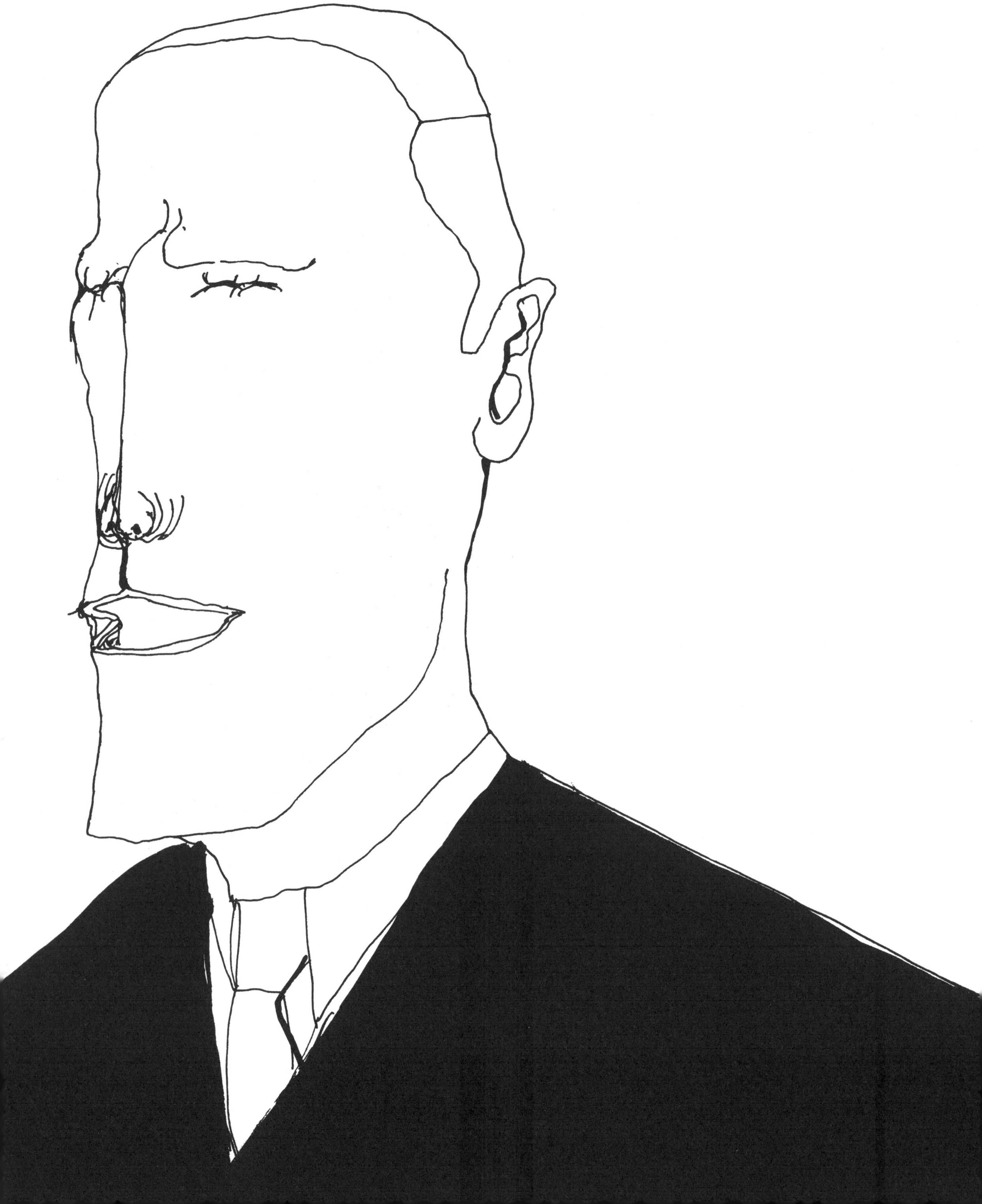

and Mrs Grey Blathers née Ratsall.

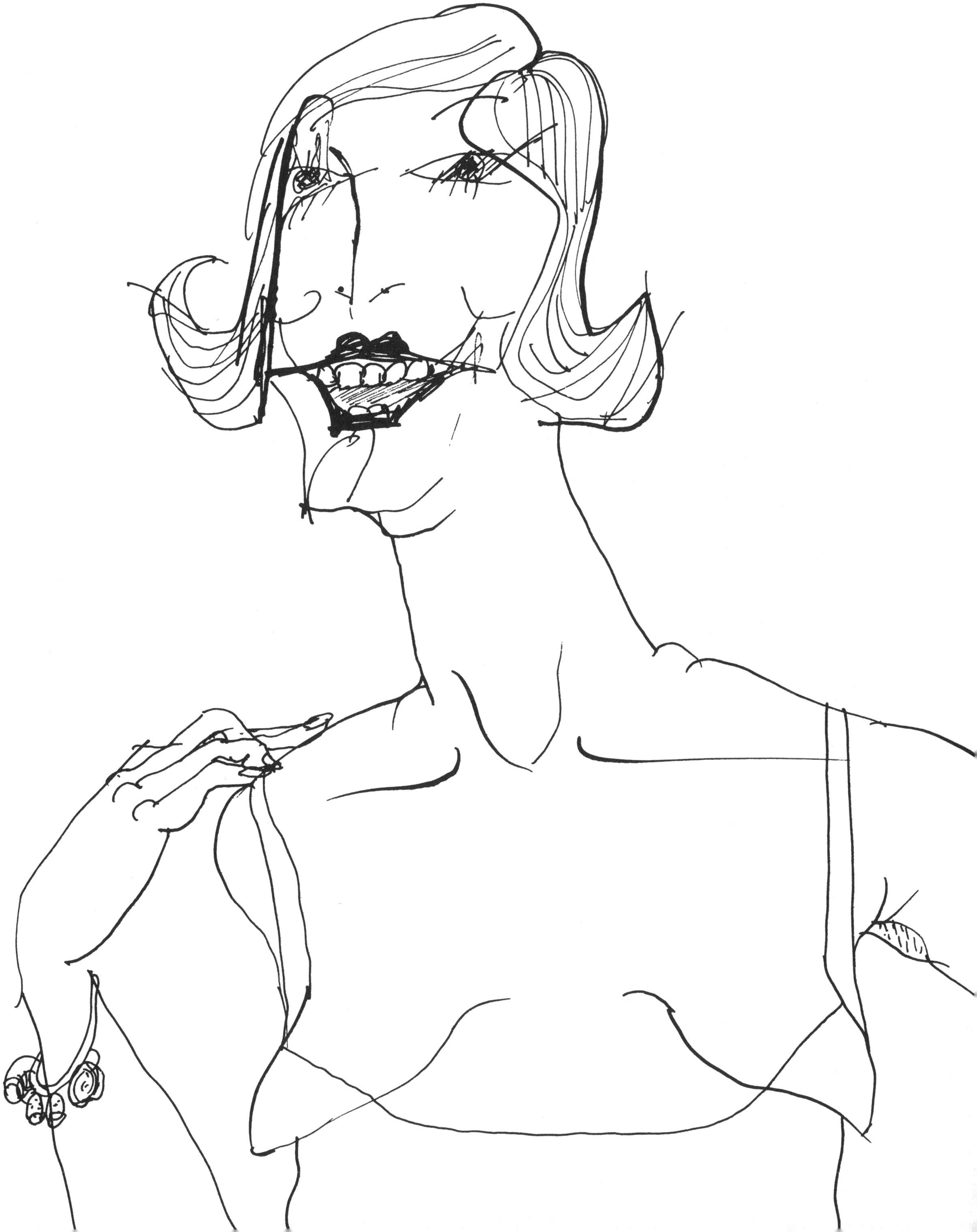

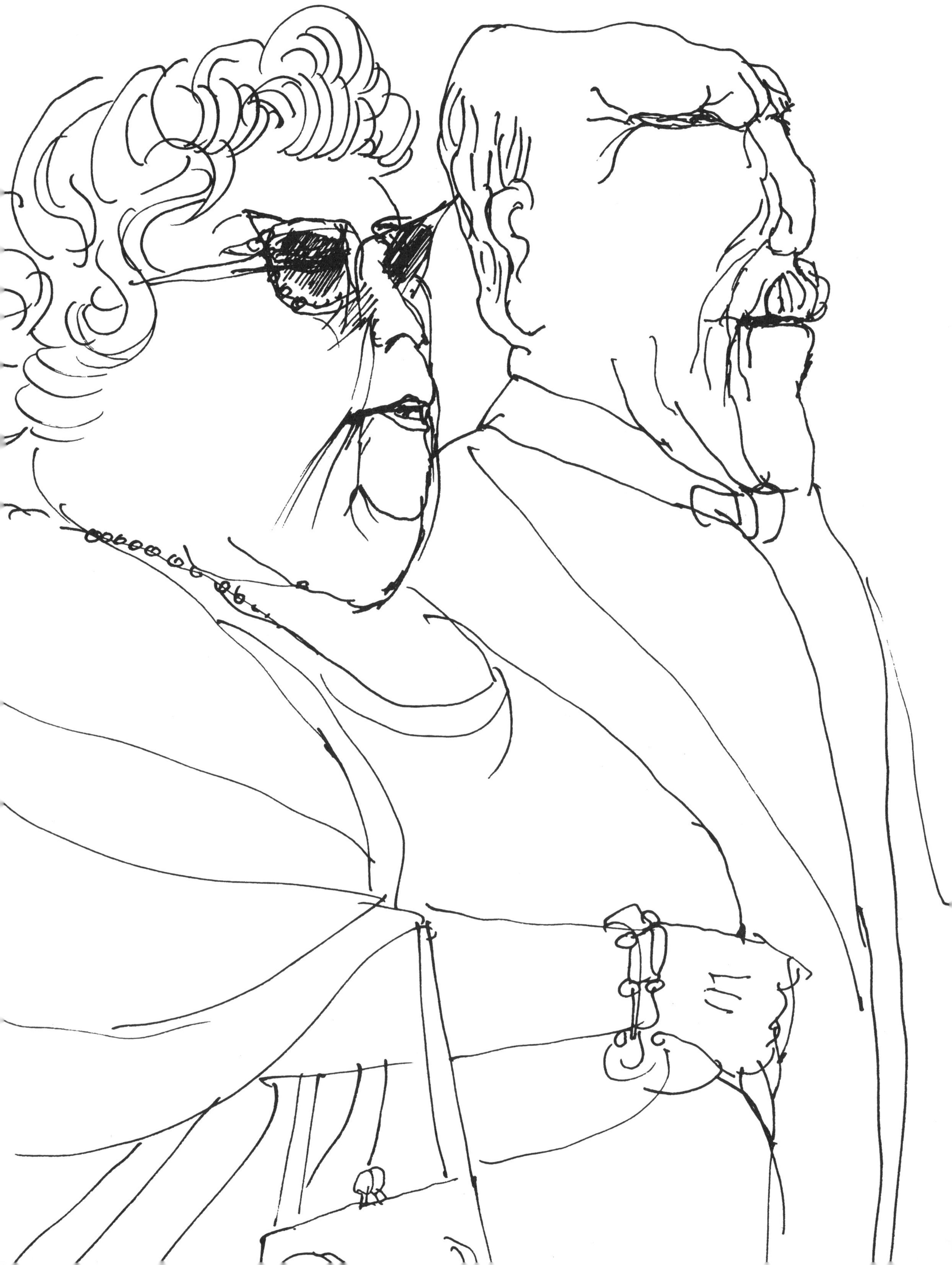

Mrs. Jocelyn Leperscum introducing her son Albert to Mr & Mrs Dean Potsworth from Palm Springs and Philadelphia.

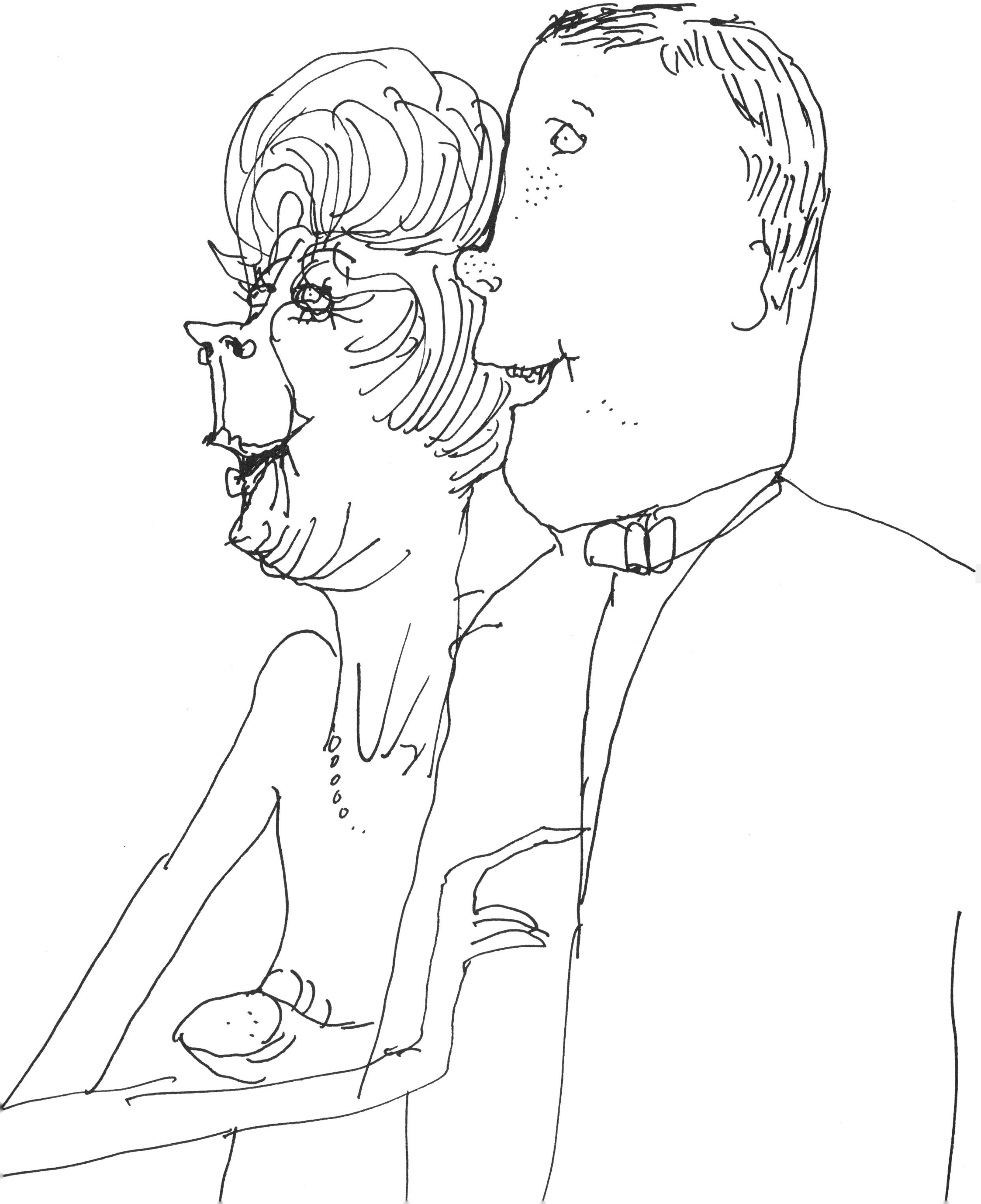

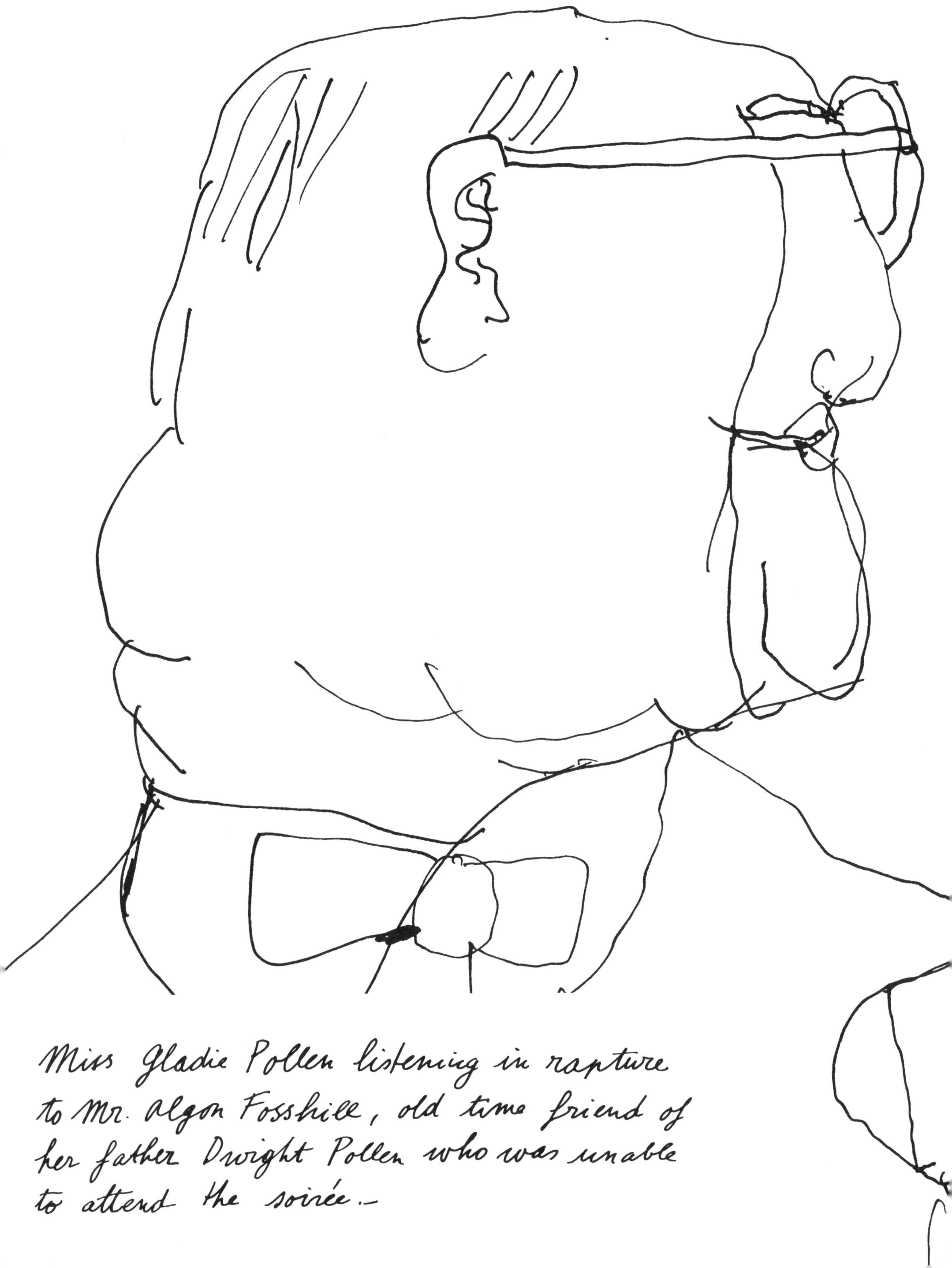

Miss Gladie Pollen listening in rapture to Mr. Algon Fosshill, old time friend of her father Dwight Pollen who was unable to attend the soirée.–

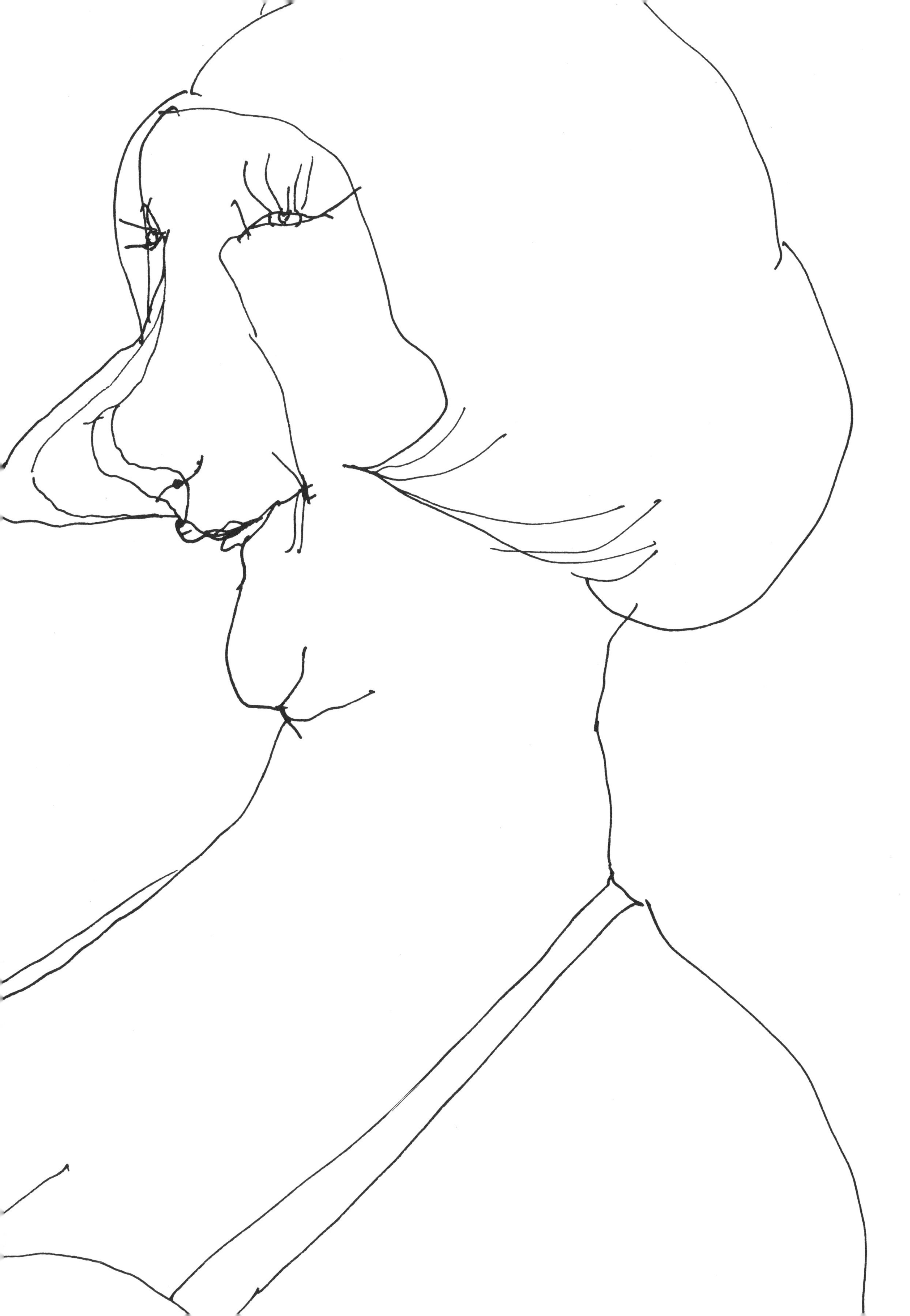

Exchange of congratulations between Henry II Boldench (left) and Mr. Bendel Bloomstein – Both Mr. Boldench and Mr. Bloomstein were featured last month in Fortune Mag. in reference to their outstanding business performances. –

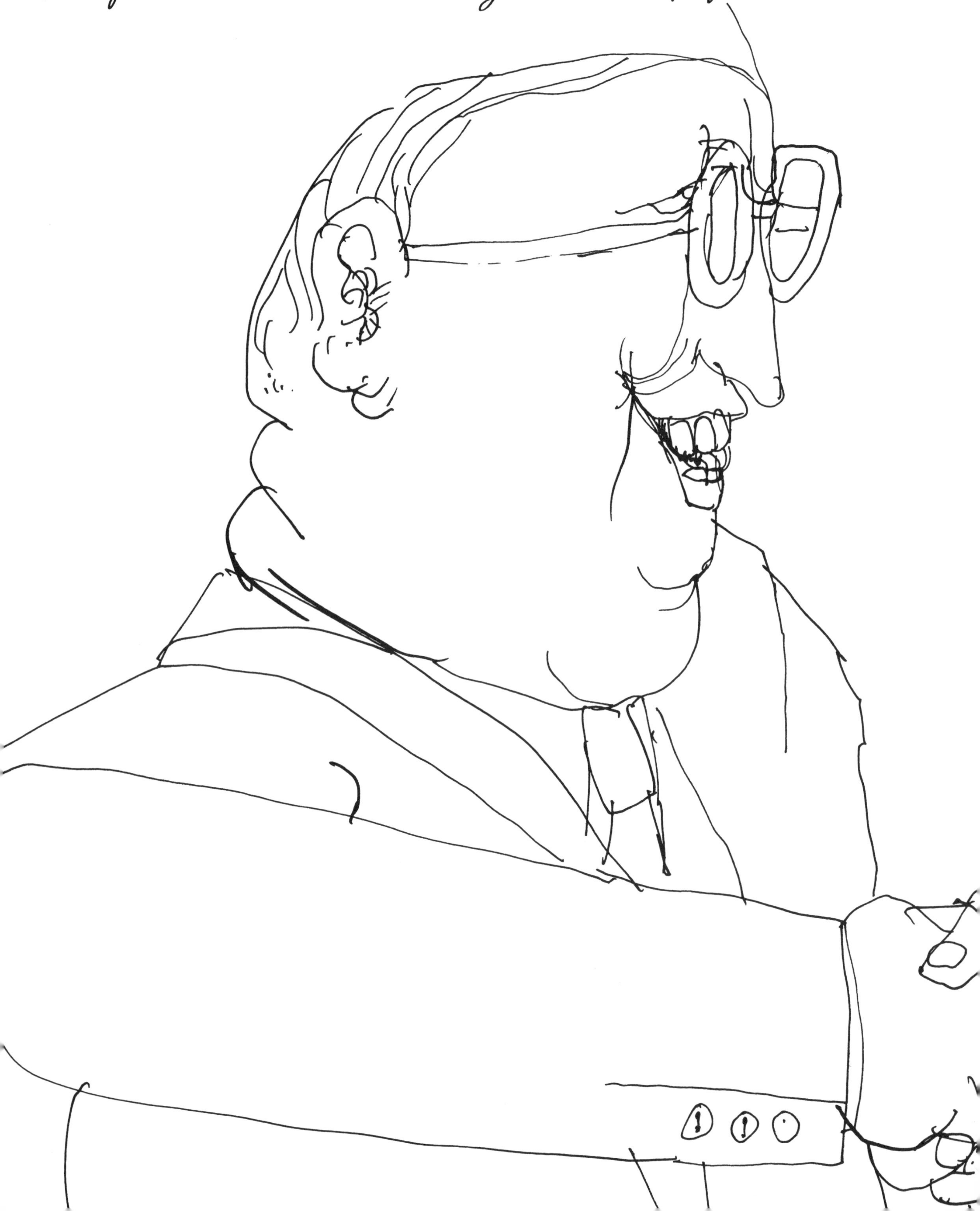

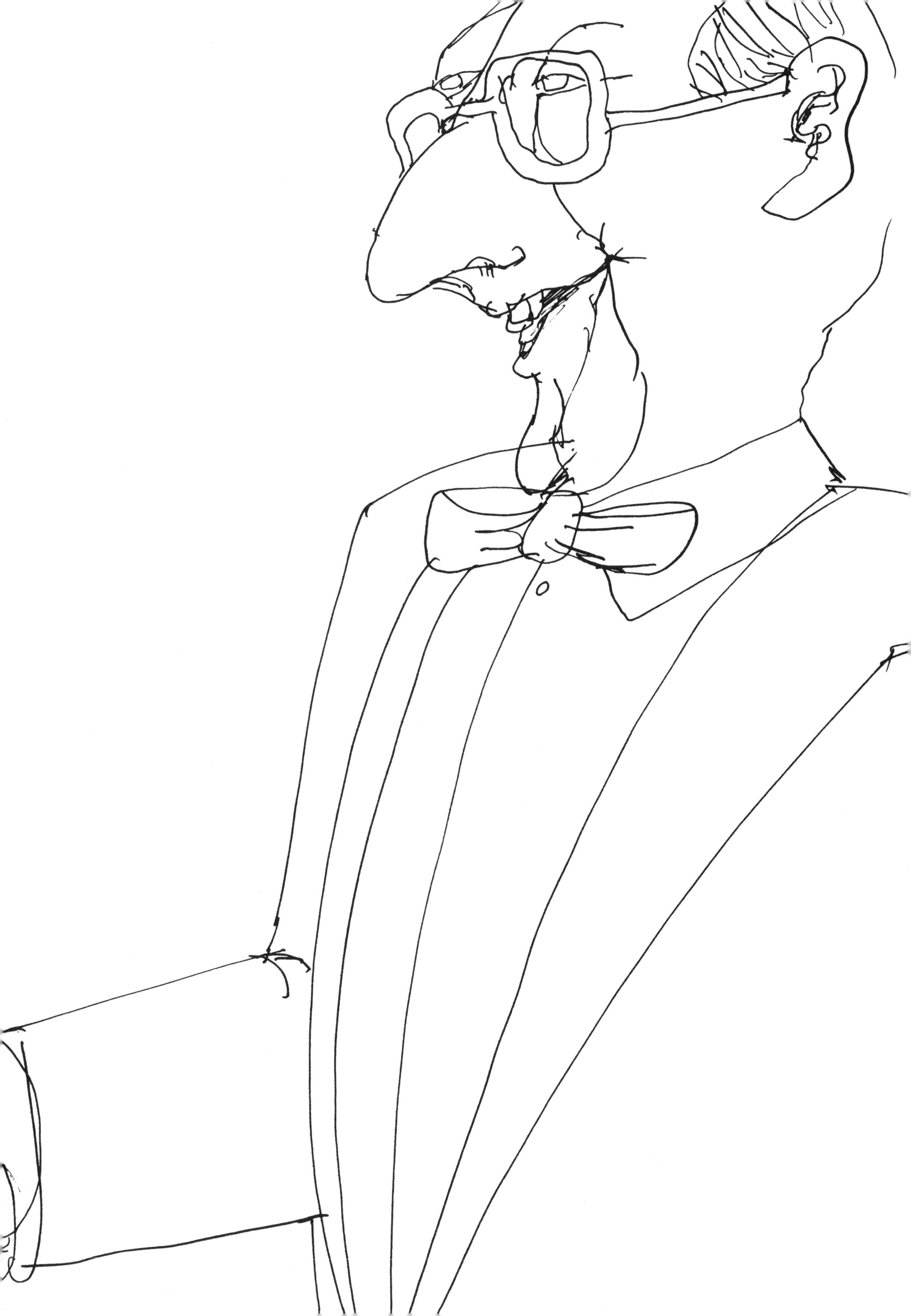

Newly weds Marjorie and Graham Spitson returning
from a three month honey moon on the continent.
Mr. Spitson is a young executive at J. Waddler thompson
His wife born Spoony graduated from Barnard last year.

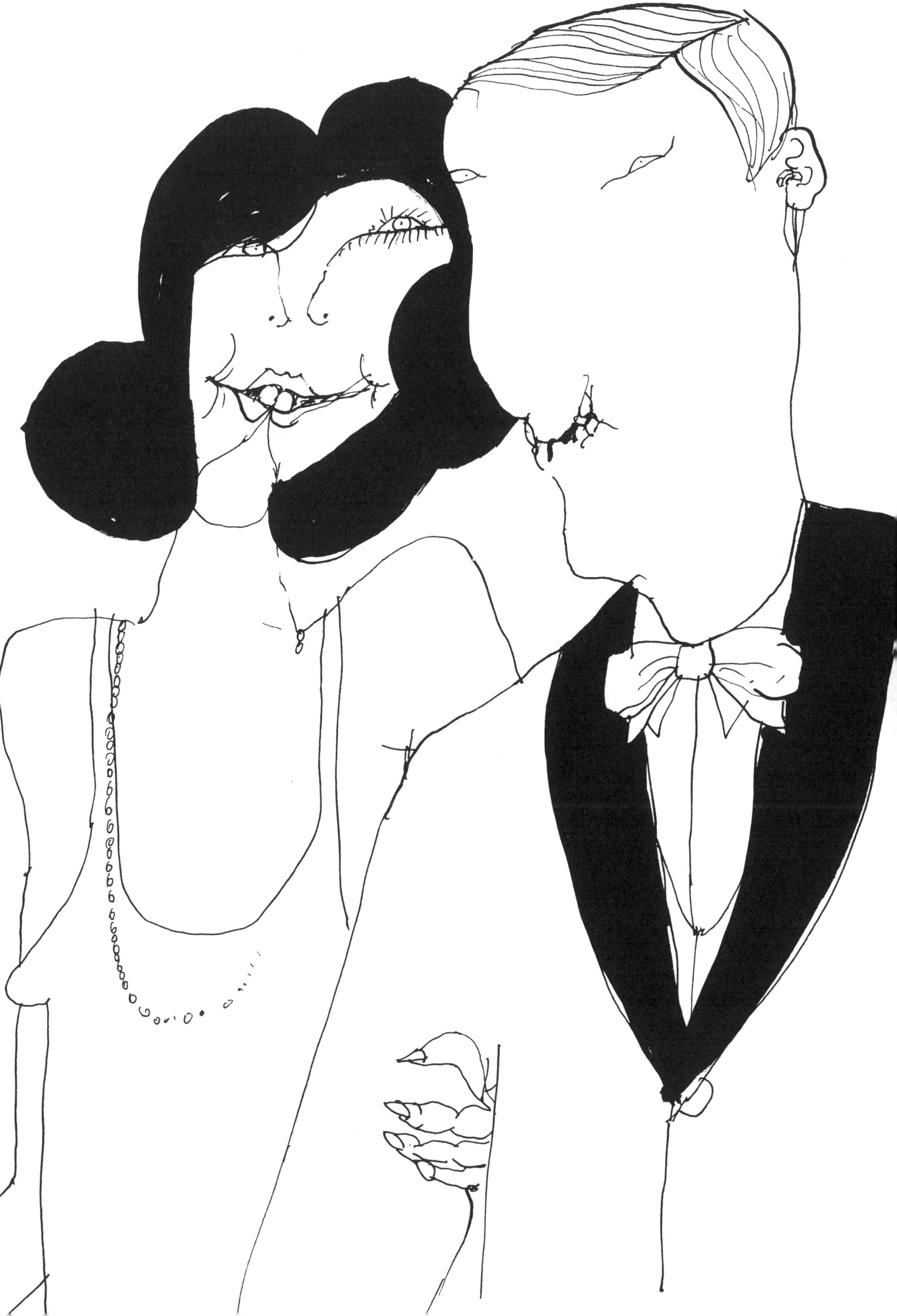

Mr. Willard McJaw from Litchfield Conn., Mr & Mrs John Spoo

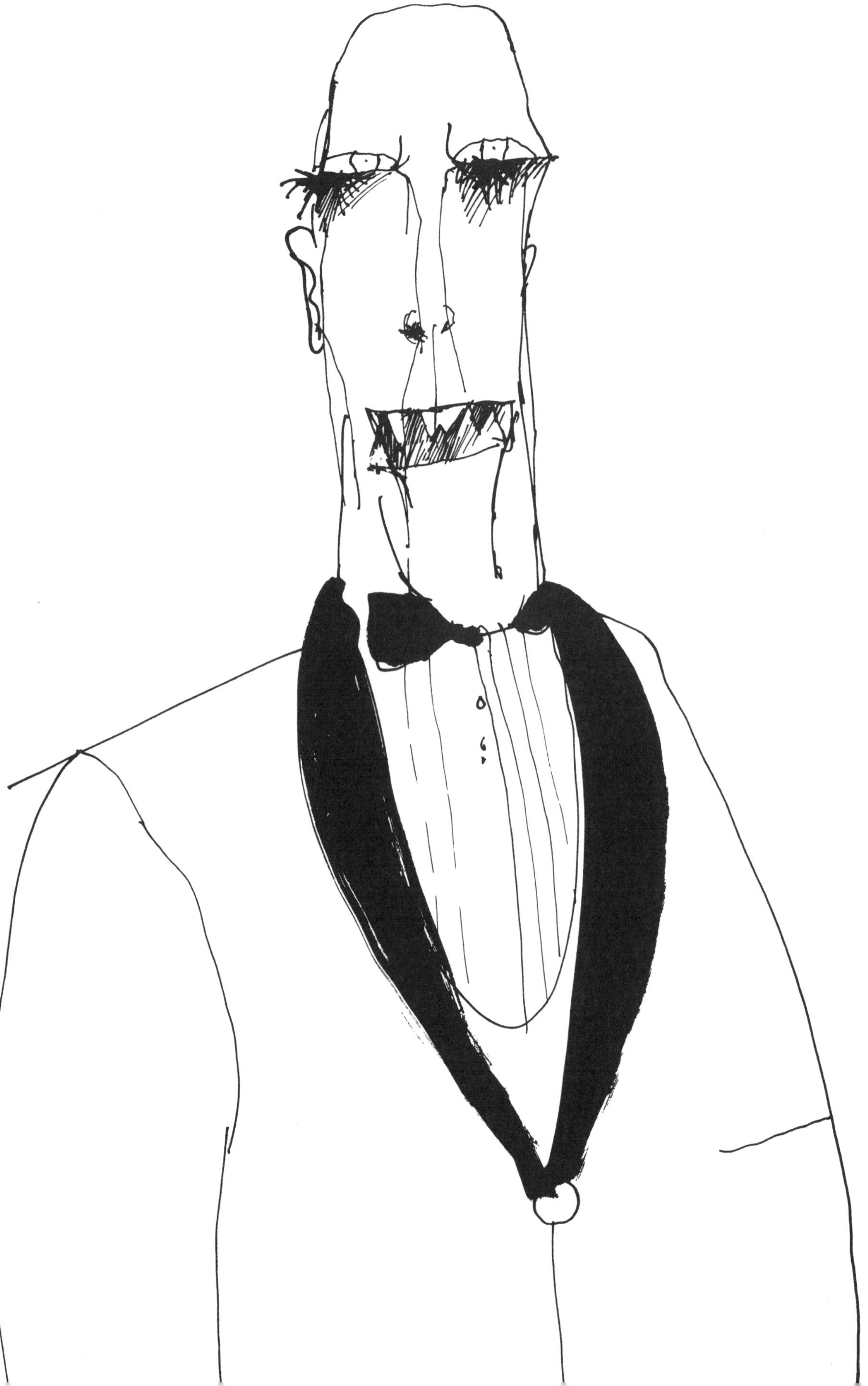

nd Mr & Mrs Hadley Fodler were there.

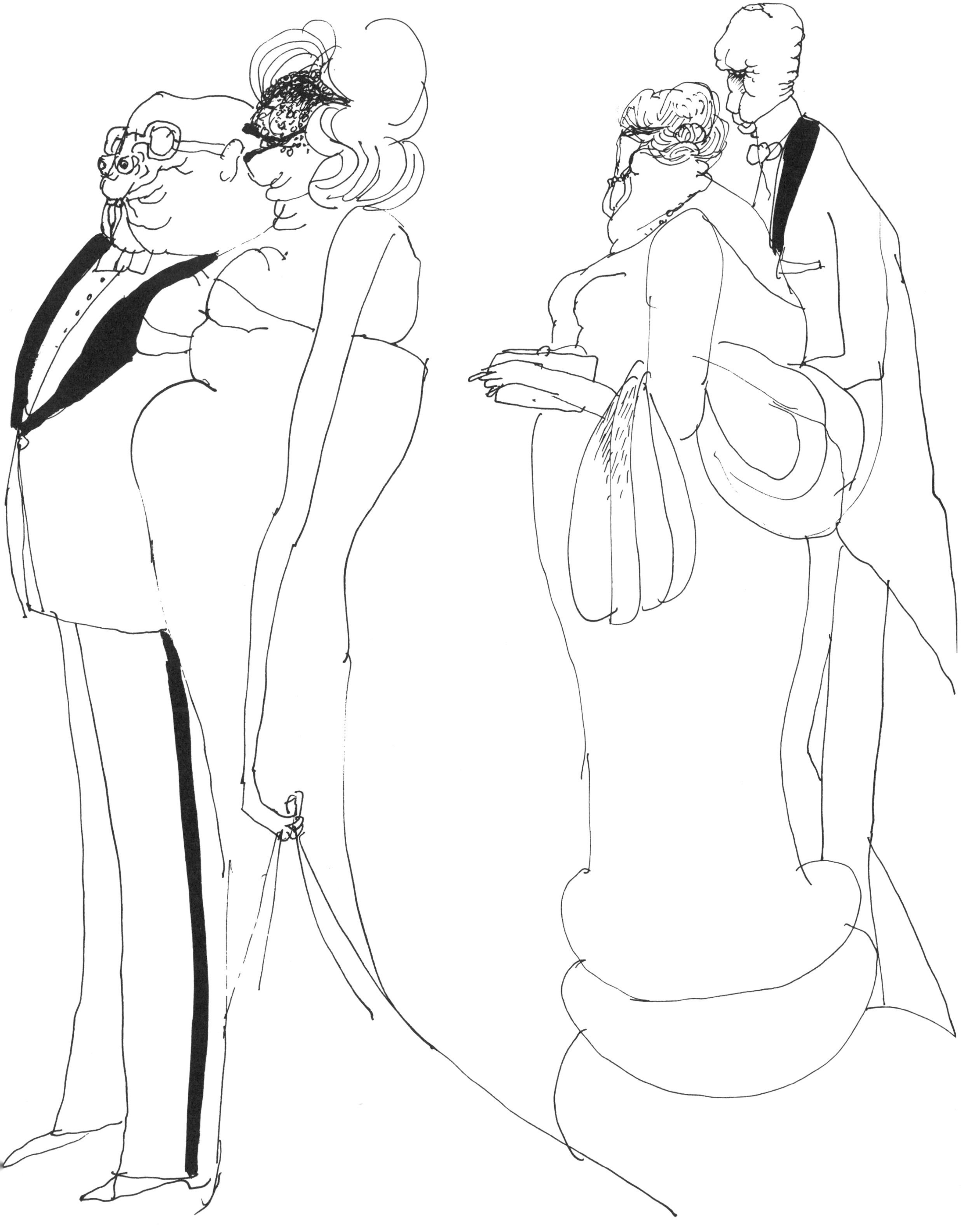

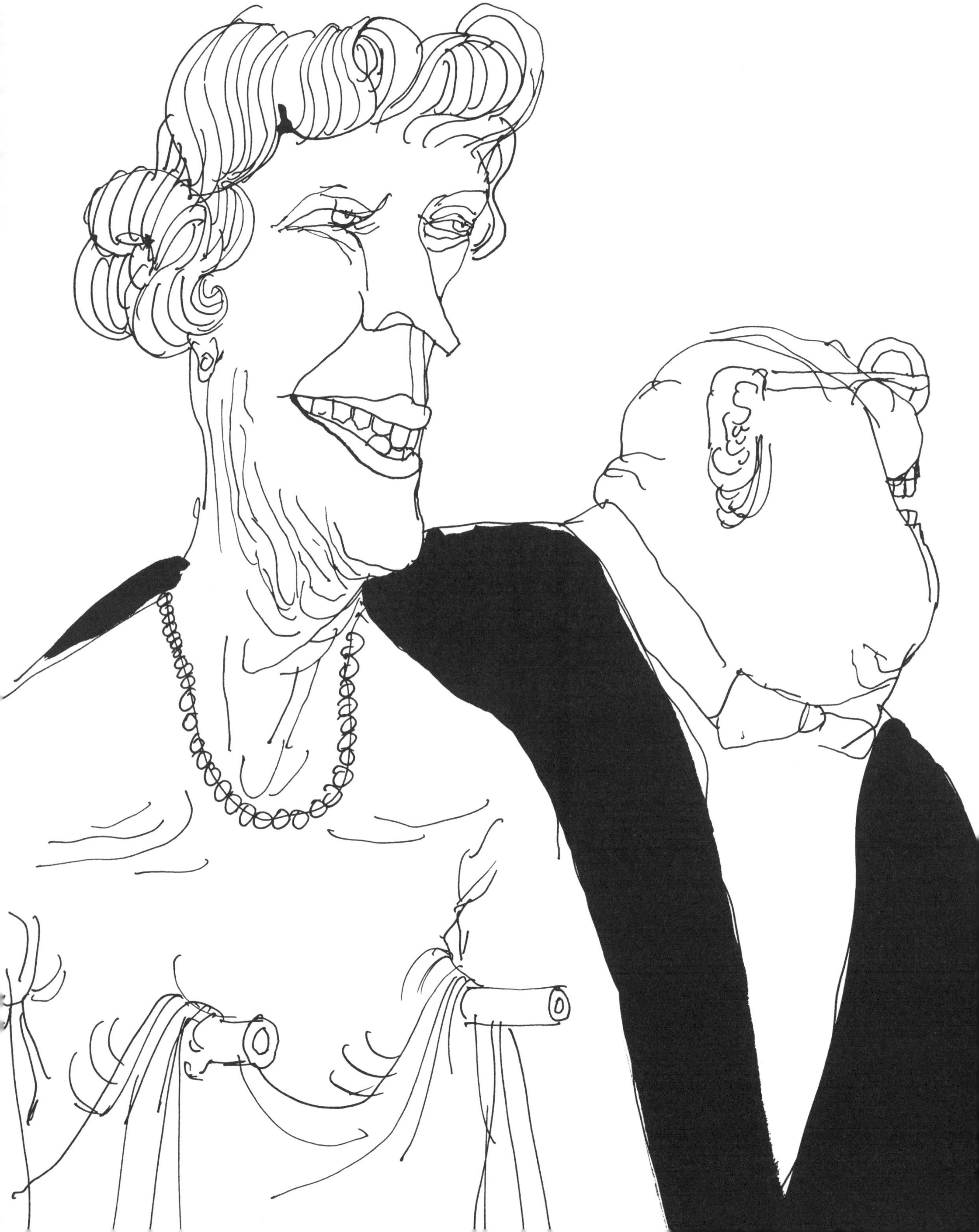

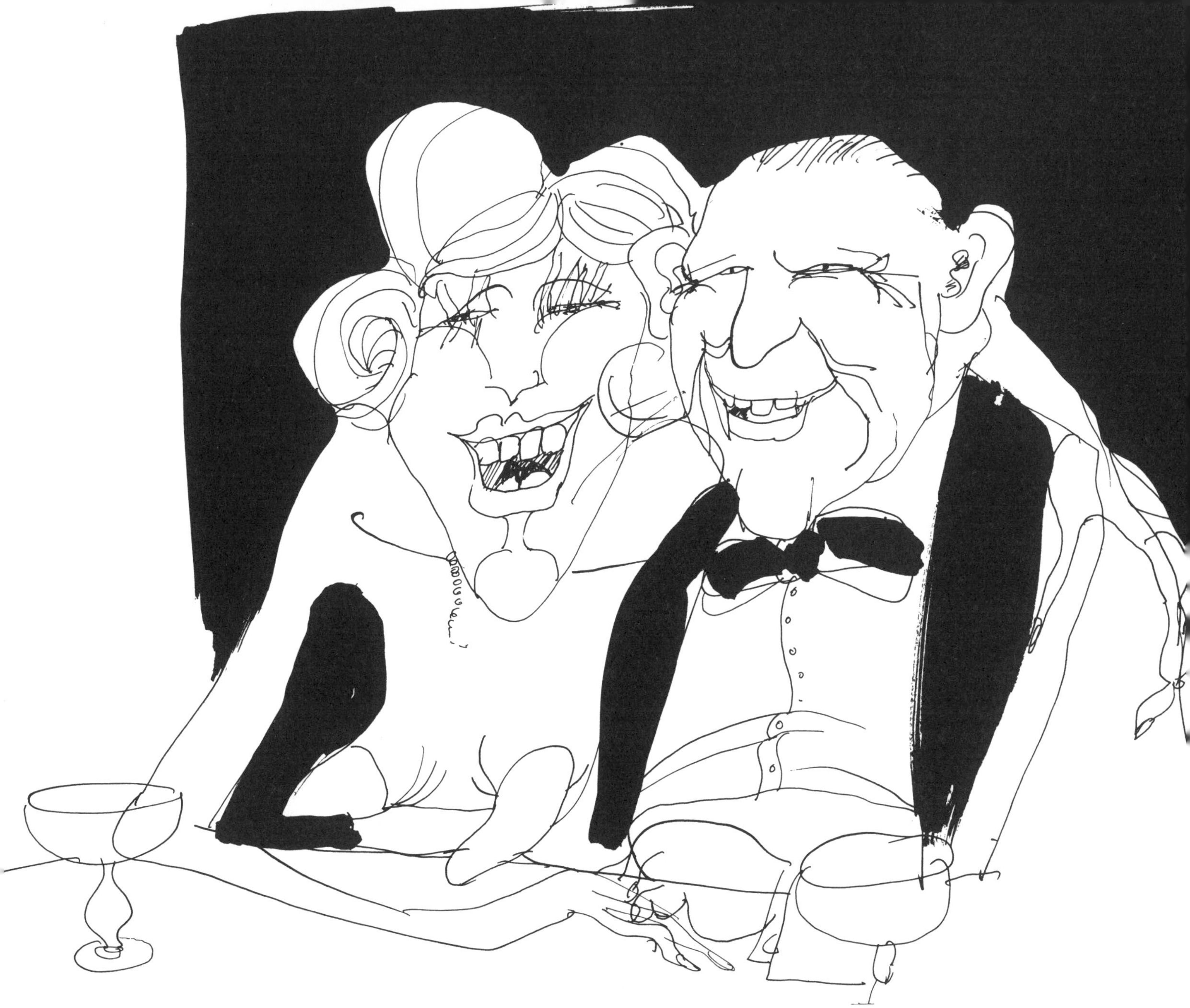

M & Mrs Jere Lugger greeting M & Mrs Bernard Ebbstein—
Both Mr. Lugger and Mr. Ebbstein are patrons of the arts,
as well as trustees of the Fuggenheim board of fellowships—

Mrs. Loomis. Van der Schmutz (middle) with her german guests Graff Otto von Lochimhund and his wife Sigrund.

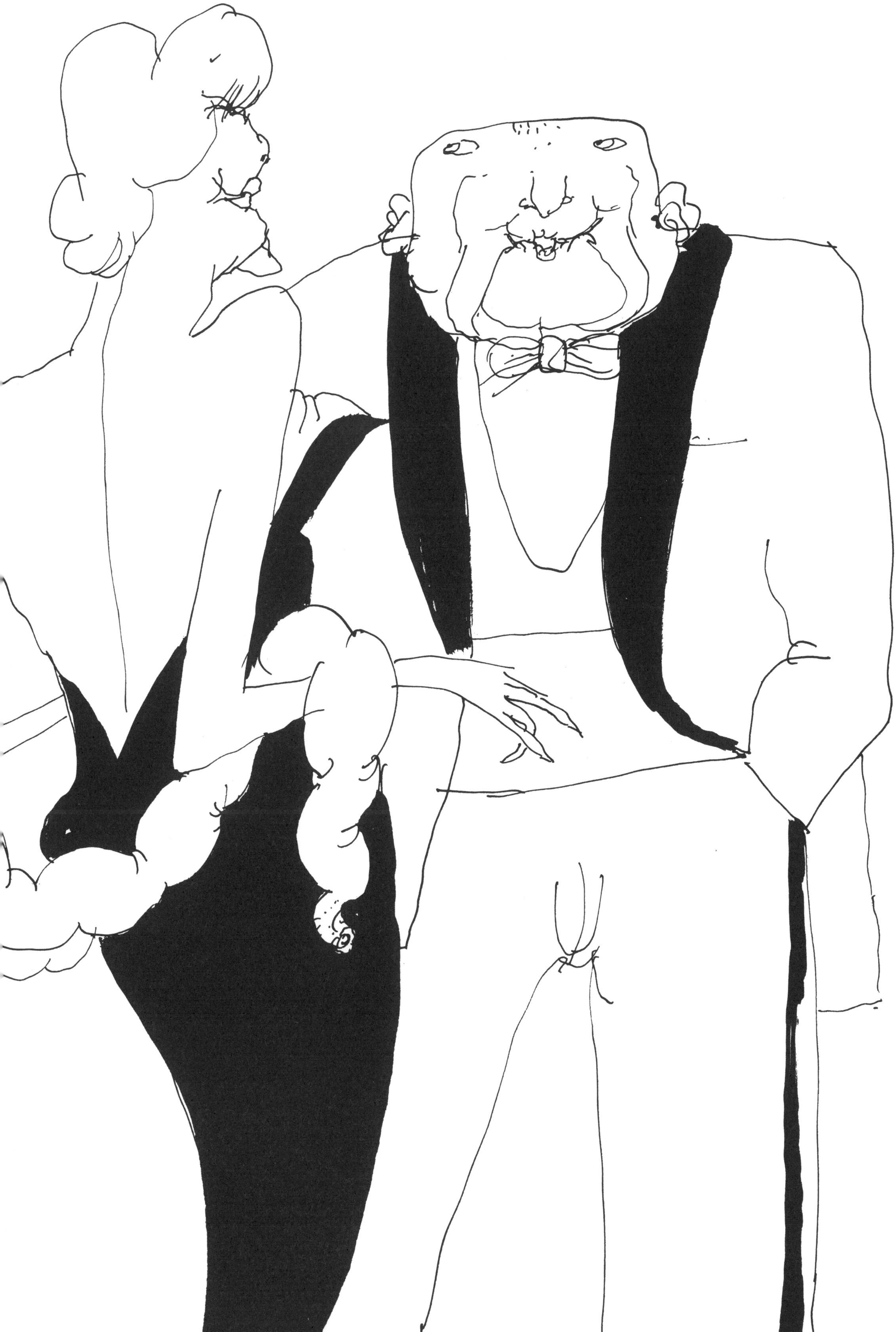

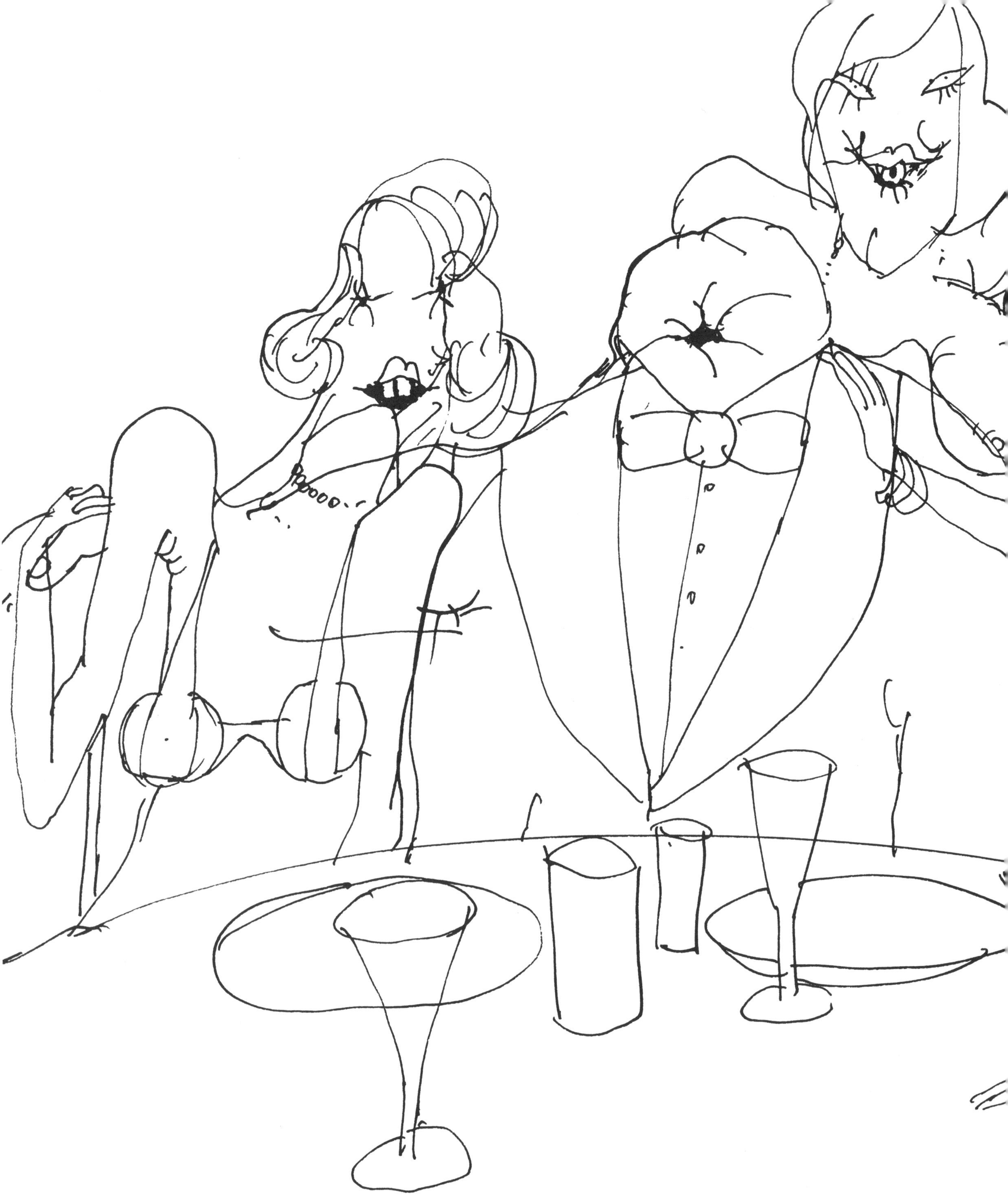

The guest of Honor. Senator Rockfester surrounded with enthusiastic admirors: Mrs Retina Wrenchall from Miami & NY. (left) Mrs Zenia Kimpel (mid) and M & Mrs David Bloats.–

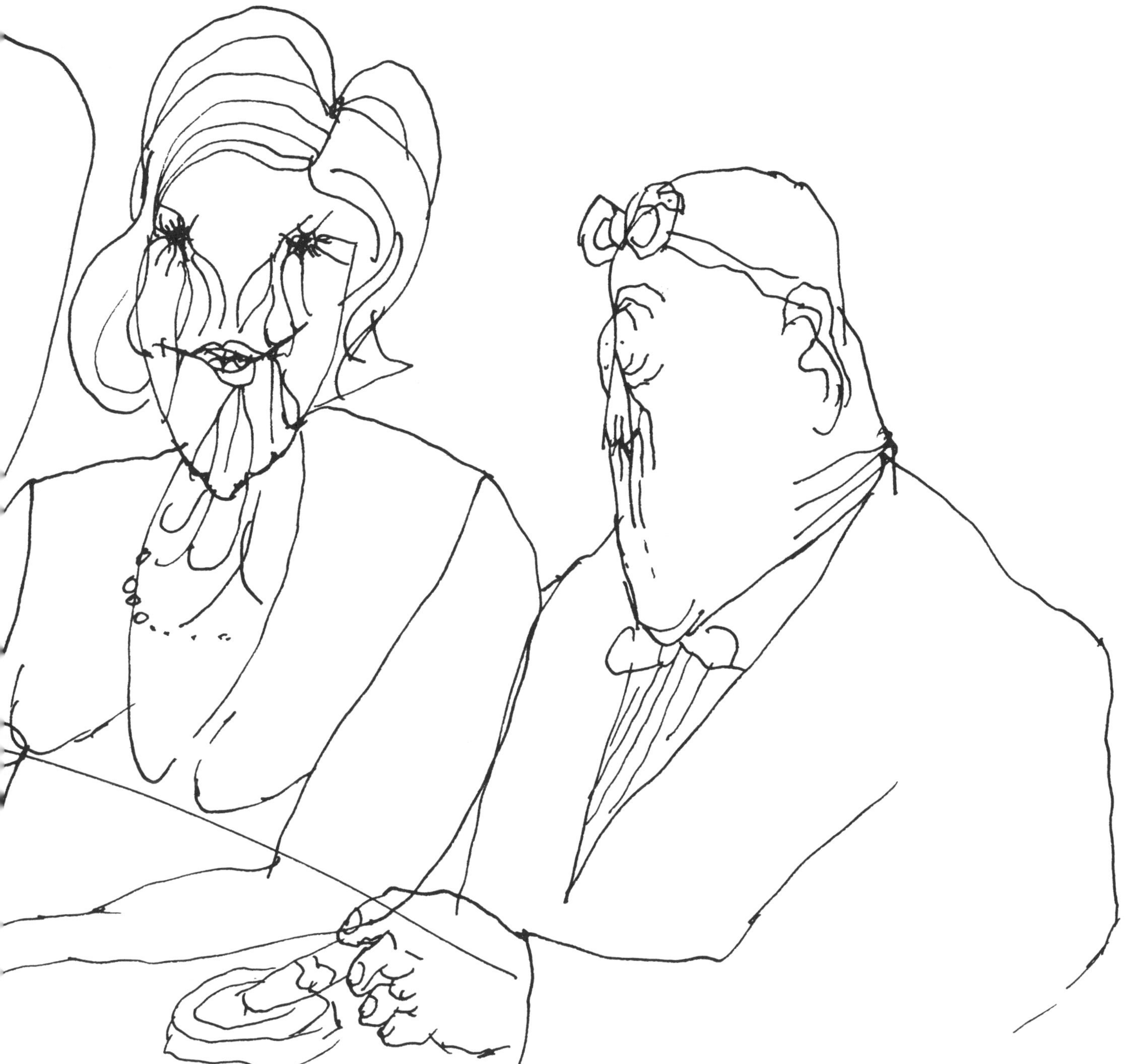

Mrs. Bernice Limp the distinguished wife of former Mass. representative Dougald Limp is plunging headlong into the Social Summer Season (S.S.S.) of the Hamptons.

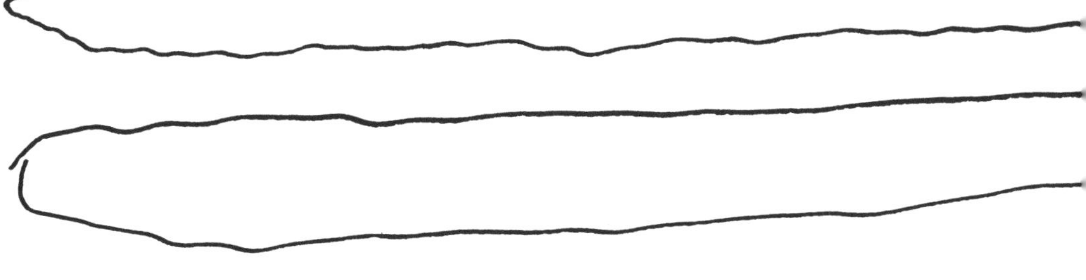

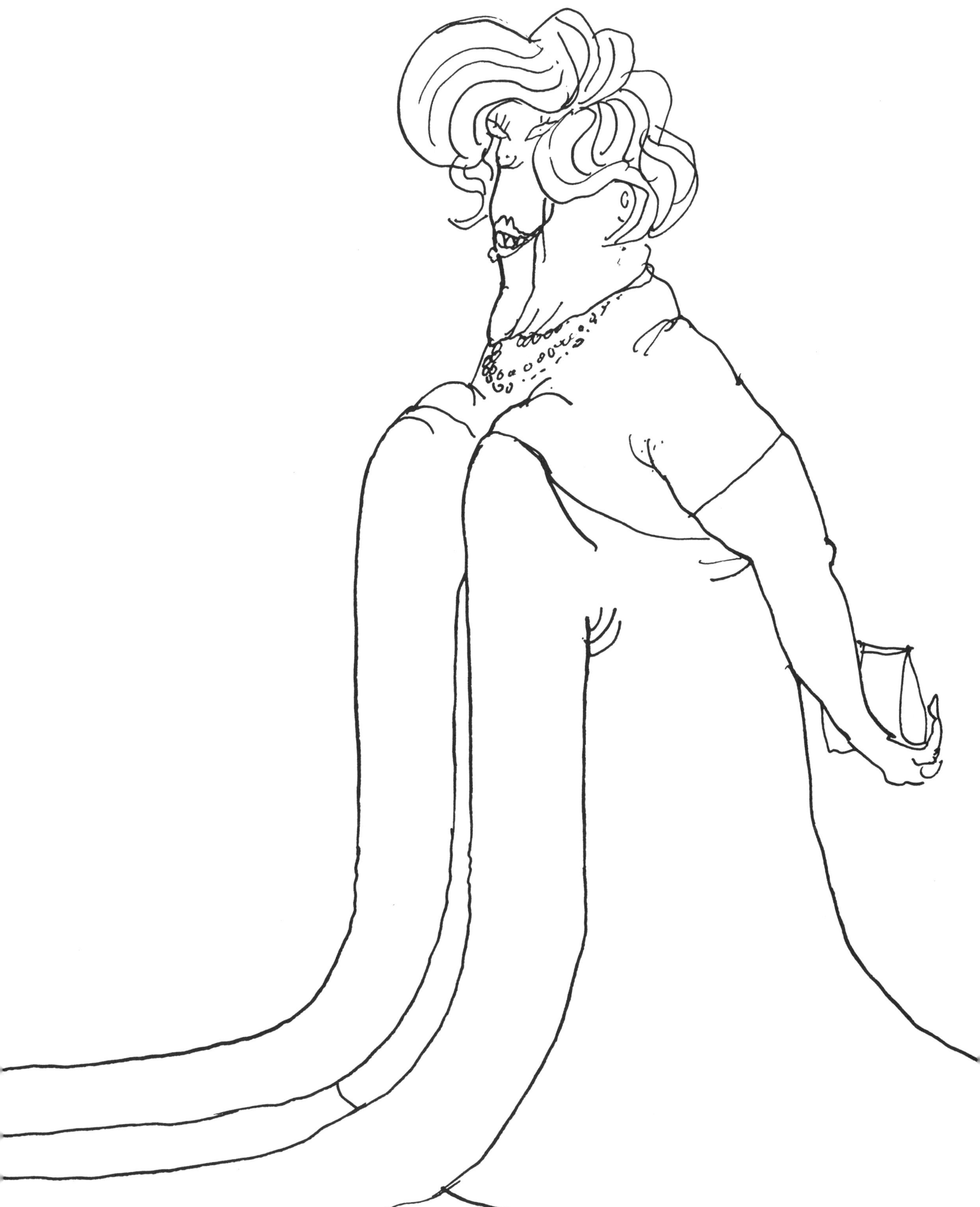

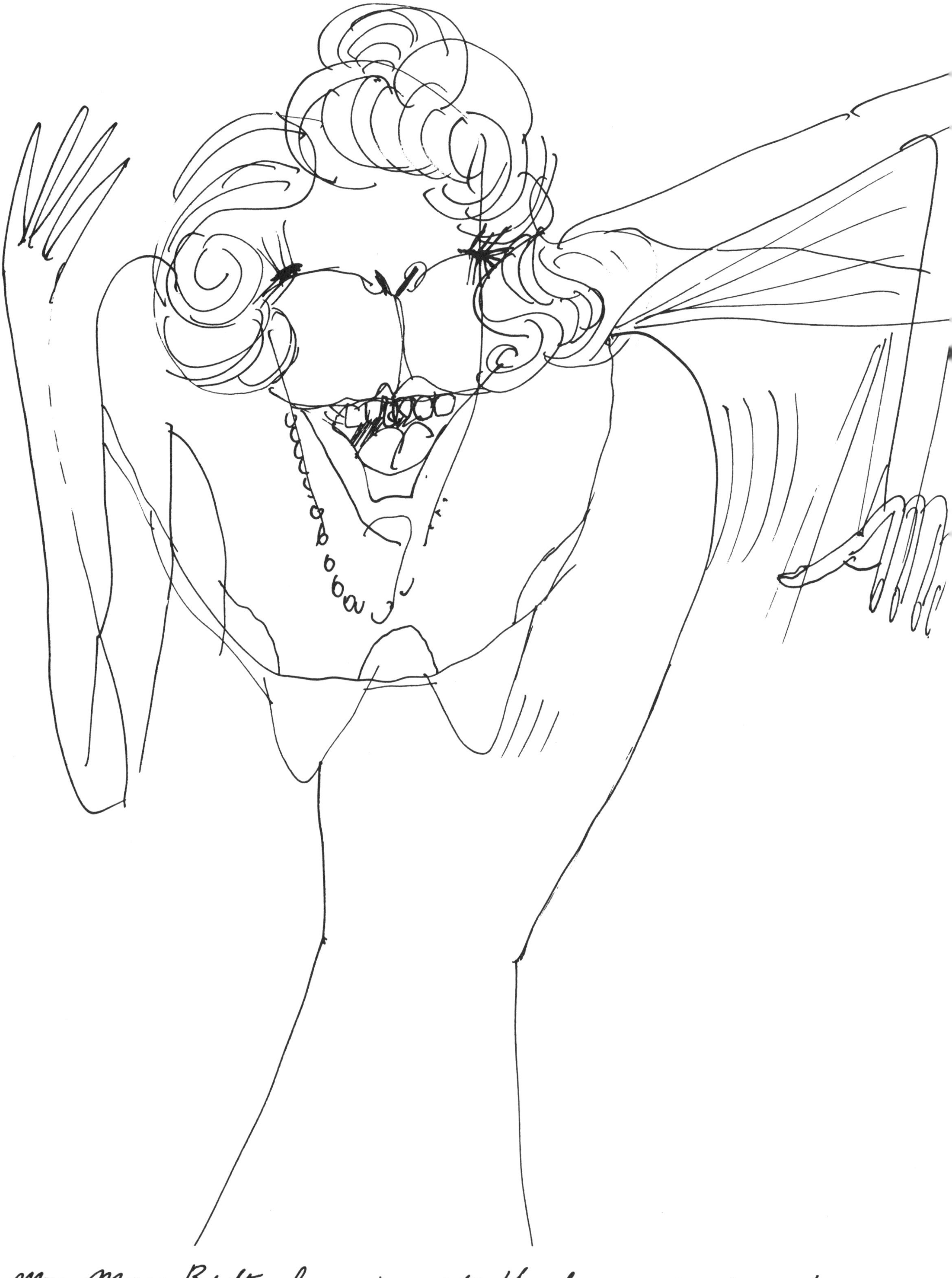

Mrs. May Butt frugging at the dynamic sound of a local Teen Band.

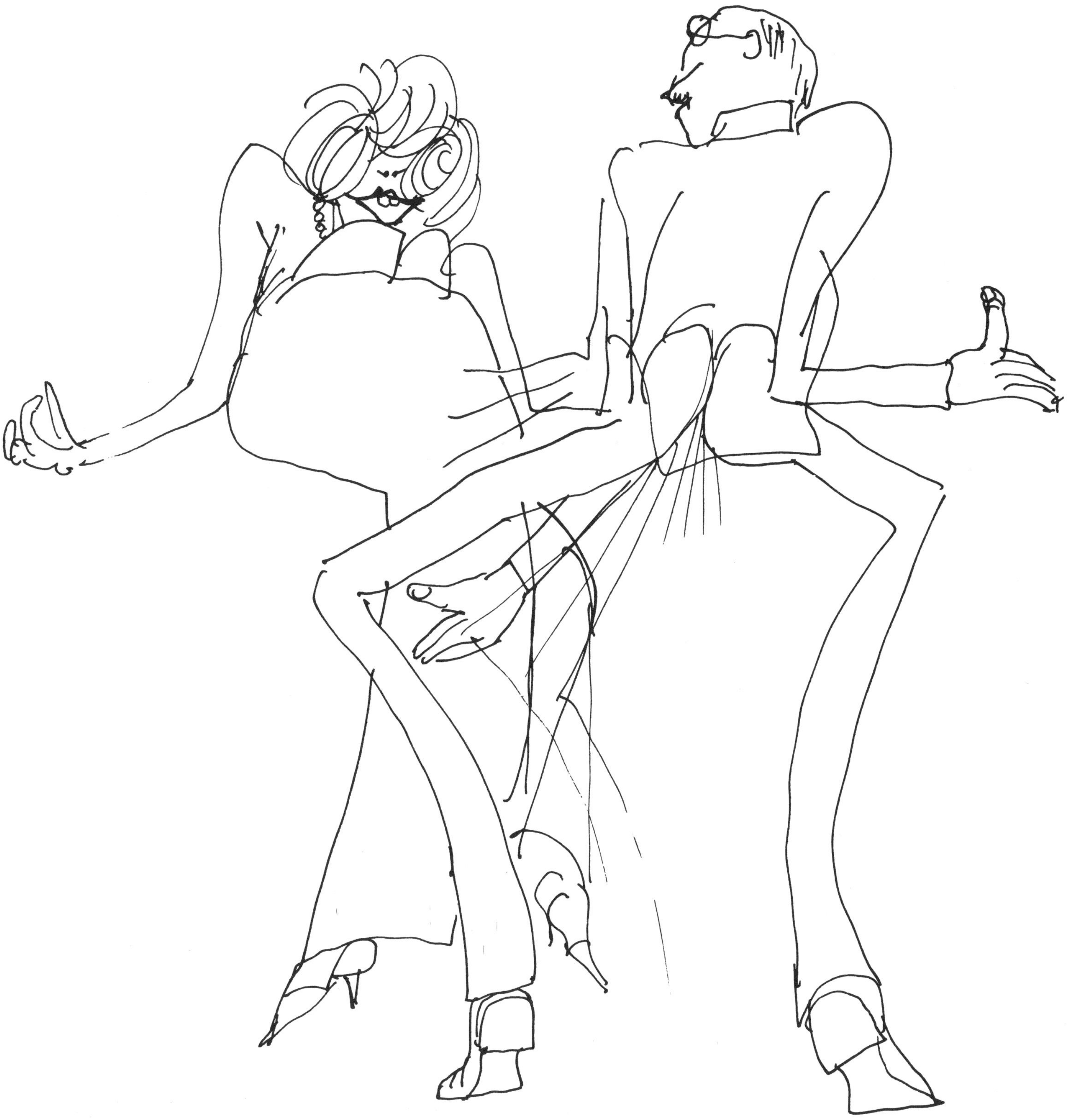

Miss Annie Chasm finds a more then competent partner in the person of Mr. Hugh Ballright.

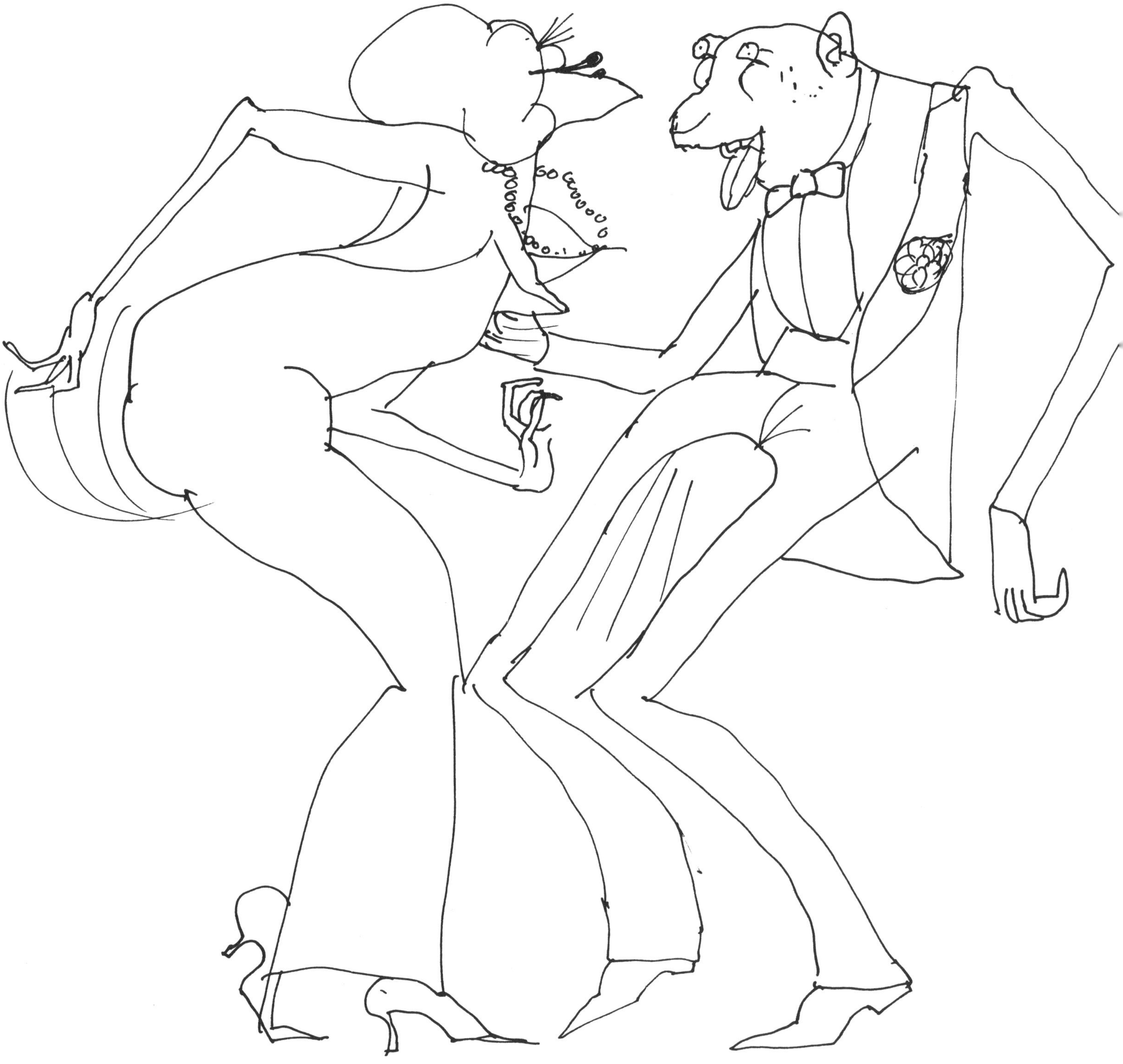

Recklessly joining the fun are Mrs. Dee Flaps, John (jojo) Gibbons, Miss Flannery Rump and Bertand Gland Jun.

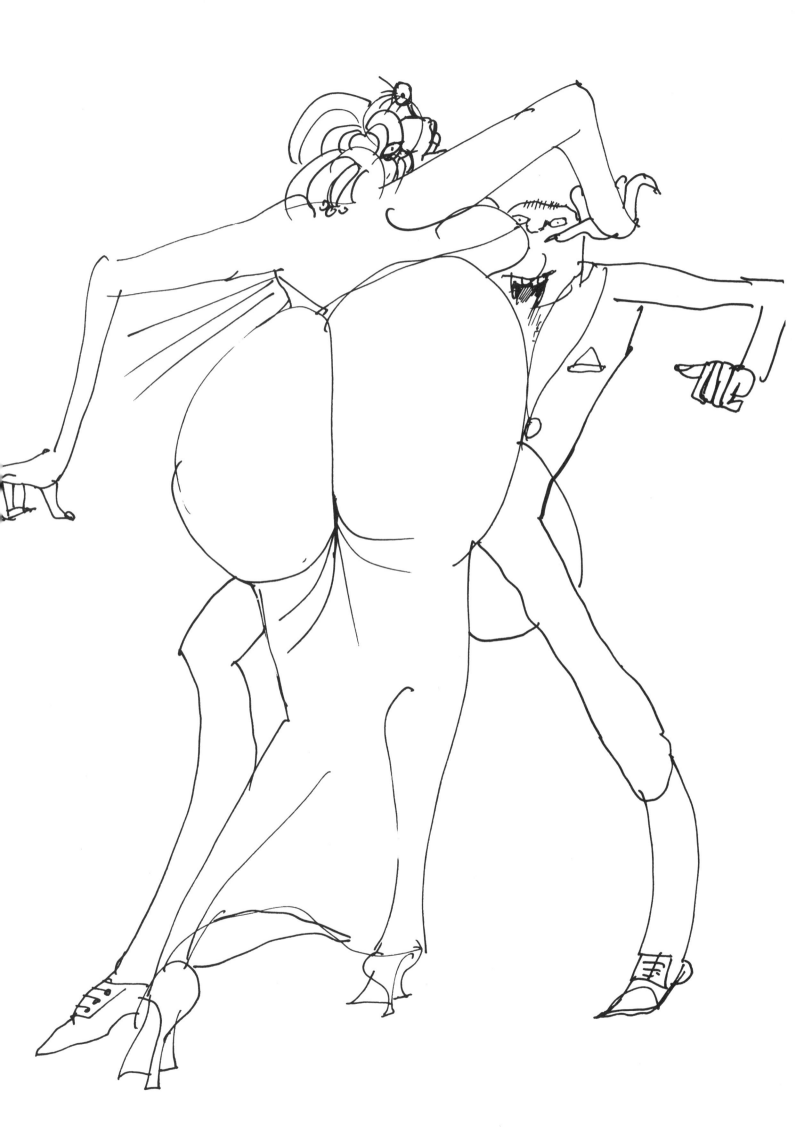

Mr. Bennett Roach & Miss Emerald Flank returning from the dance floor, exhausted but elated.

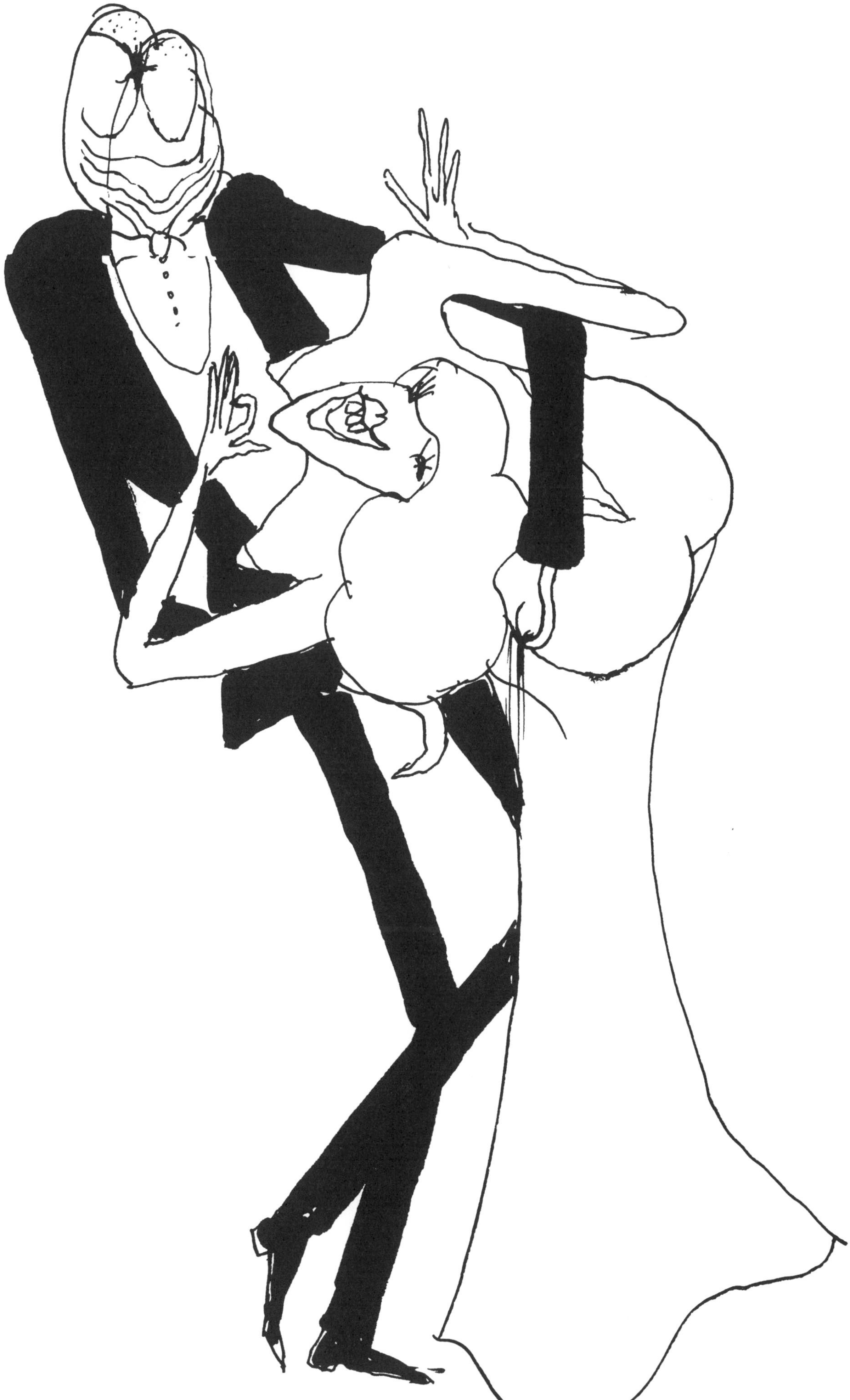

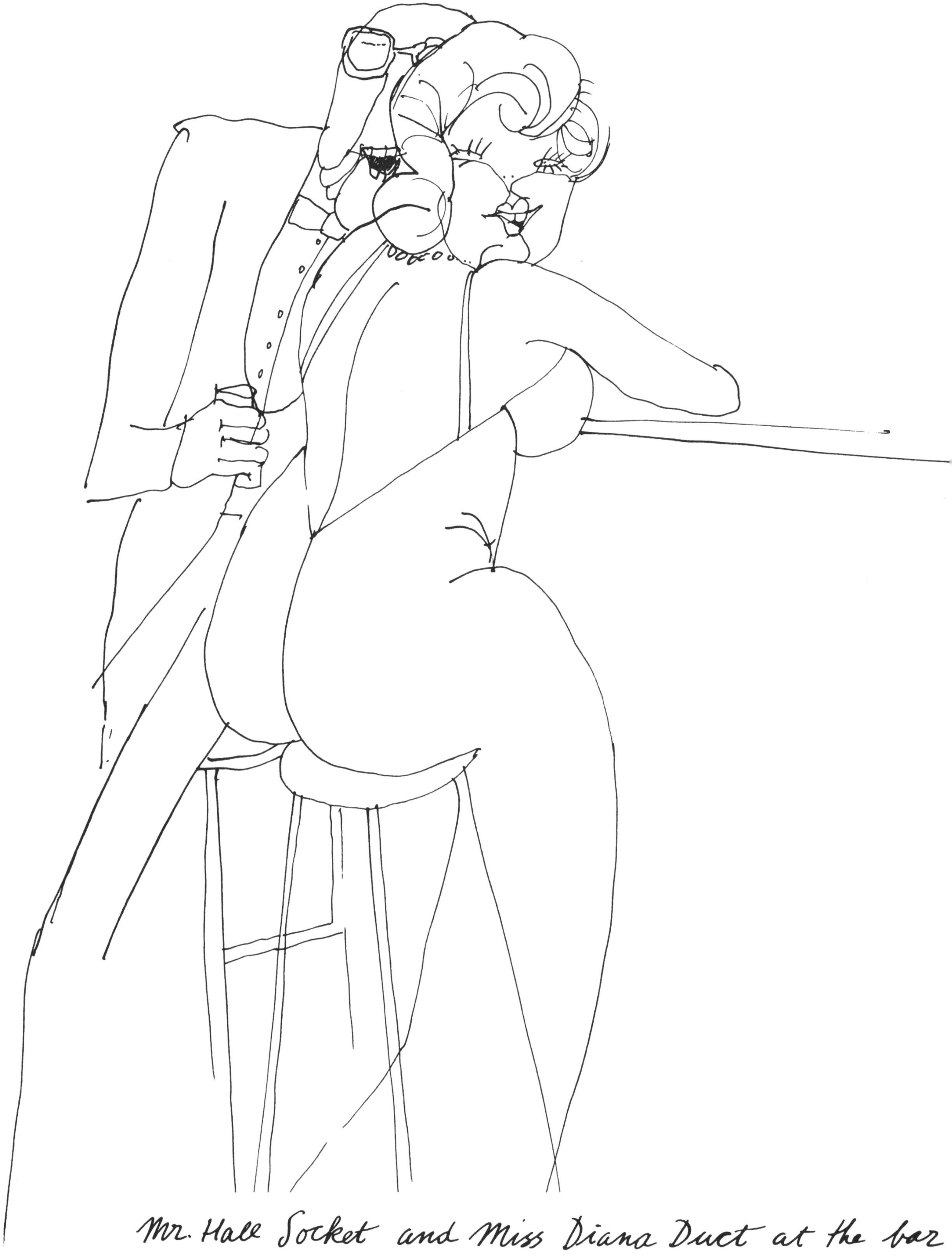

Mr. Hall Socket and Miss Diana Duct at the bar

French educated Celia Whipswood exchanging views with Canadian magnate Alton Scumson.

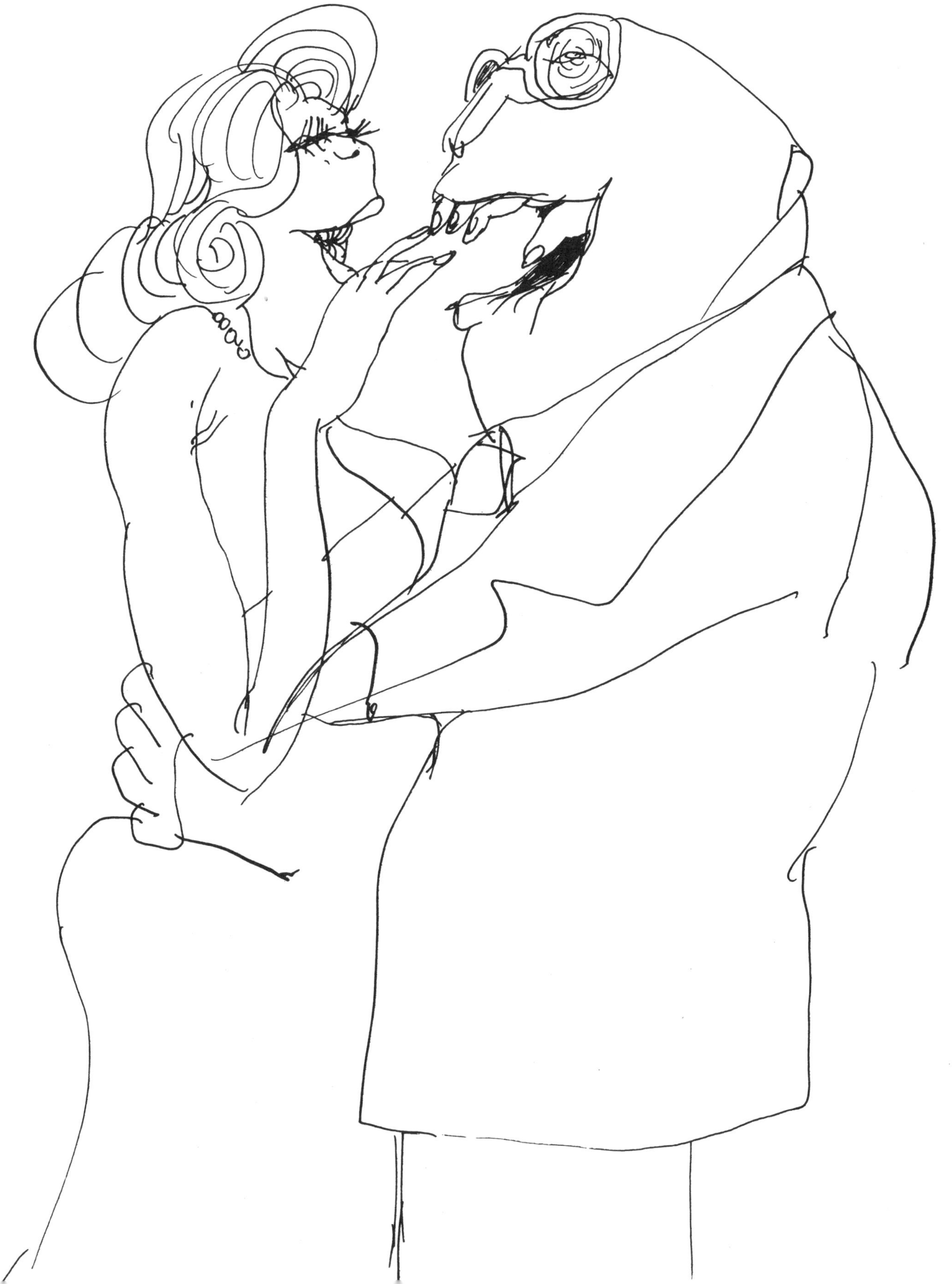

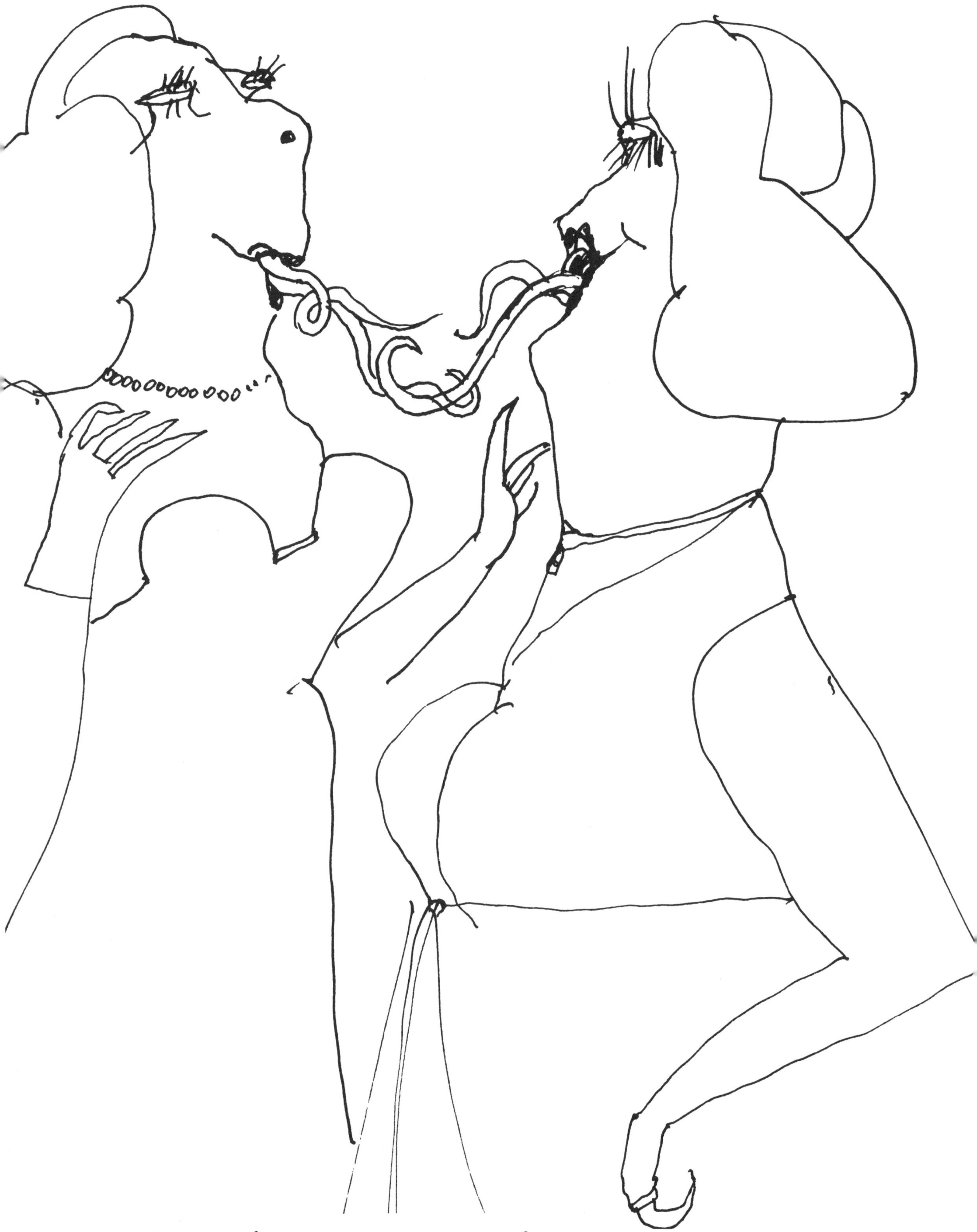

Mrs. Concha Rancid and Mrs. Lucille Pistill.

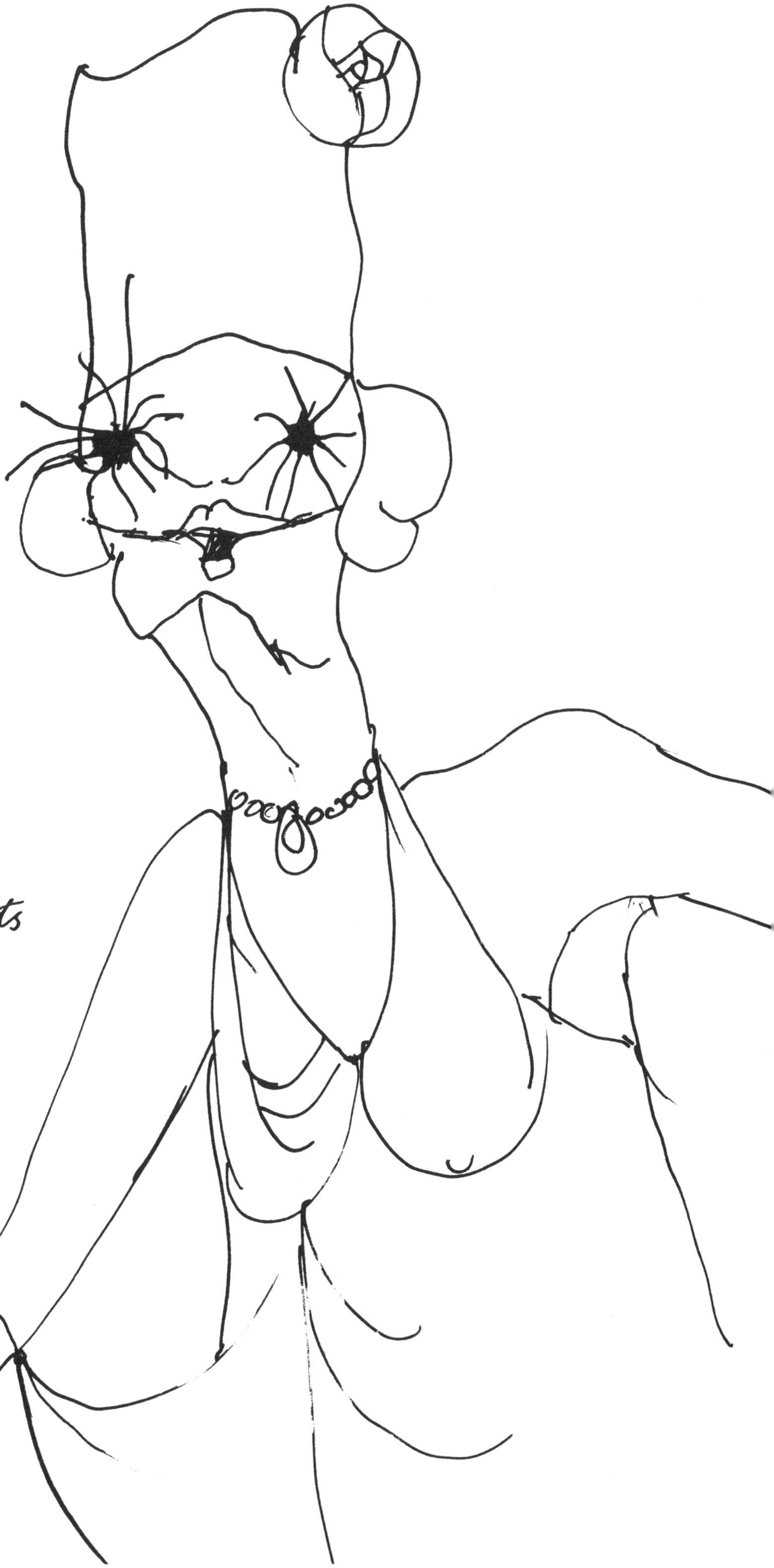

Mrs Esther Rickets
from London.

Graff Gunther von Hinter newly appointed embassador of Liptenstein with his wife Flavia geb. von Fuchs garnicht making their entrance — Graff von Hinter has served in the diplomatic corpse of his country for many years. He is remembered for his role as mediator in the Hispano-Burmese conflict three years ago

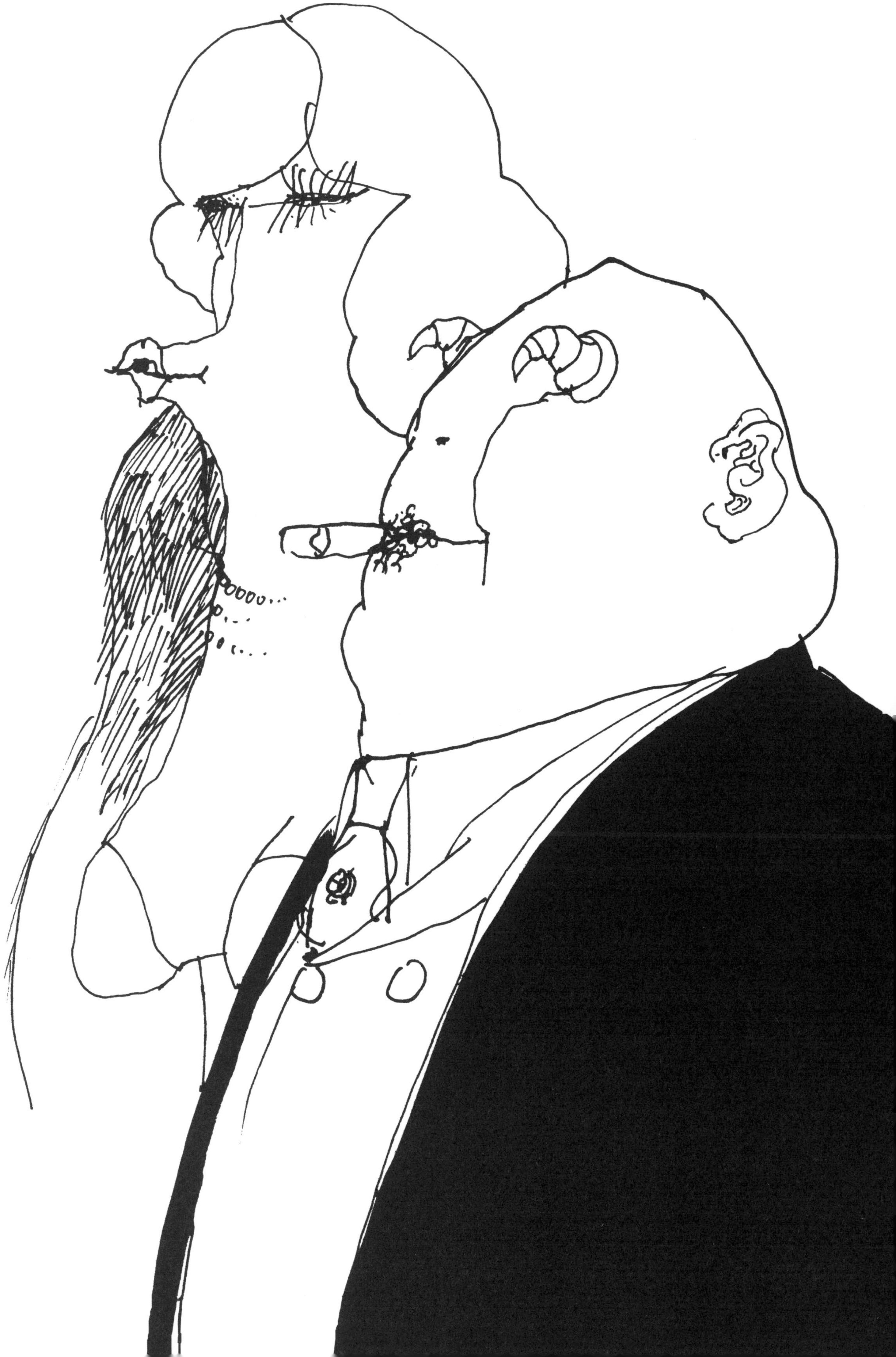

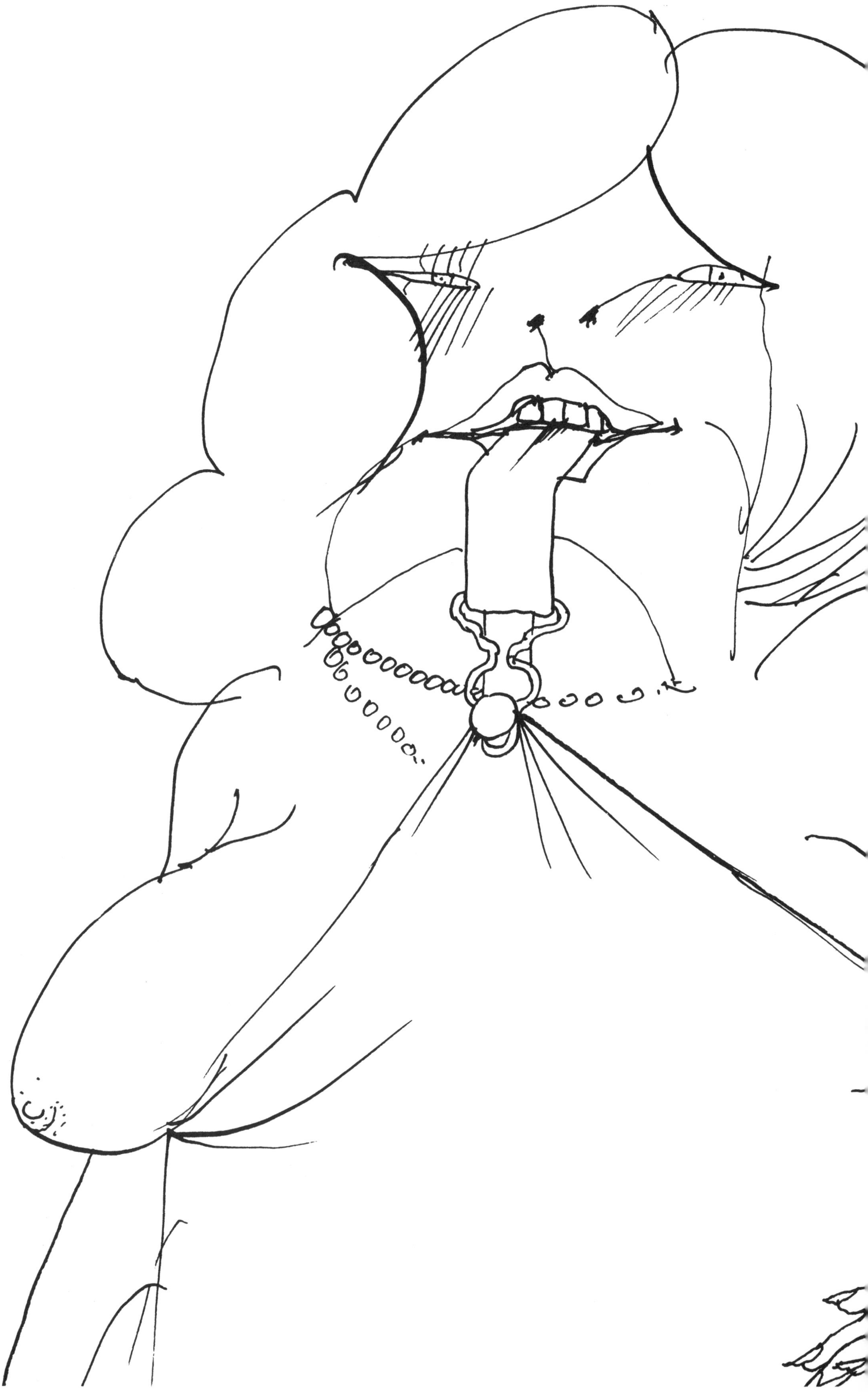

Miss Mollie Follicle heiress to the Spanflex fortune.

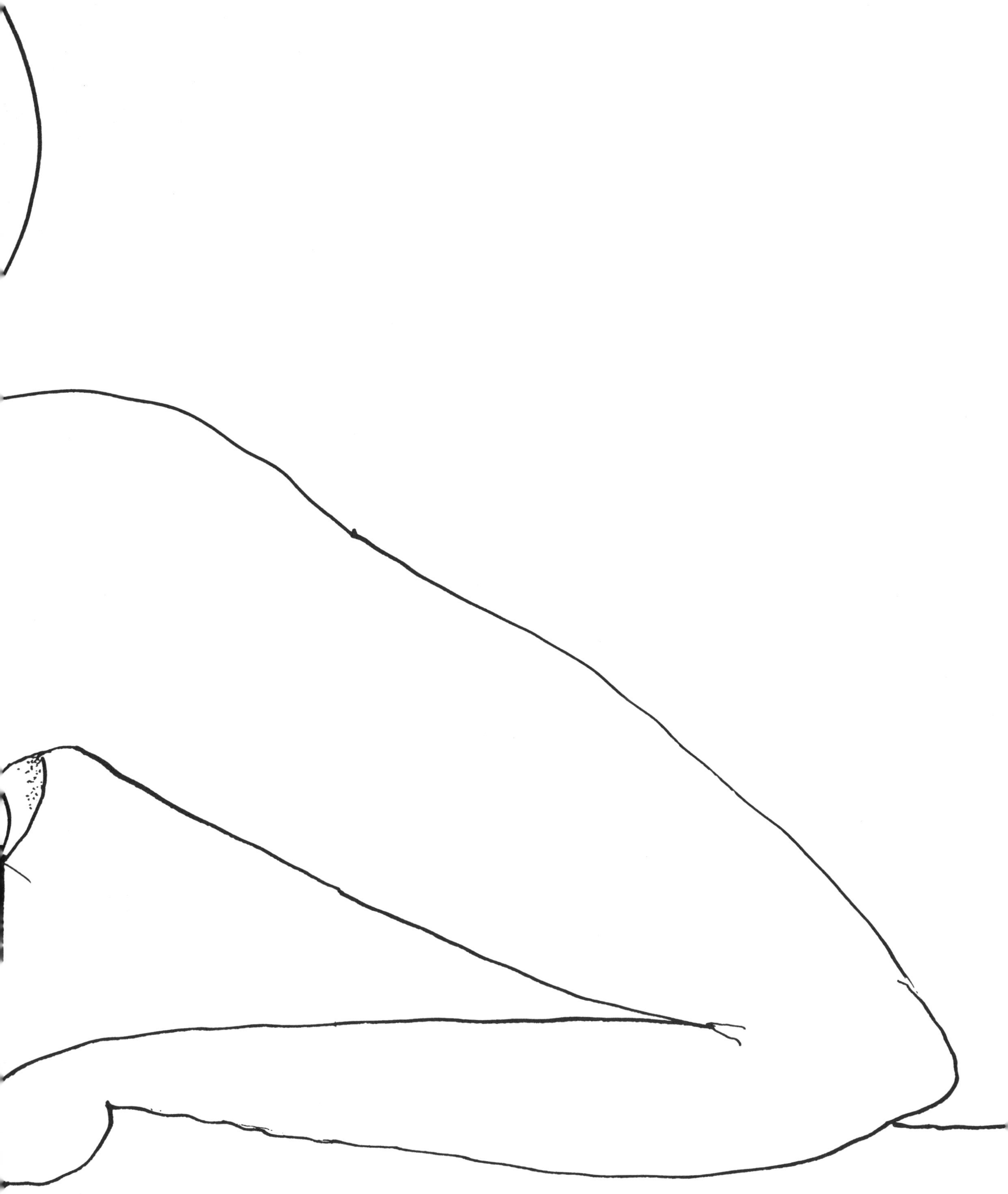

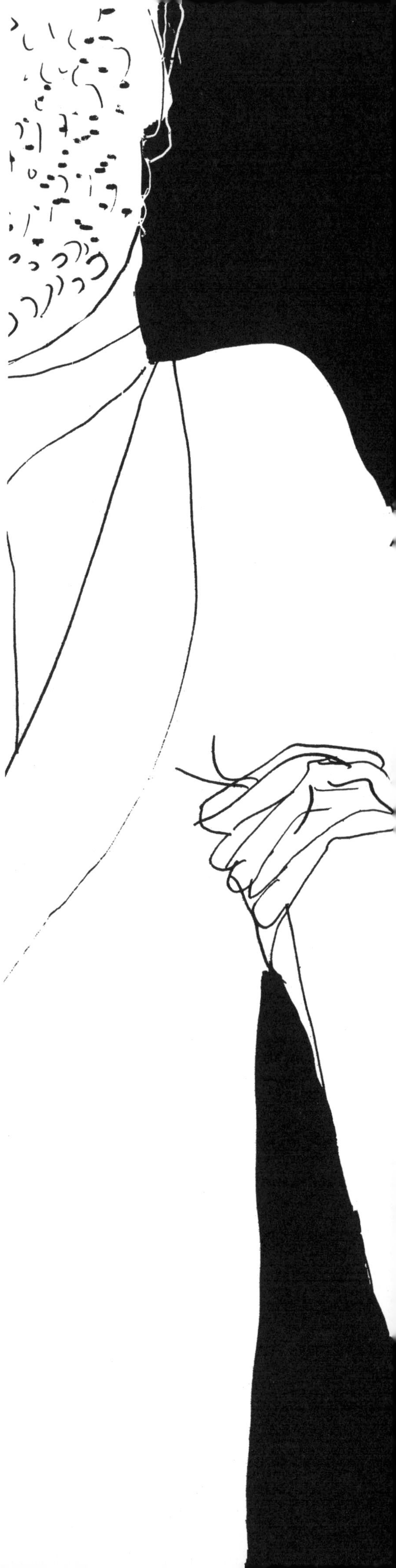

Mrs Dahlia Doberman introducing her husband Mitri Scrophulos, greek entrepreneur who is new to our shores -

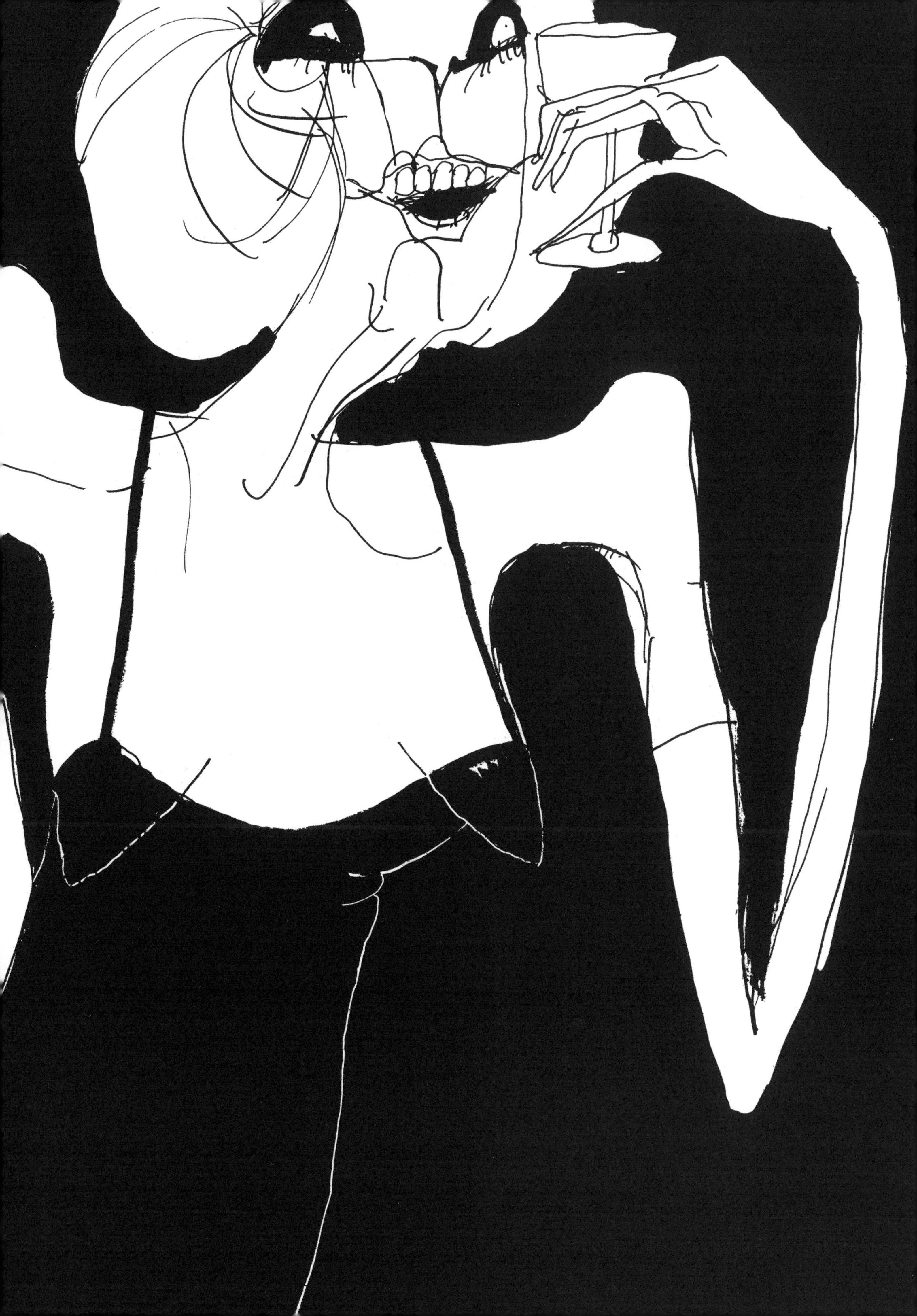

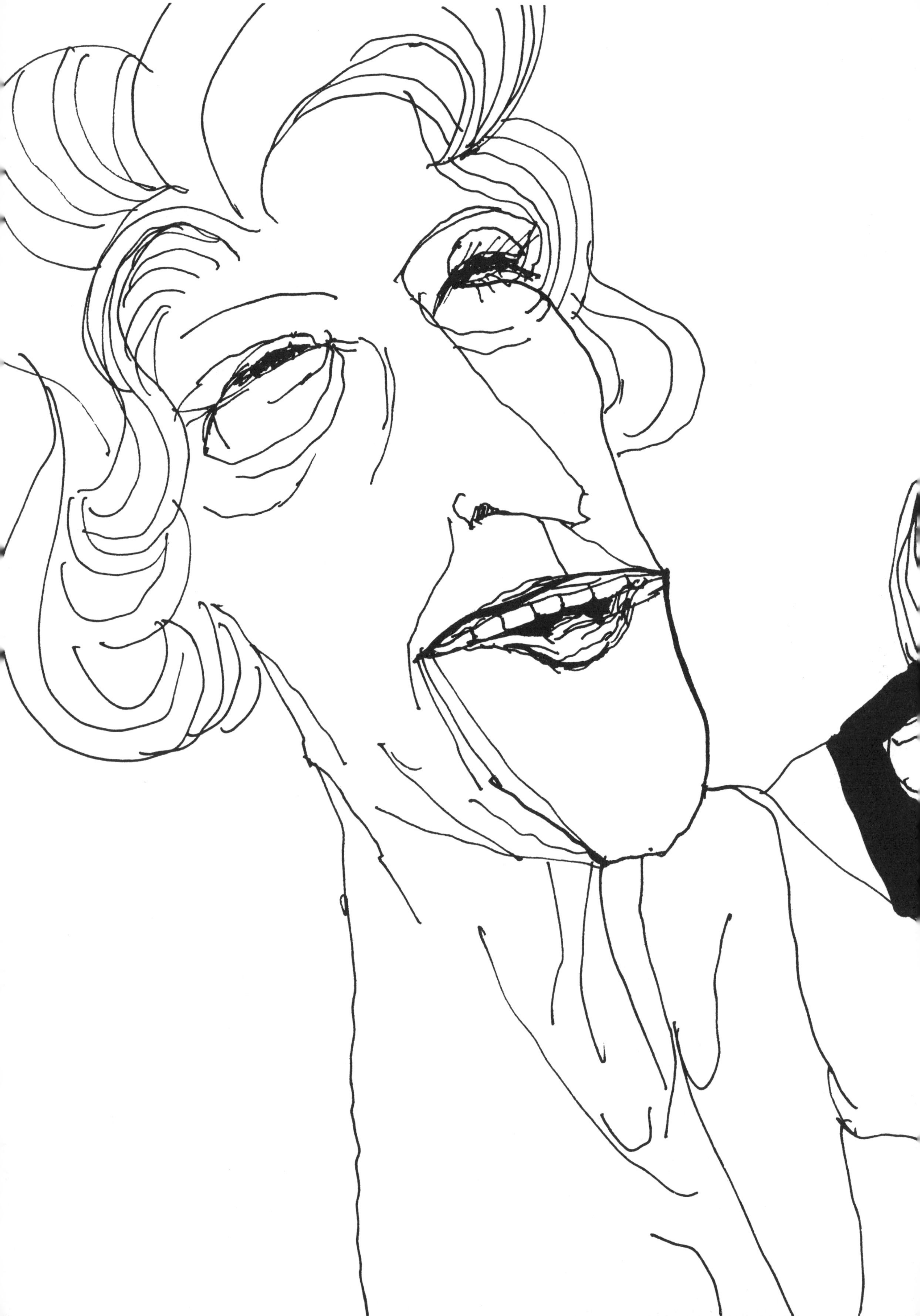

Mrs. Uvula Rottenham at dinner with Mr. Julius Grunt, irrepressible Pittsburgh financier

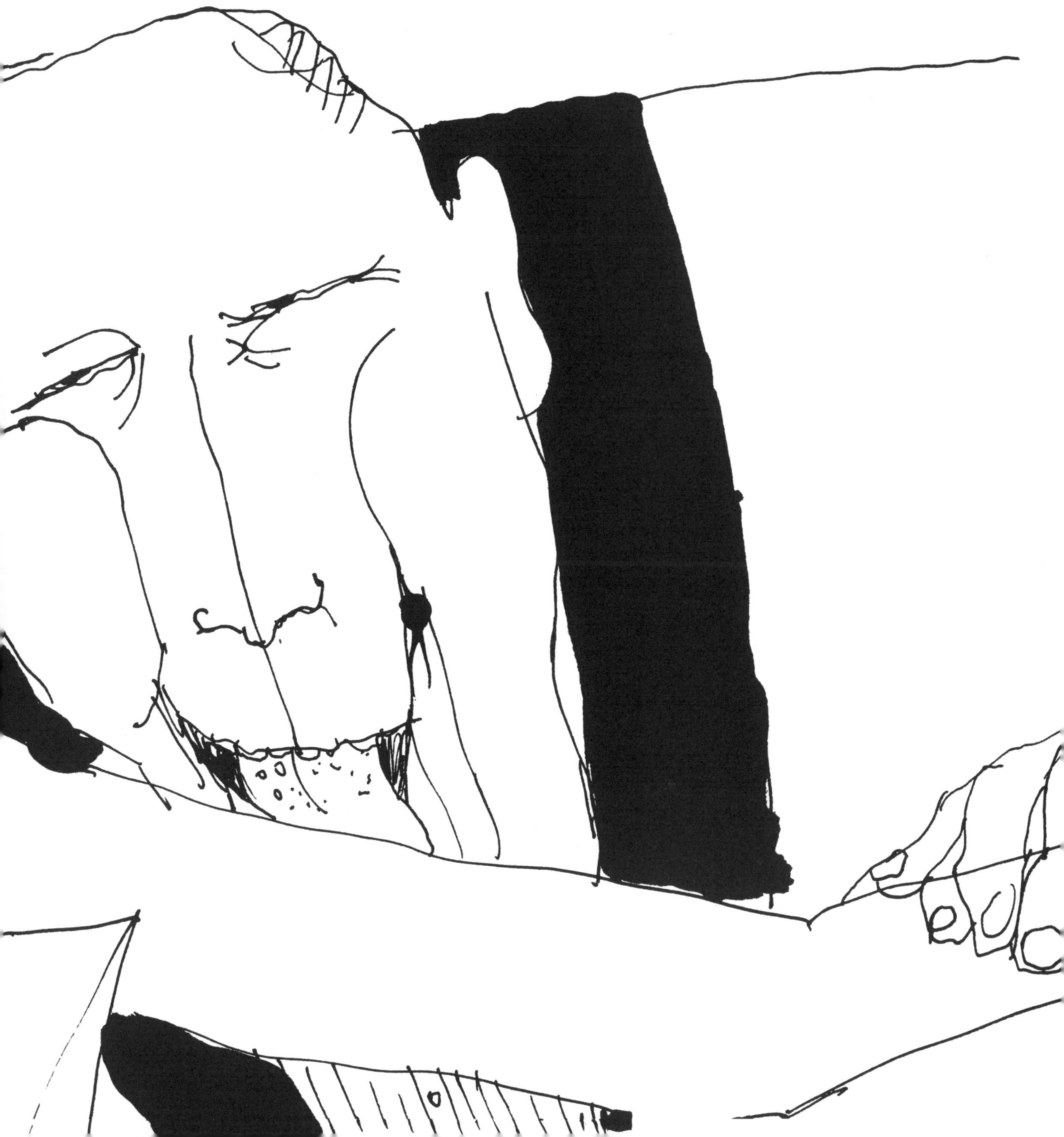

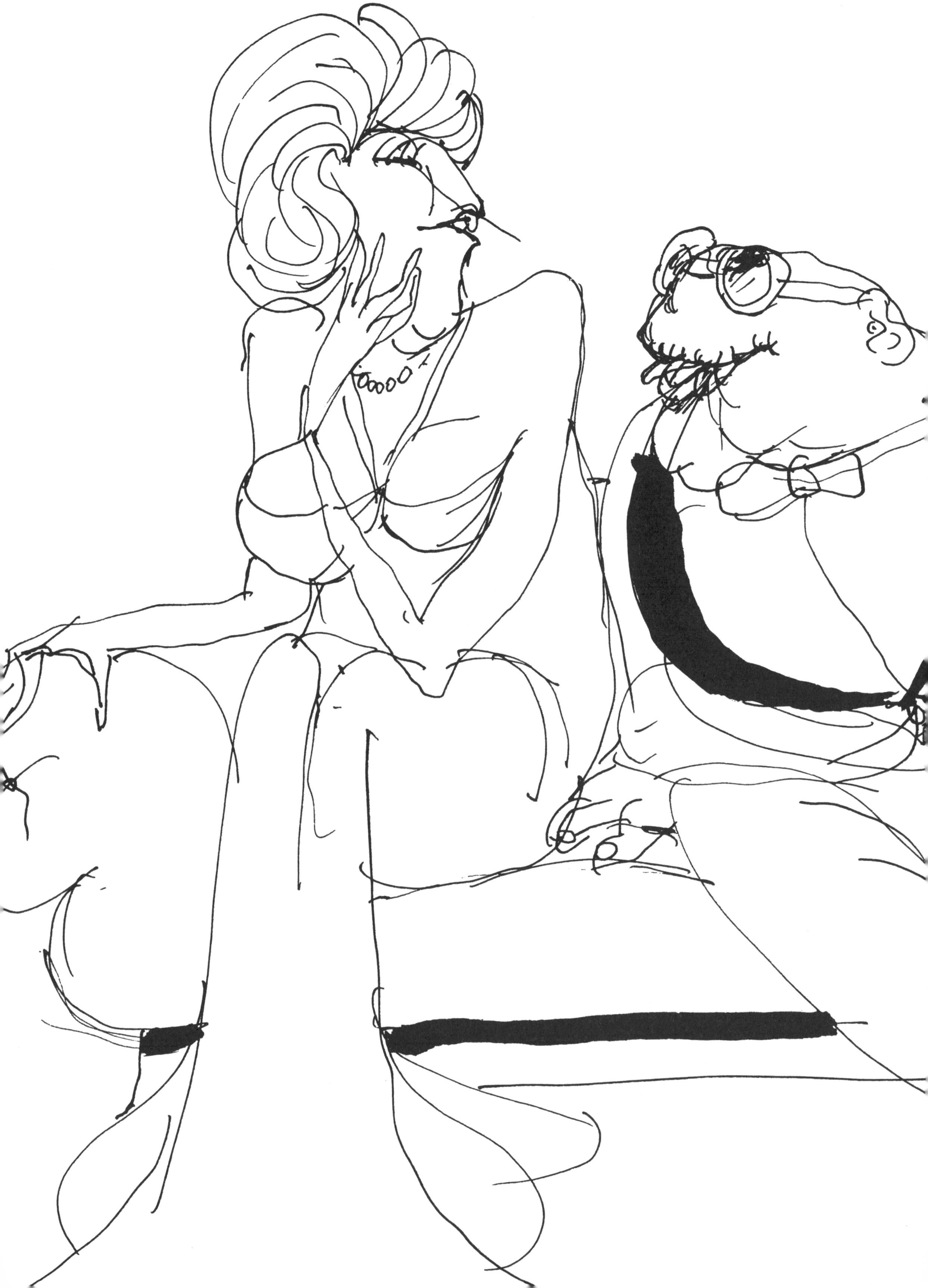

Mr. Alex Groin paying tribute to Countessa Papilla de Fogorza who was wearing a most attractive turquoise gown by Salmain—

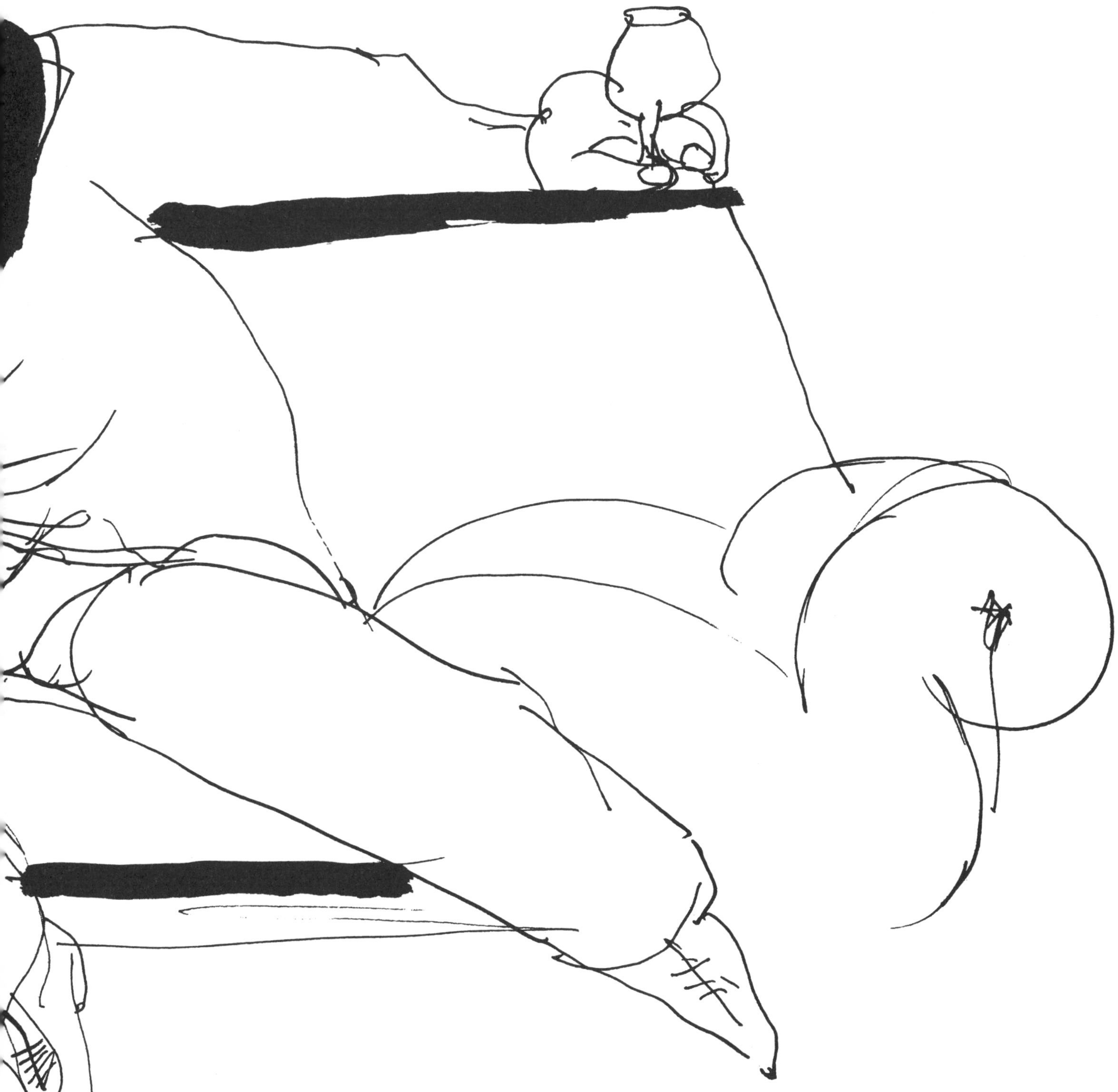

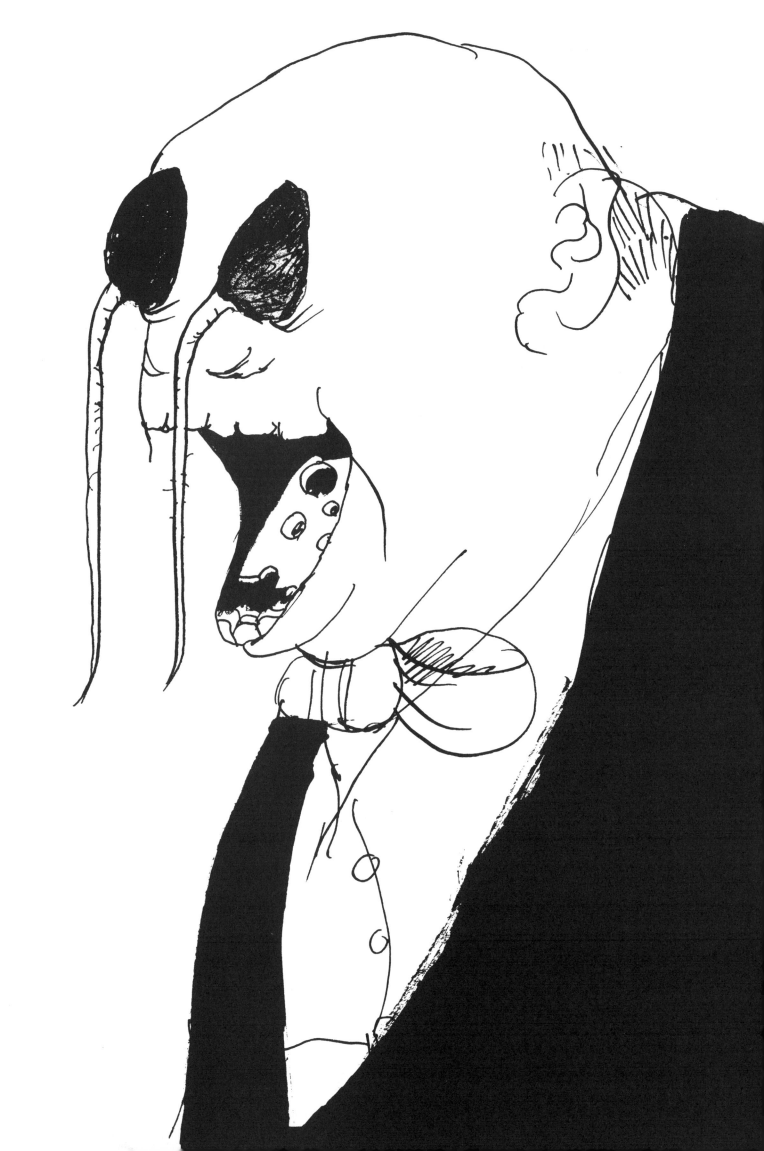

Juge Willard goiterson from Dallas about to propose
a toast to his old friend (Harvard 1915) Sen. Rockfester.

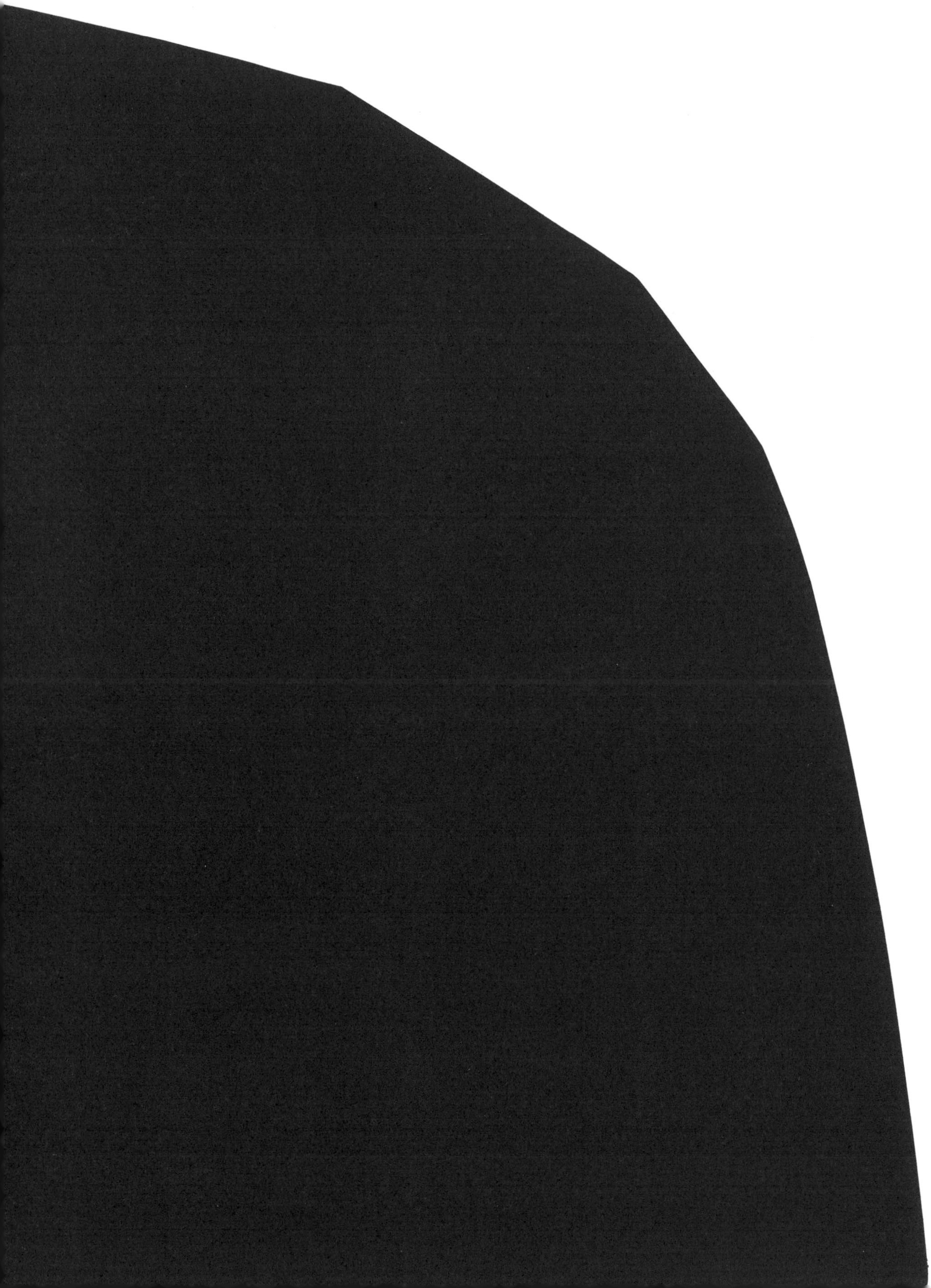

Prince Serge Rimsk-Turdovsky seen observing the scene as Lady Bronwin Sorab and Mrs Alma Crawford exit to the terrace for a breath of fresh sea-air.

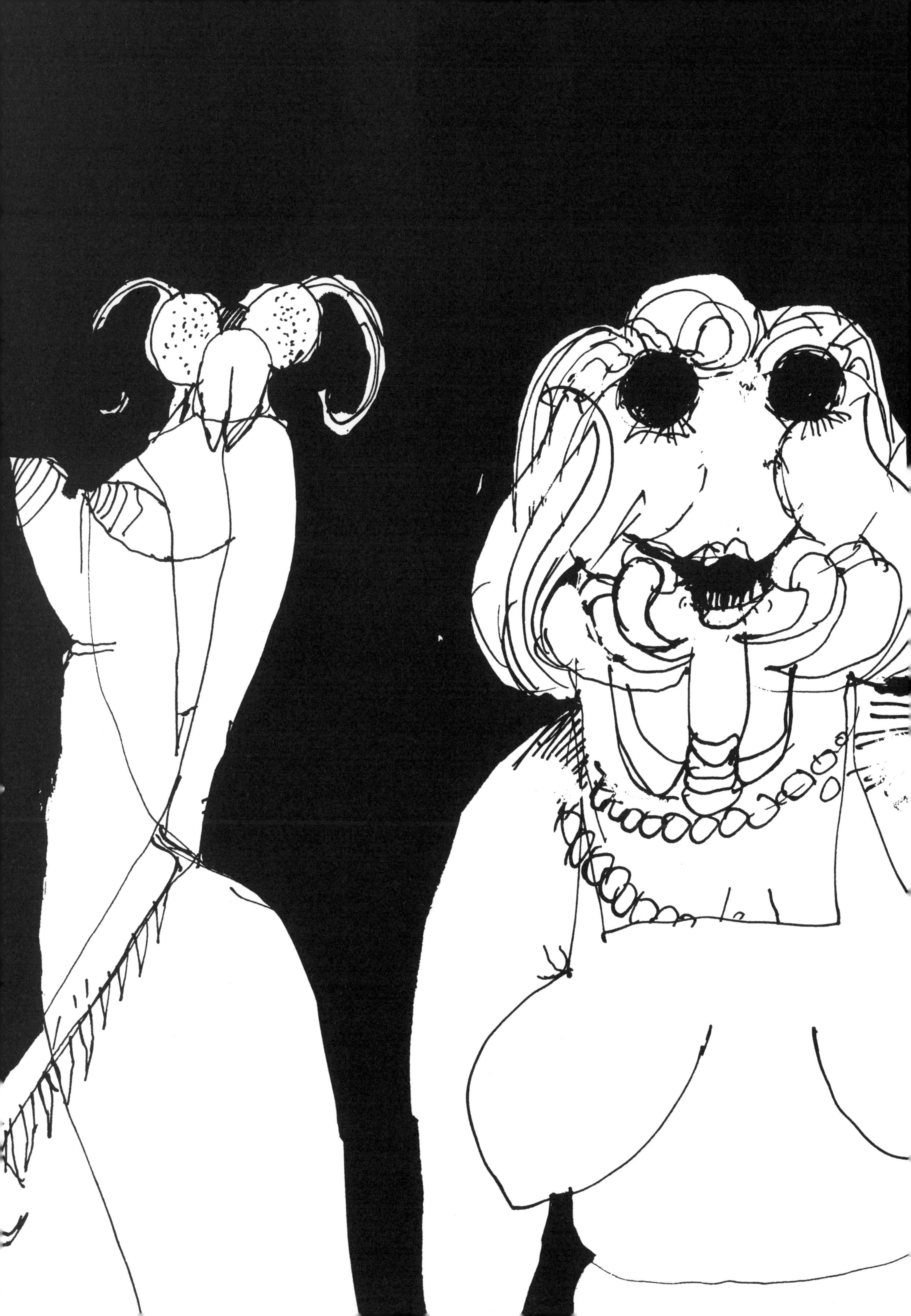

Mr. Gideon Milton Rotlieb, Los-Angeles Tycoon
and sportsman. this was the first party
attended by Mr Rotlieb since his wife's death
last aprie. She was Ann Blender from Boston

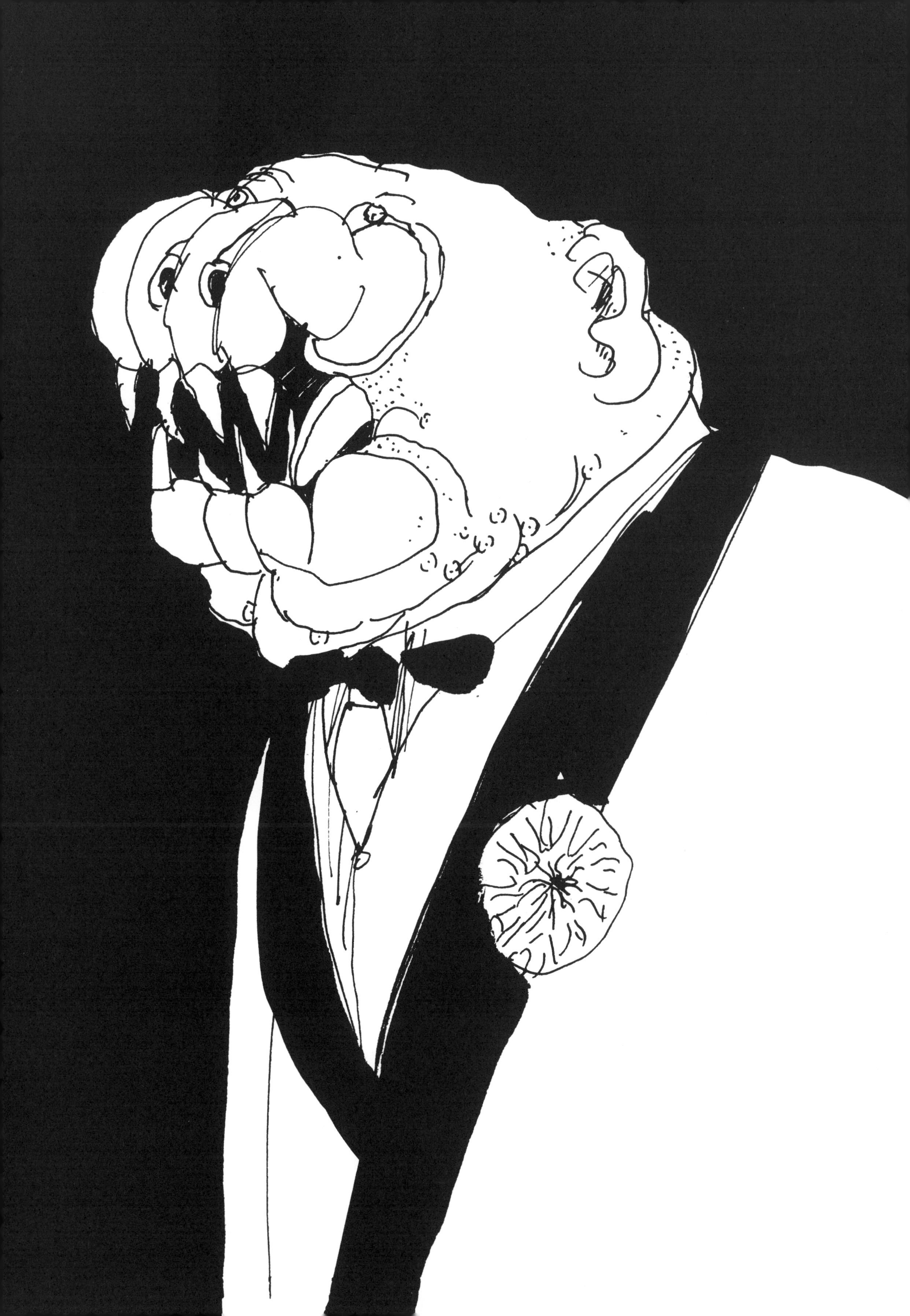

Mr. Alex Cramp Limulus and his wife Chrysales who just drove in from Manhattan.

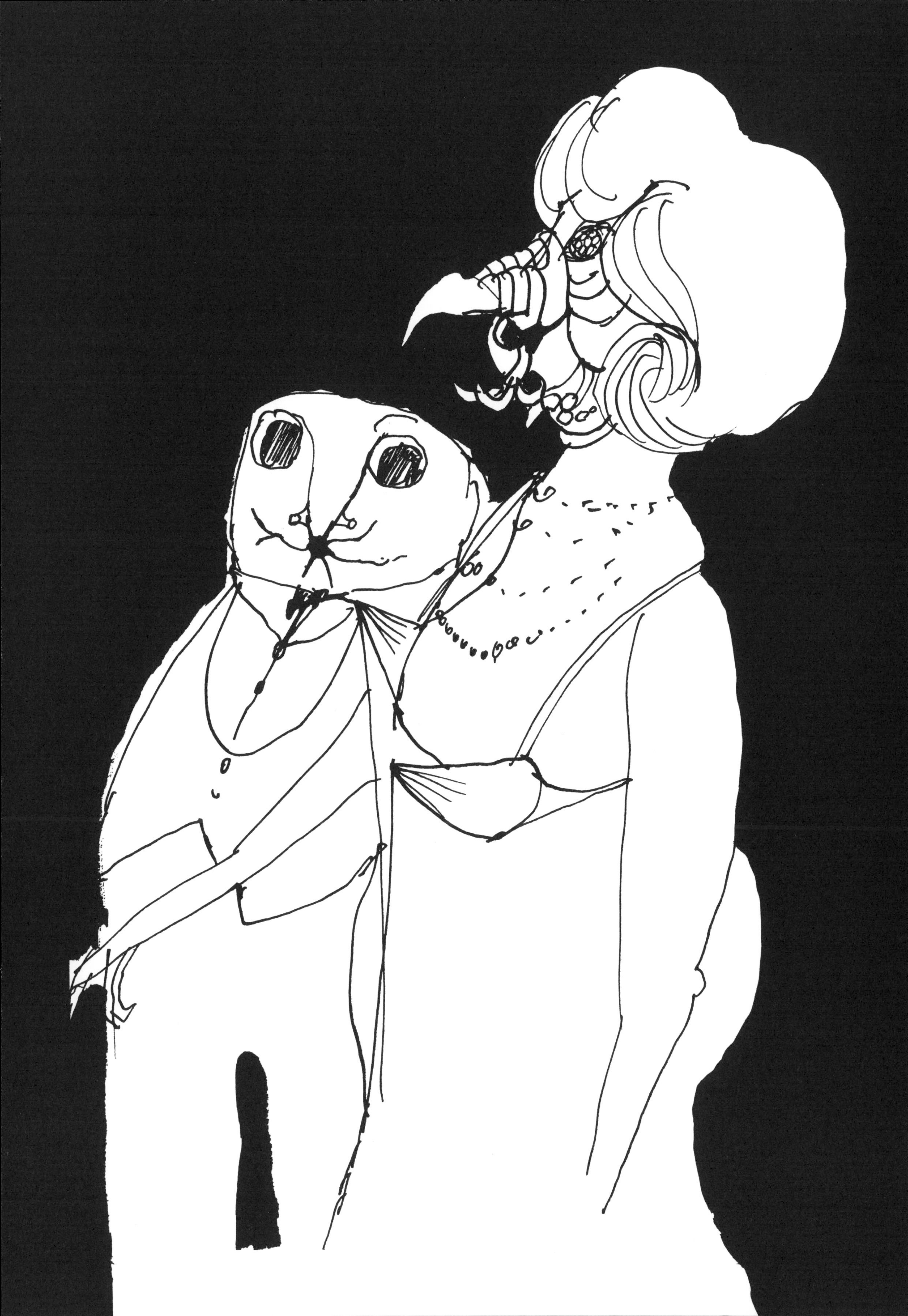

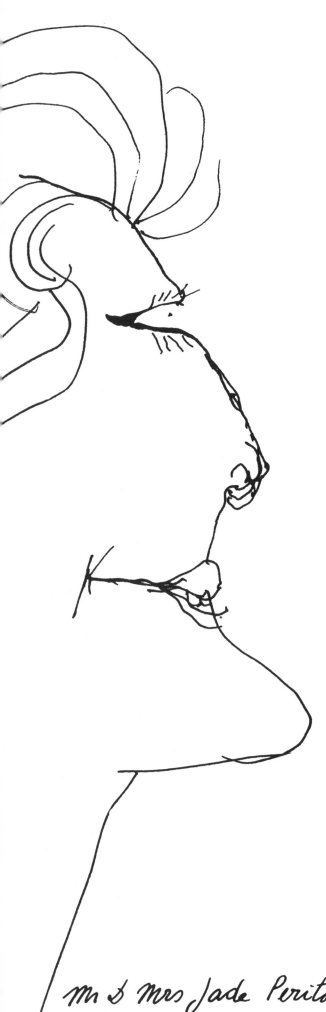

Mr & Mrs Jade Periton and Miss Pinna Scrothill (middle)
who acquainted last year in Cannes are surprised to
meet again. —

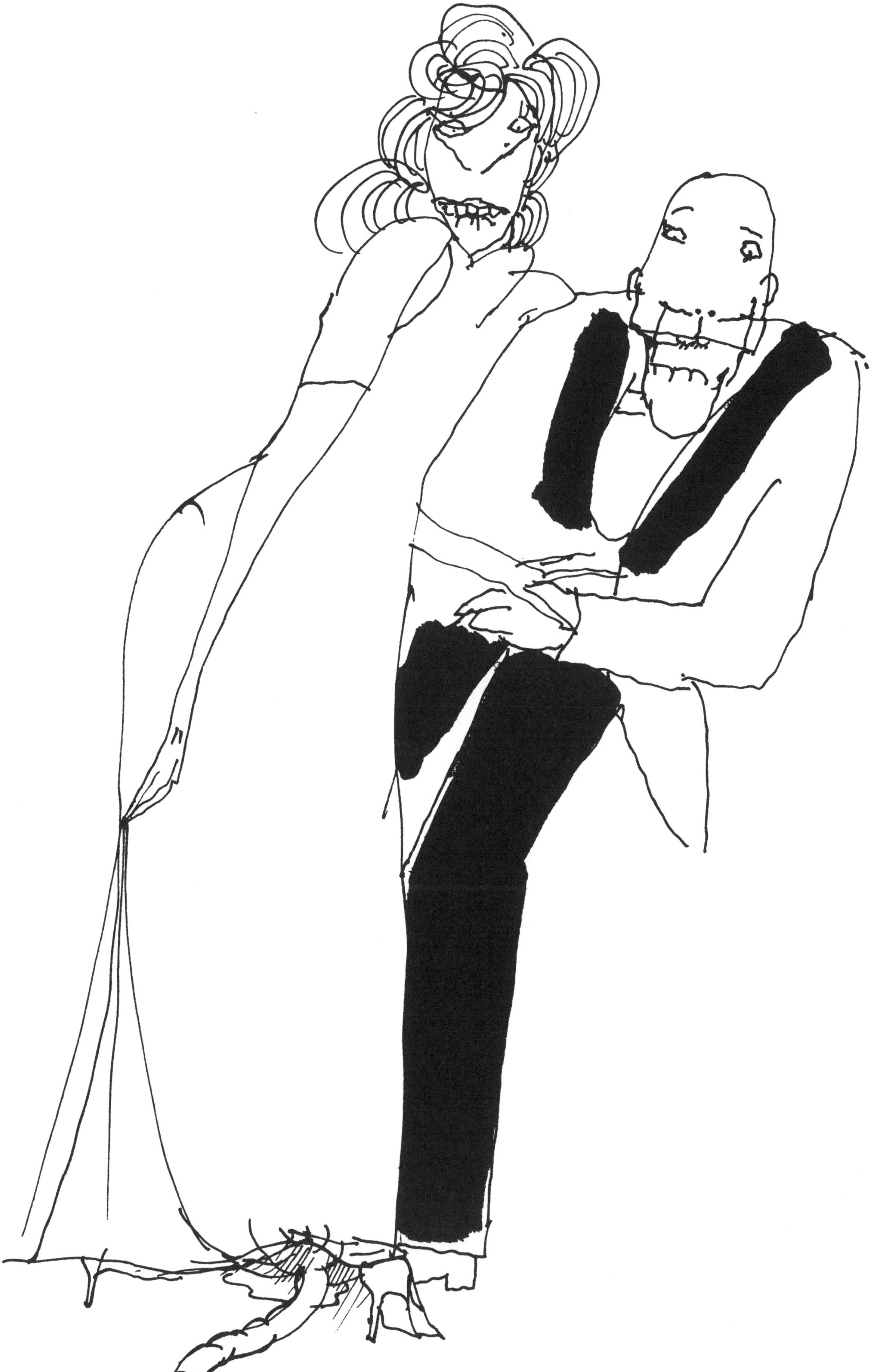

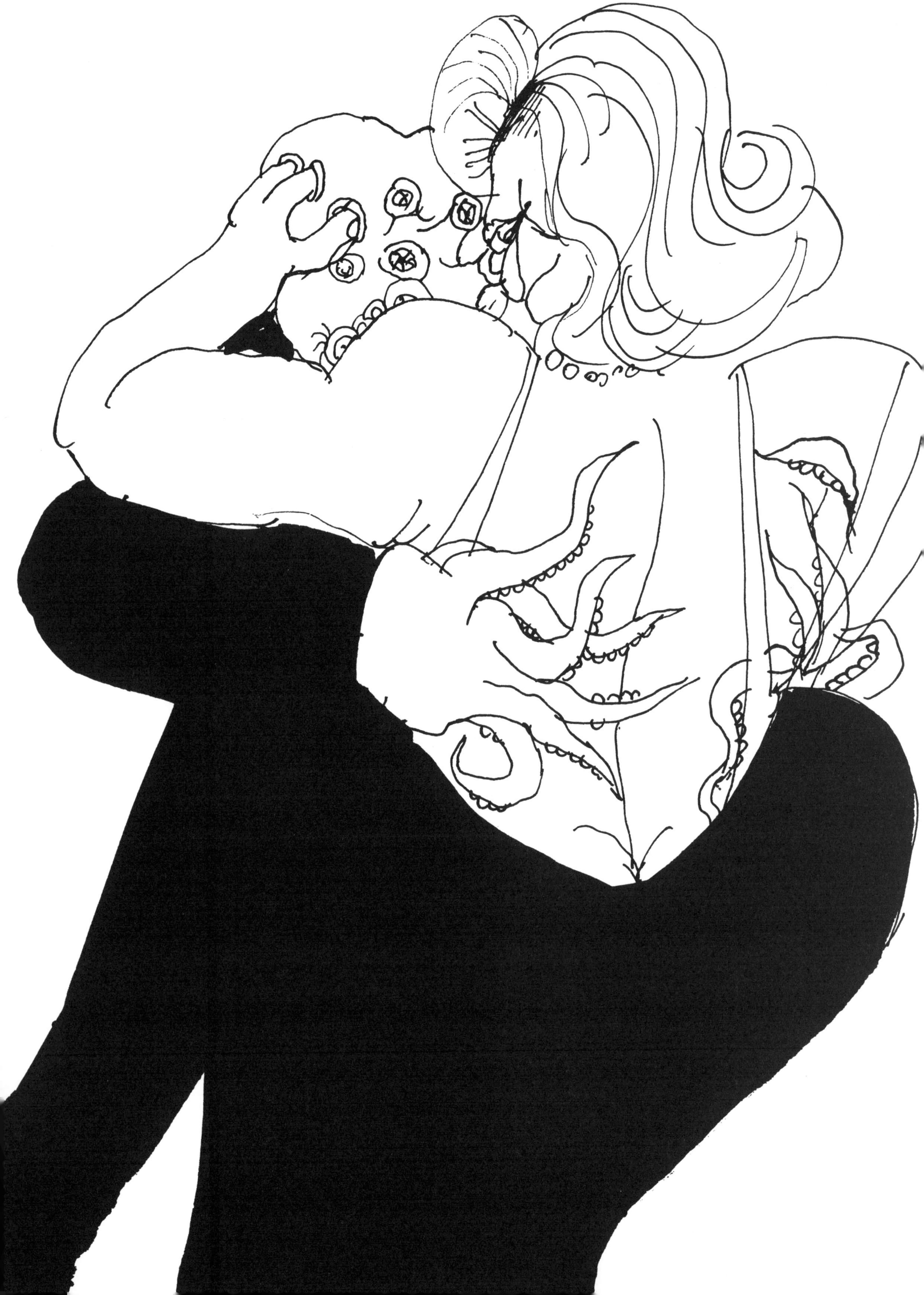

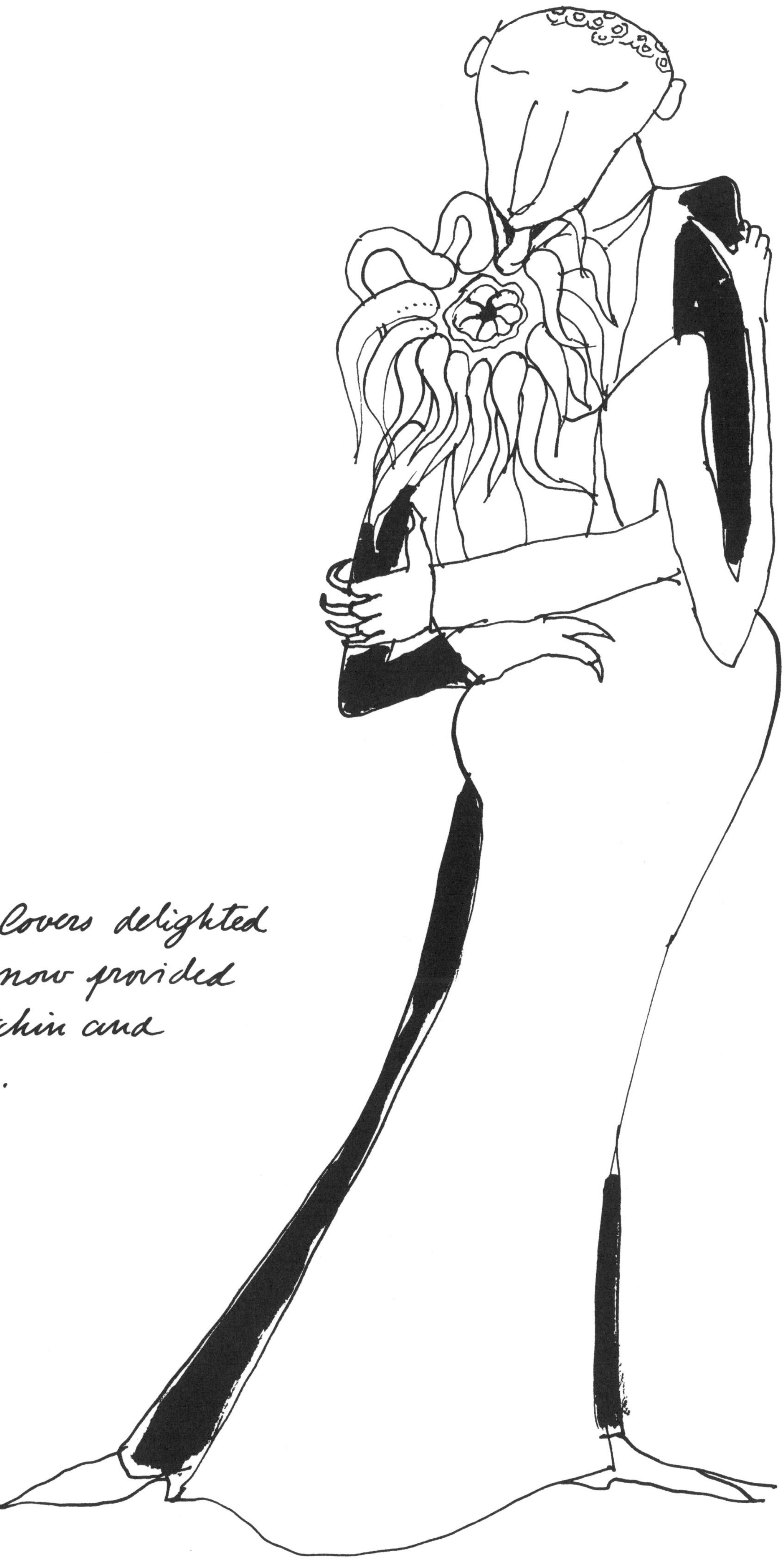

Gliding dance lovers delighted
by the moods now provided
by Peter Butchin and
his orchestra.

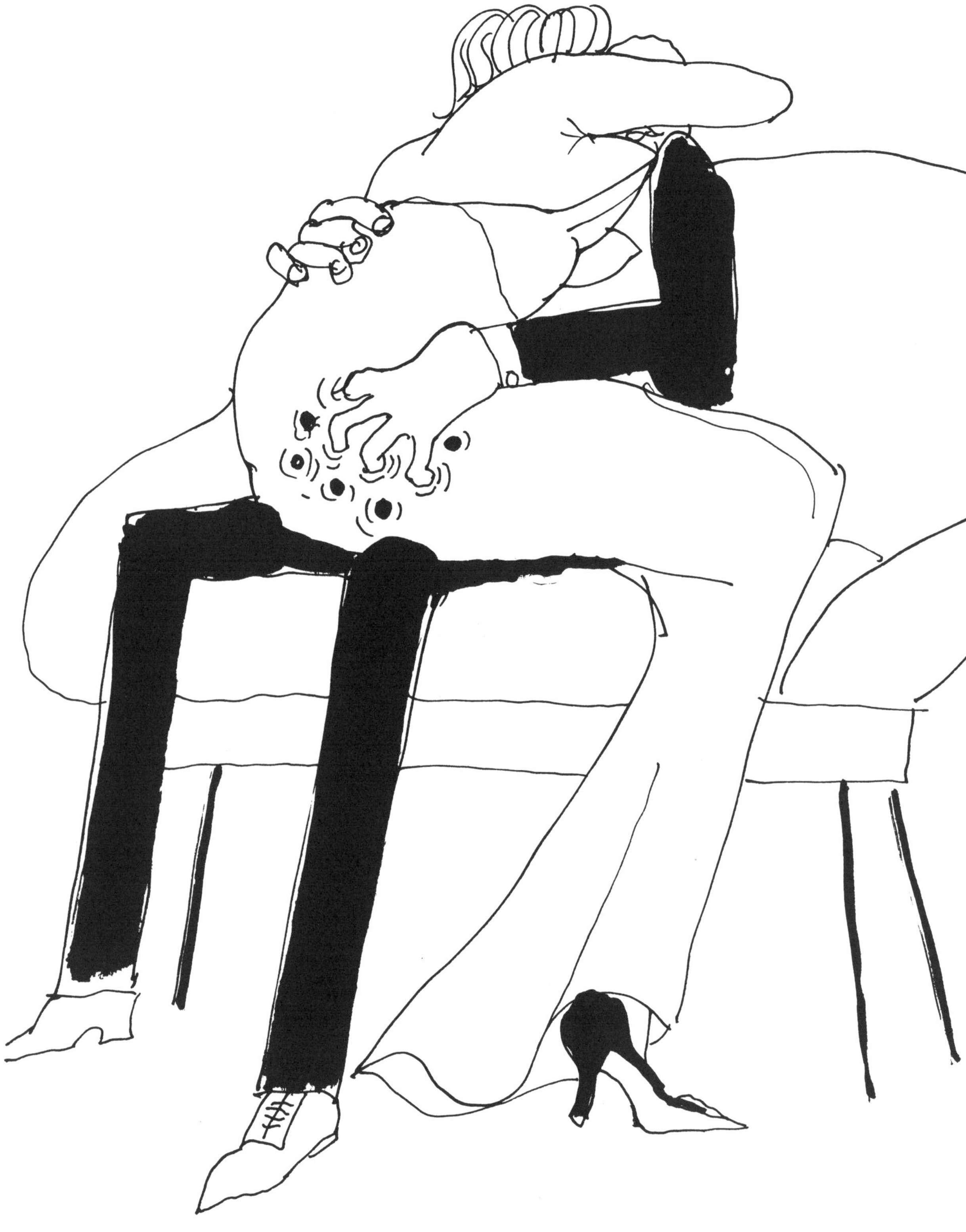

A congenial athmosphere was prevailing throughout.

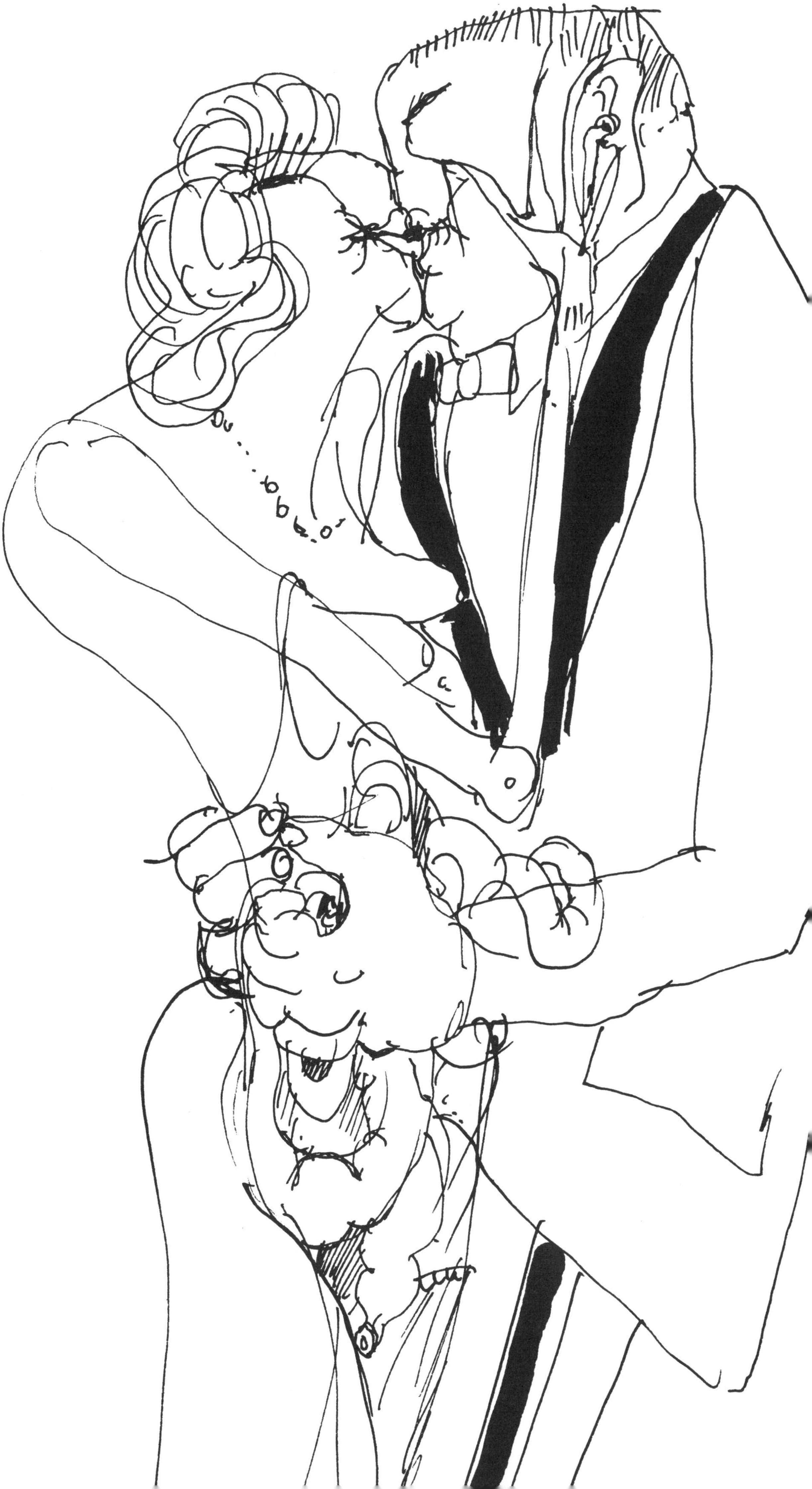

Mr. Roy Fumblethumb entertaining Mrs. Joyce Rampage with his accounts of his last trip in Japan

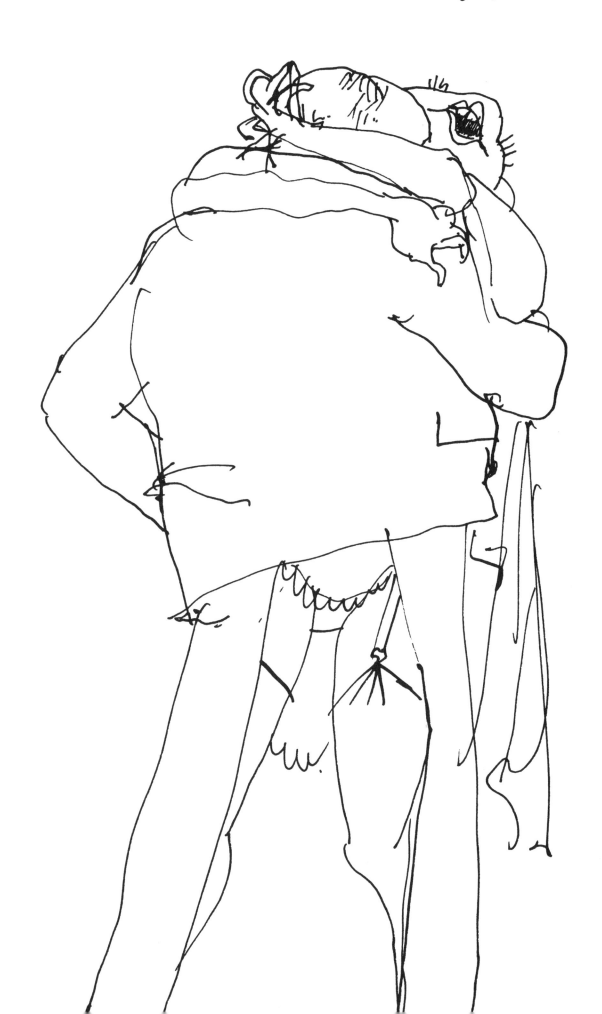

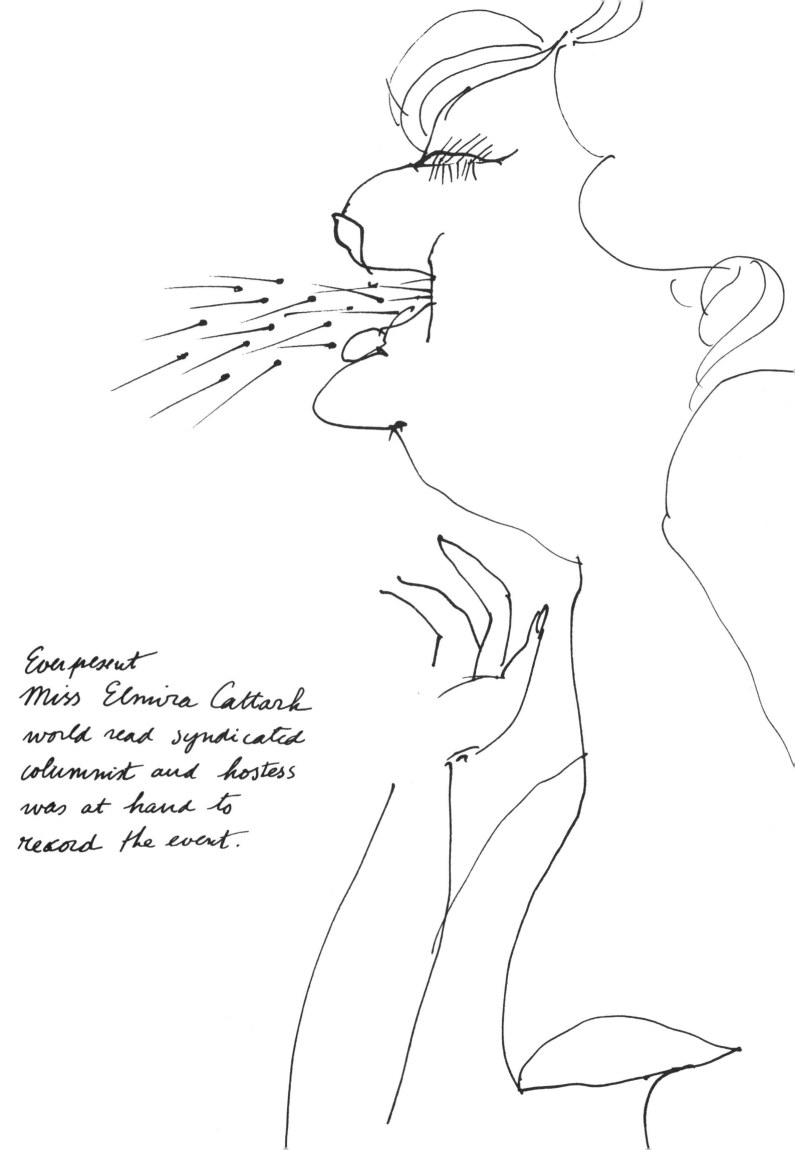

Everpresent
Miss Elmira Cattark
world read syndicated
columnist and hostess
was at hand to
record the event.

The hit of the evening provided by the impressive performance of world famous soprano Miss Inge Horn who out did herself in her famous rendering of Mimi's aria from "Fellatia Rusticana"

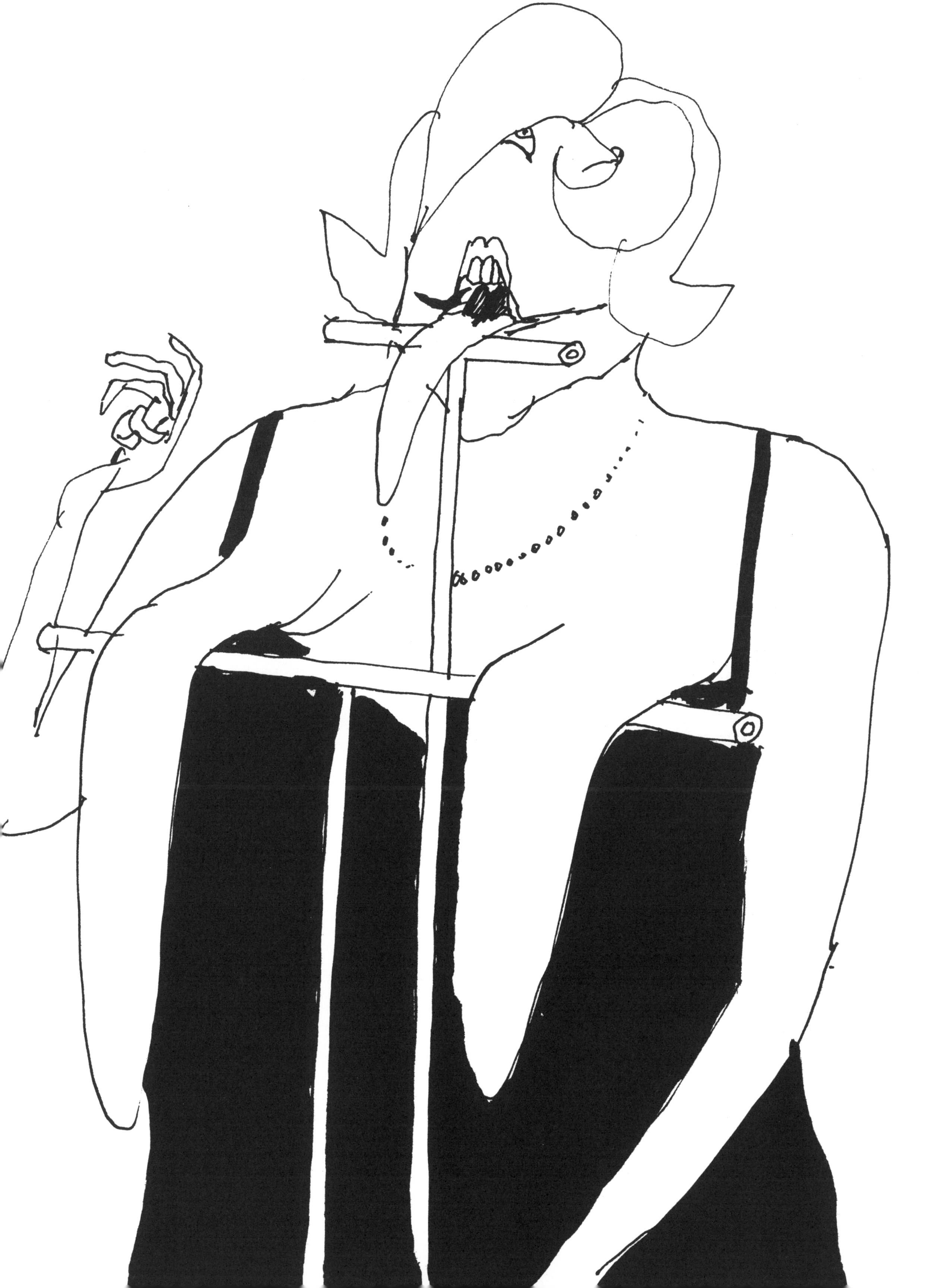

Mr. Long Folds of Houston introducing some of the lad

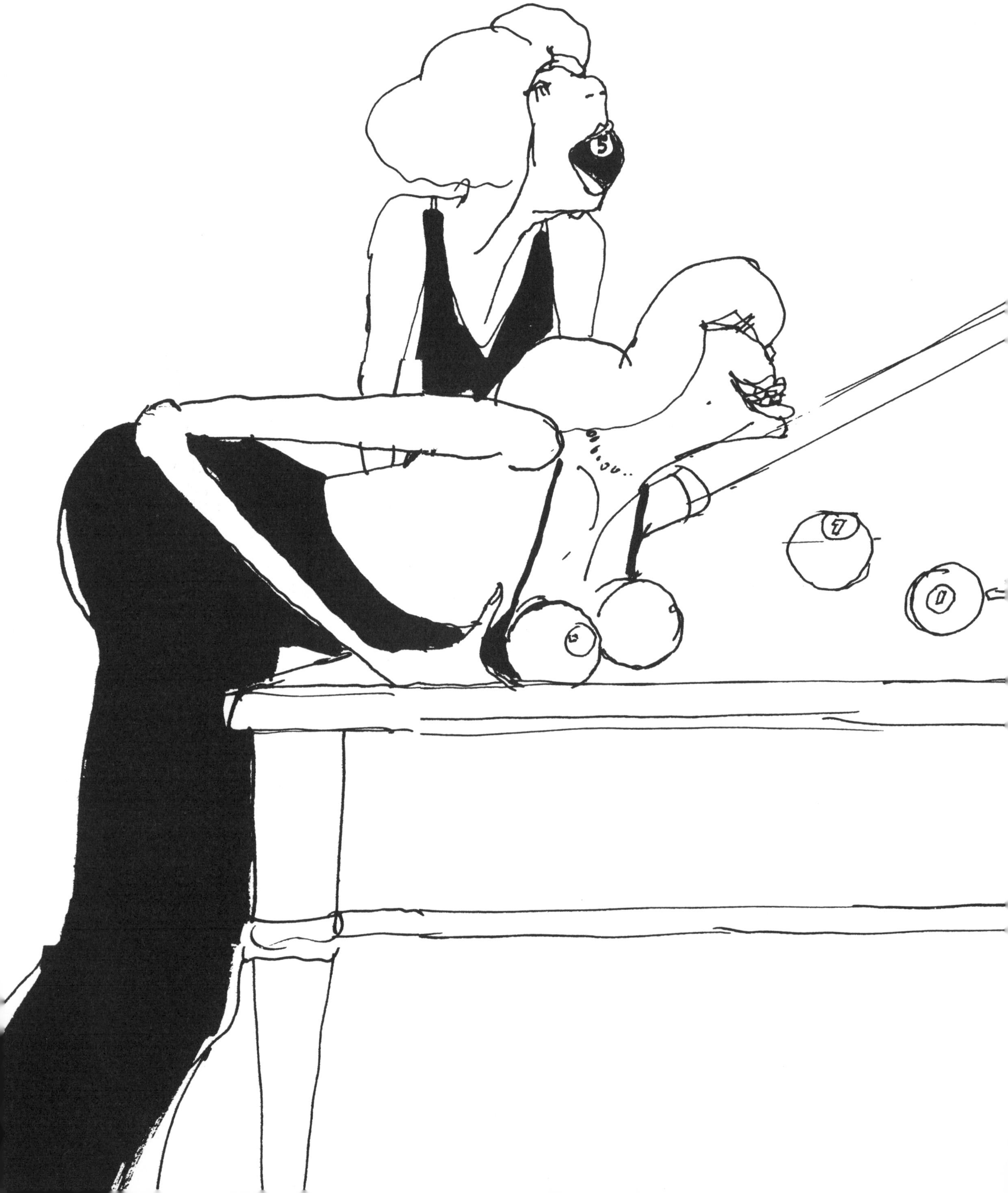
5
7
8

to the pleasures of billiards

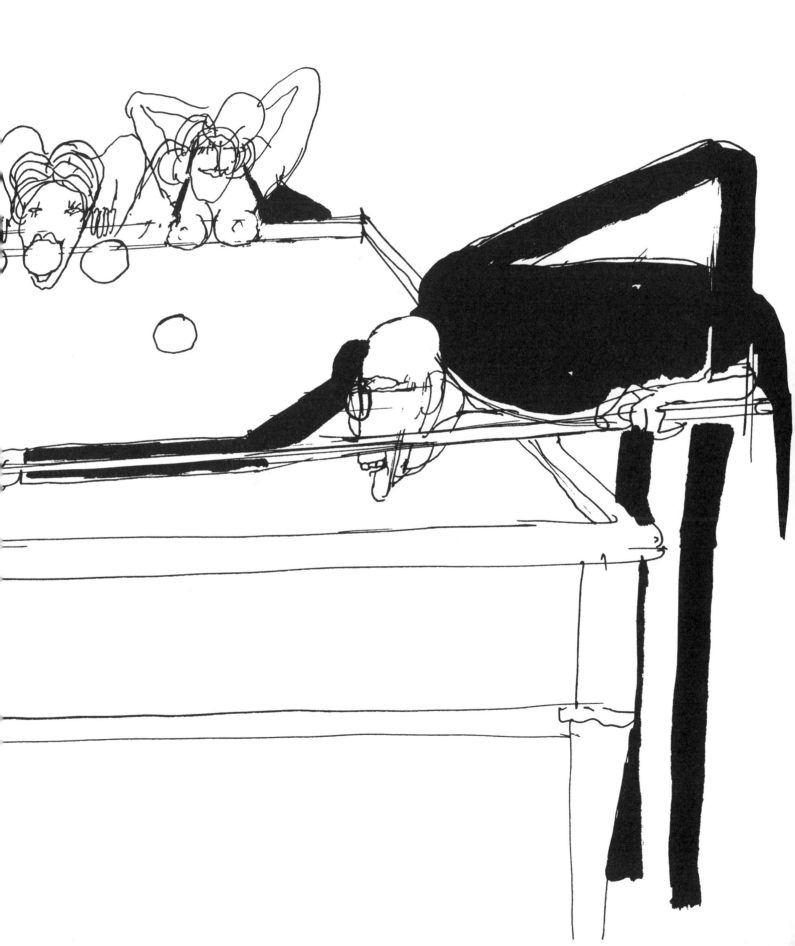

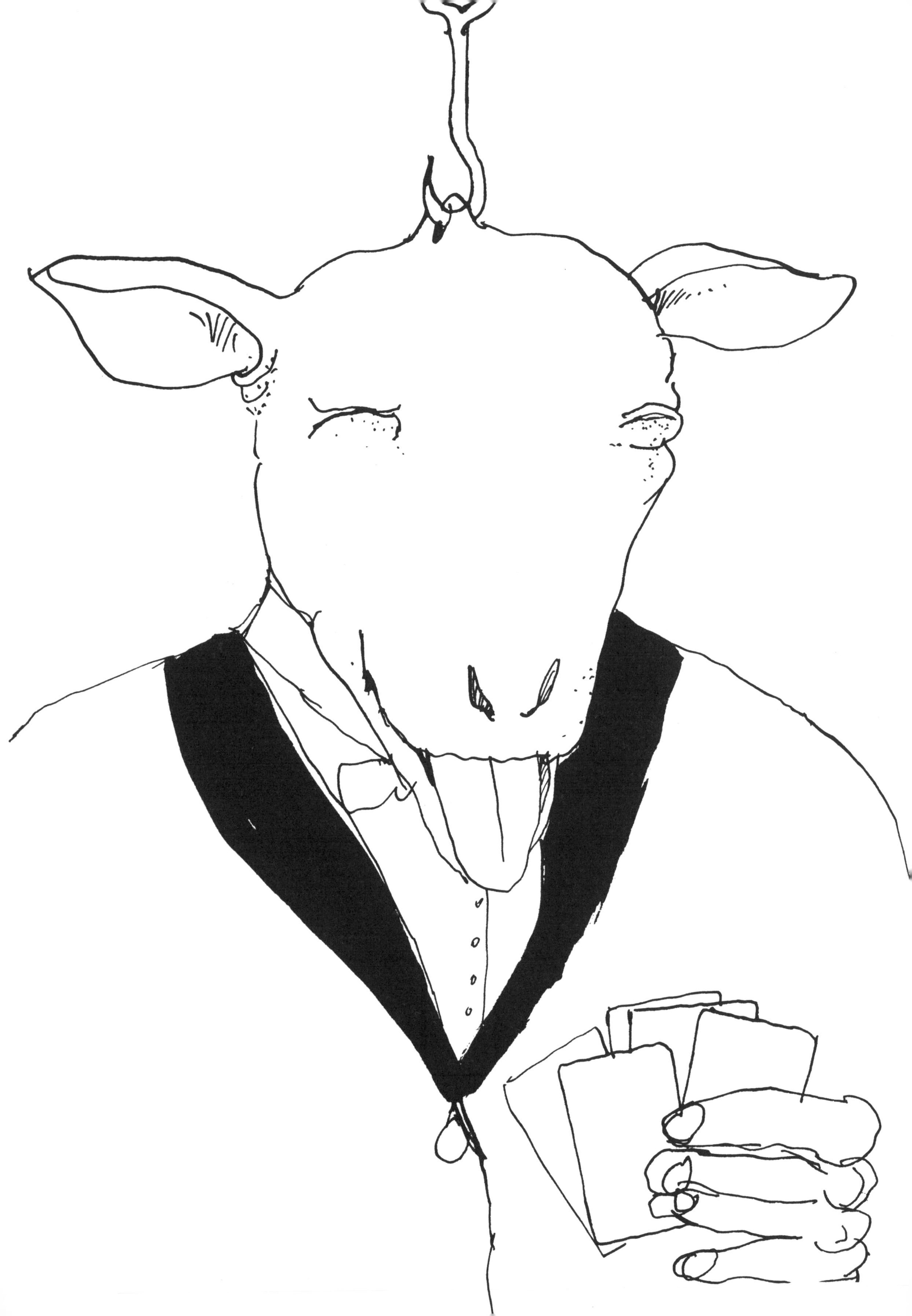

Meatpacking magnate Herman Urpel
at the bridge table..

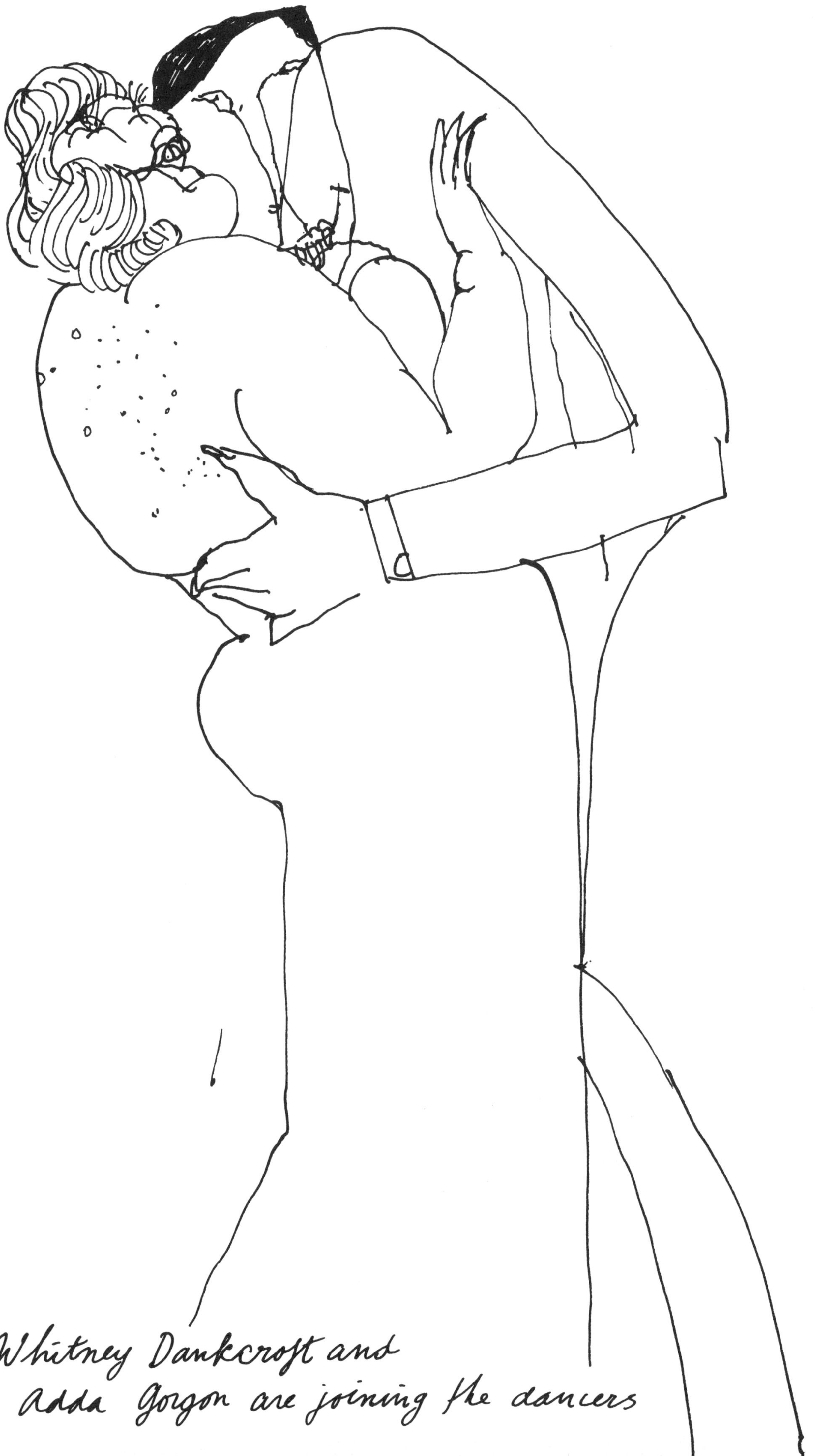

Mr. Whitney Dankcroft and
Mrs Adda Gorgon are joining the dancers

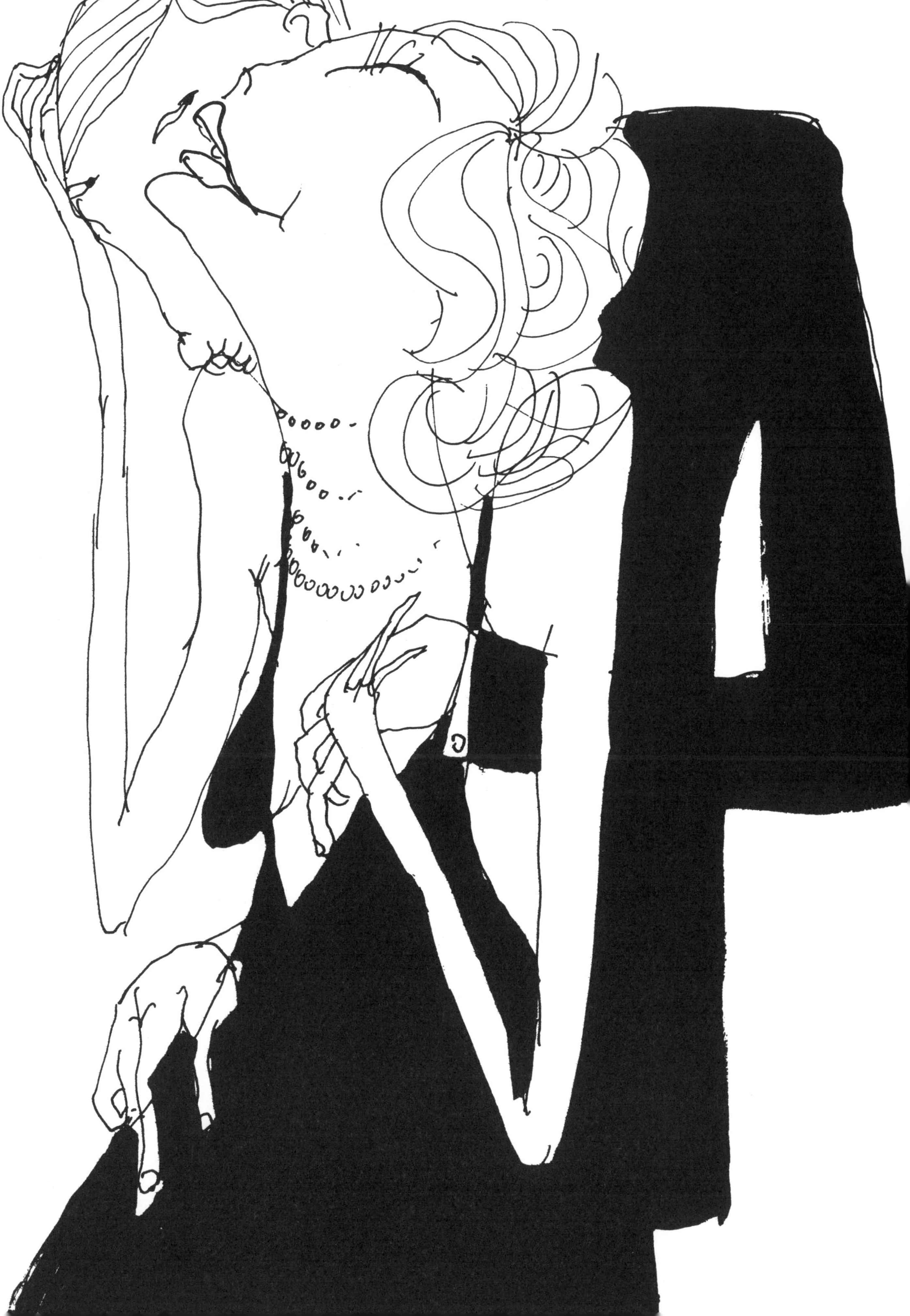

Jay C. Meatus & Miss Sophie Derm
listening to the music
in a quiet moment

Miss Dana Hogpuss Hohldeck
distinguished fashion leader is discussing new
trends in Evening wear

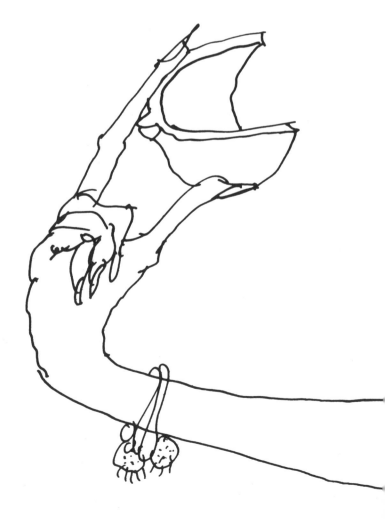

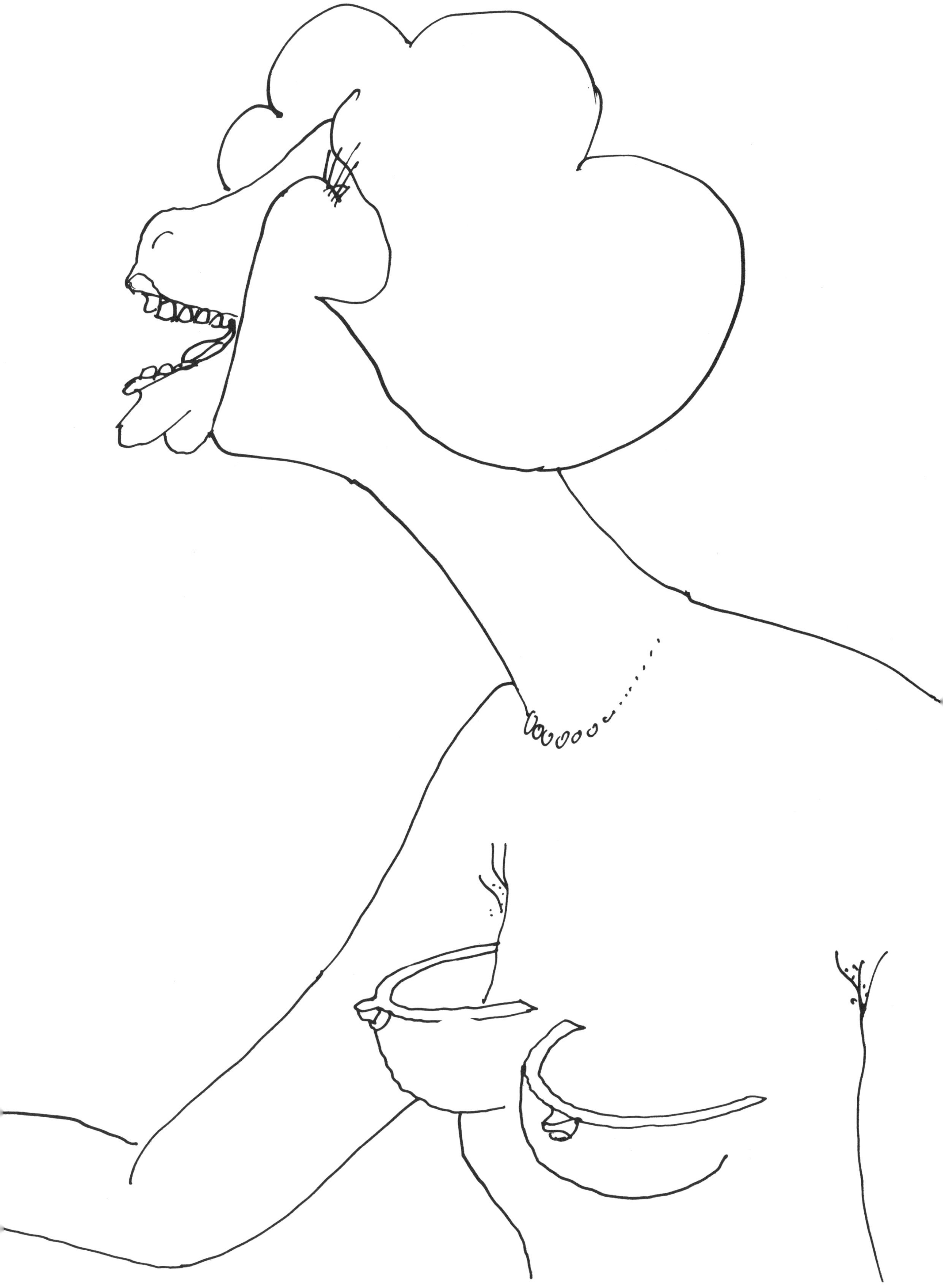

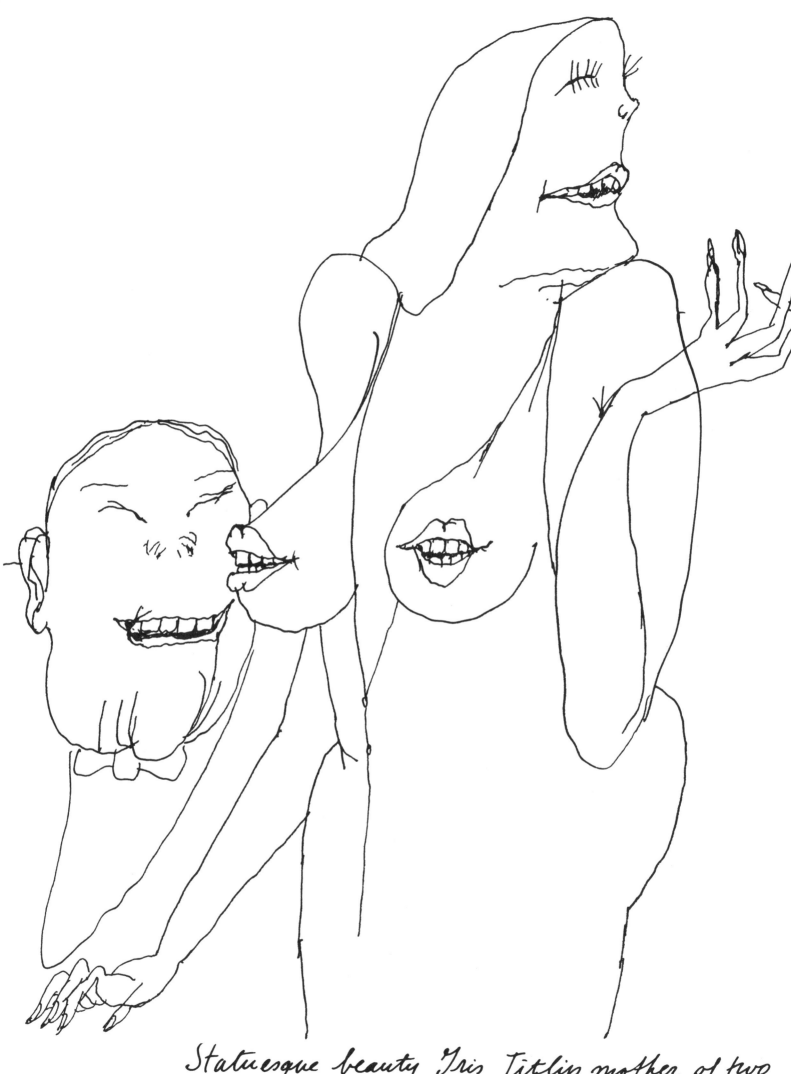

Statuesque beauty Iris Titlip mother of two

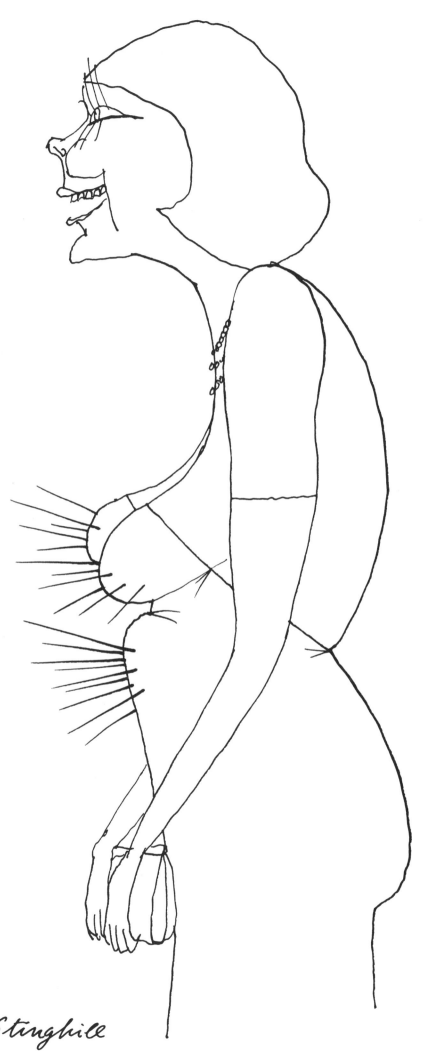

and her sister Spina Stinghill

A delicious midnight buffet provided by the kitchens of world famous „ Papillion „ restaurant in Manhattan.

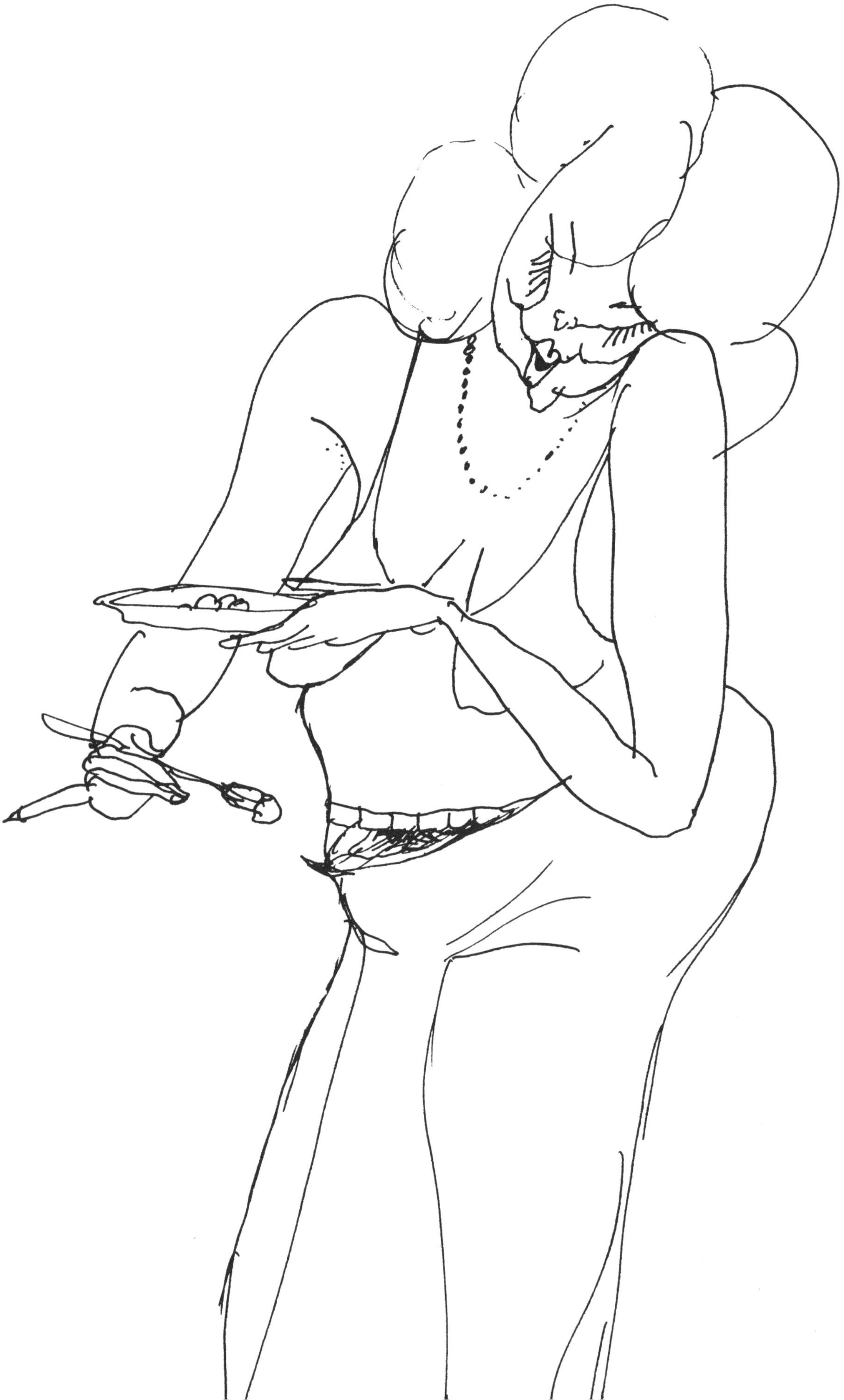

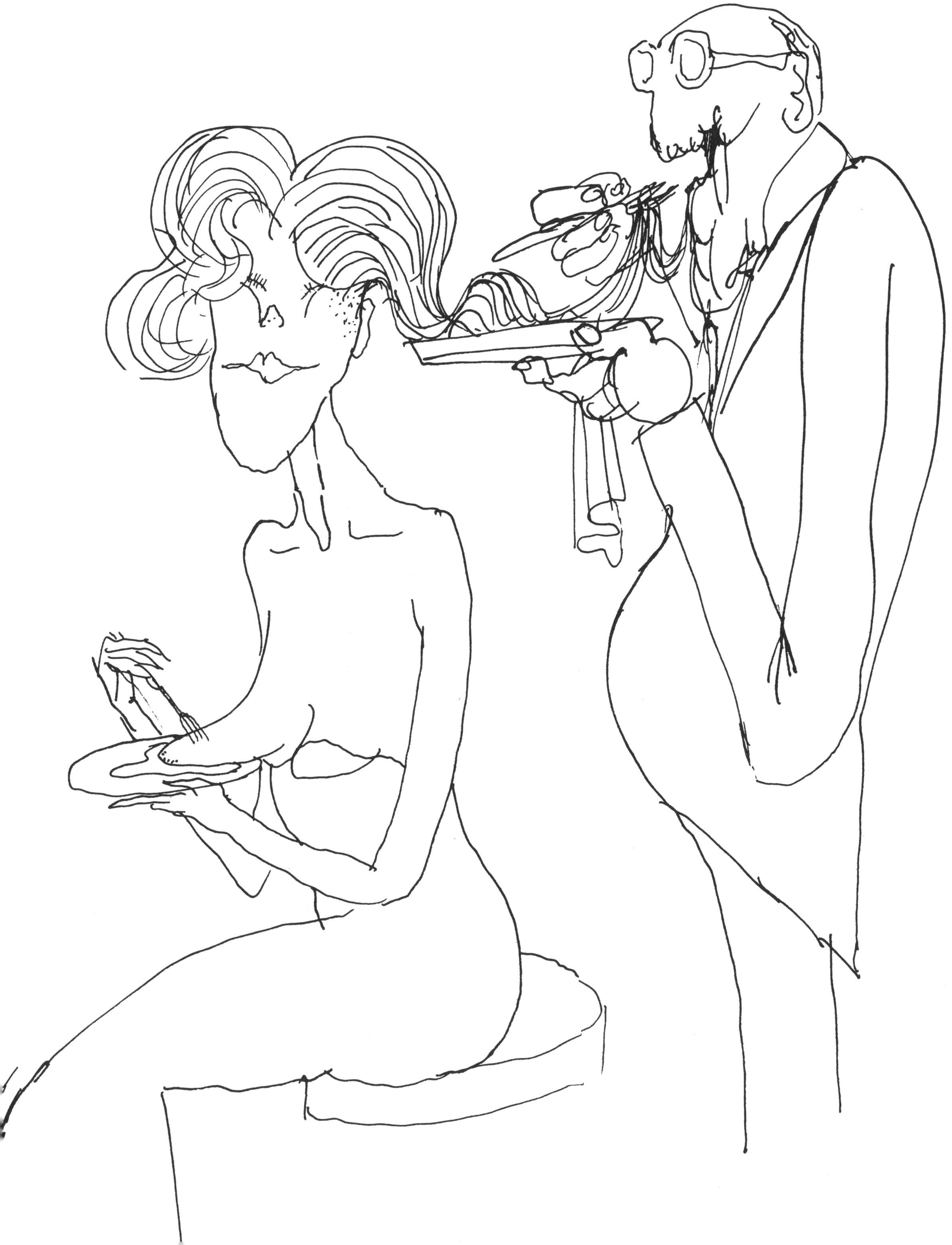

A personal touch of hospitality provided by
Mrs. Day Gutney-Sprawling passing hors d'oeuvres.
Mrs Gutney-Sprawling is the sister of the hosters and
will be spending the summer here in East Hampton.

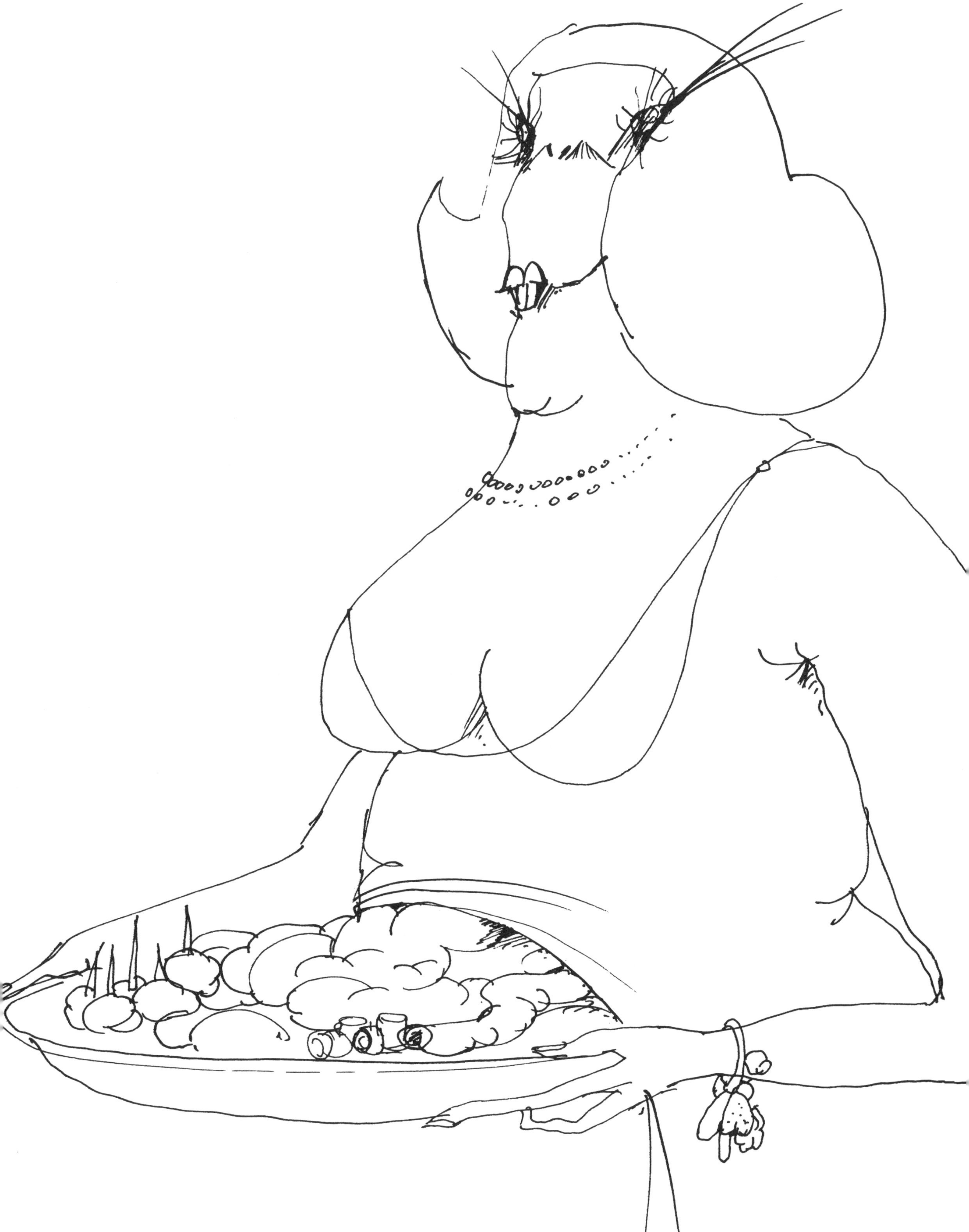

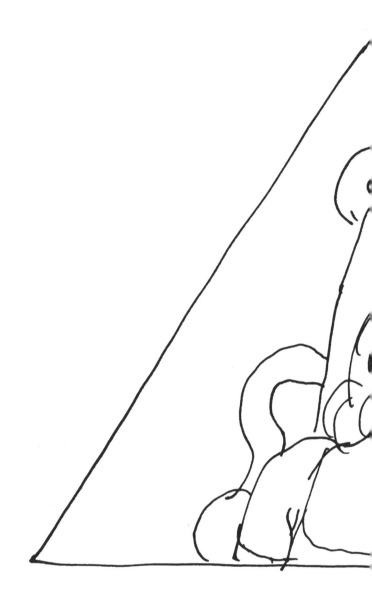

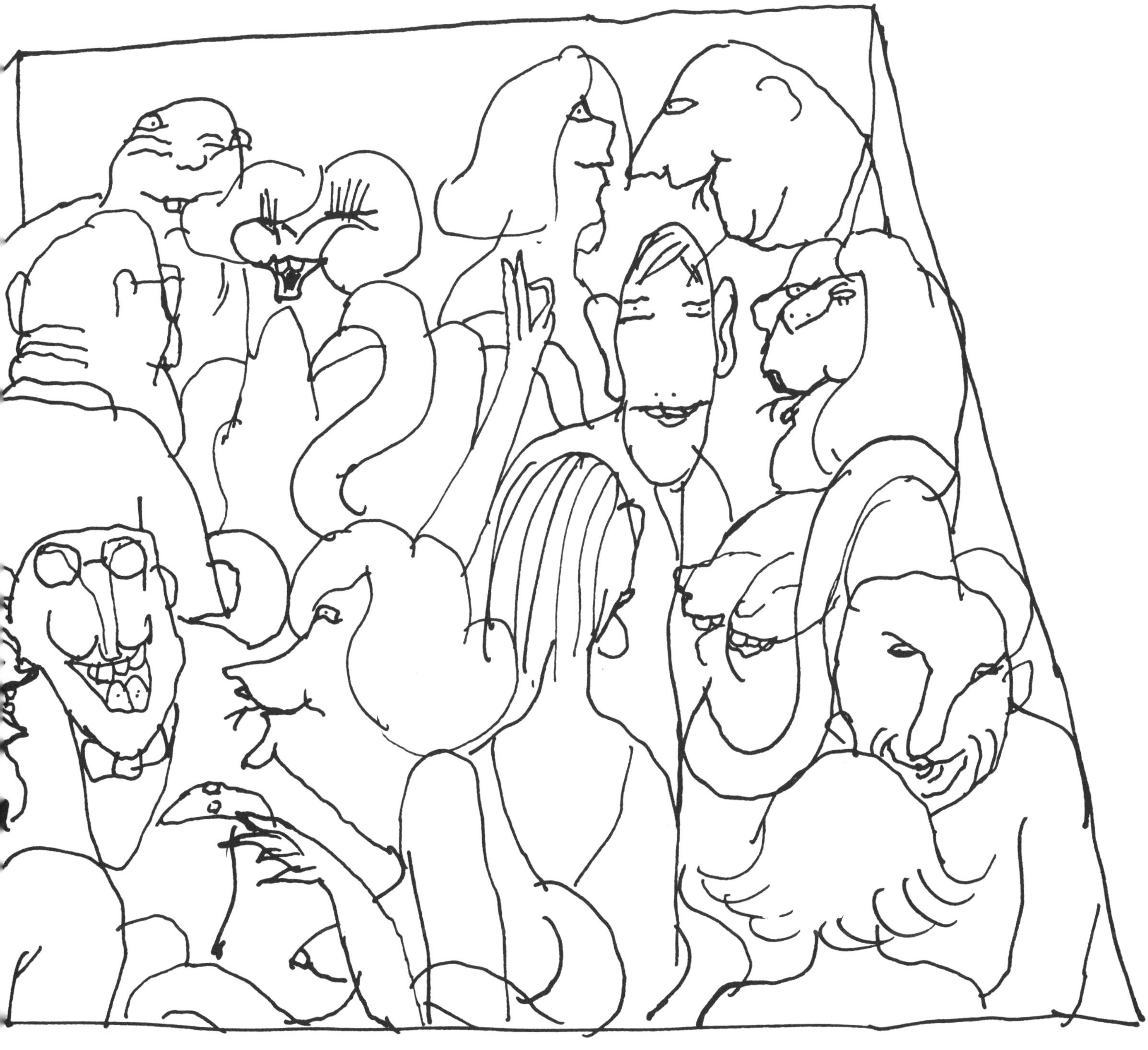

Busy-bee conversations in the den where personalities of the litterary world seem to have gathered.

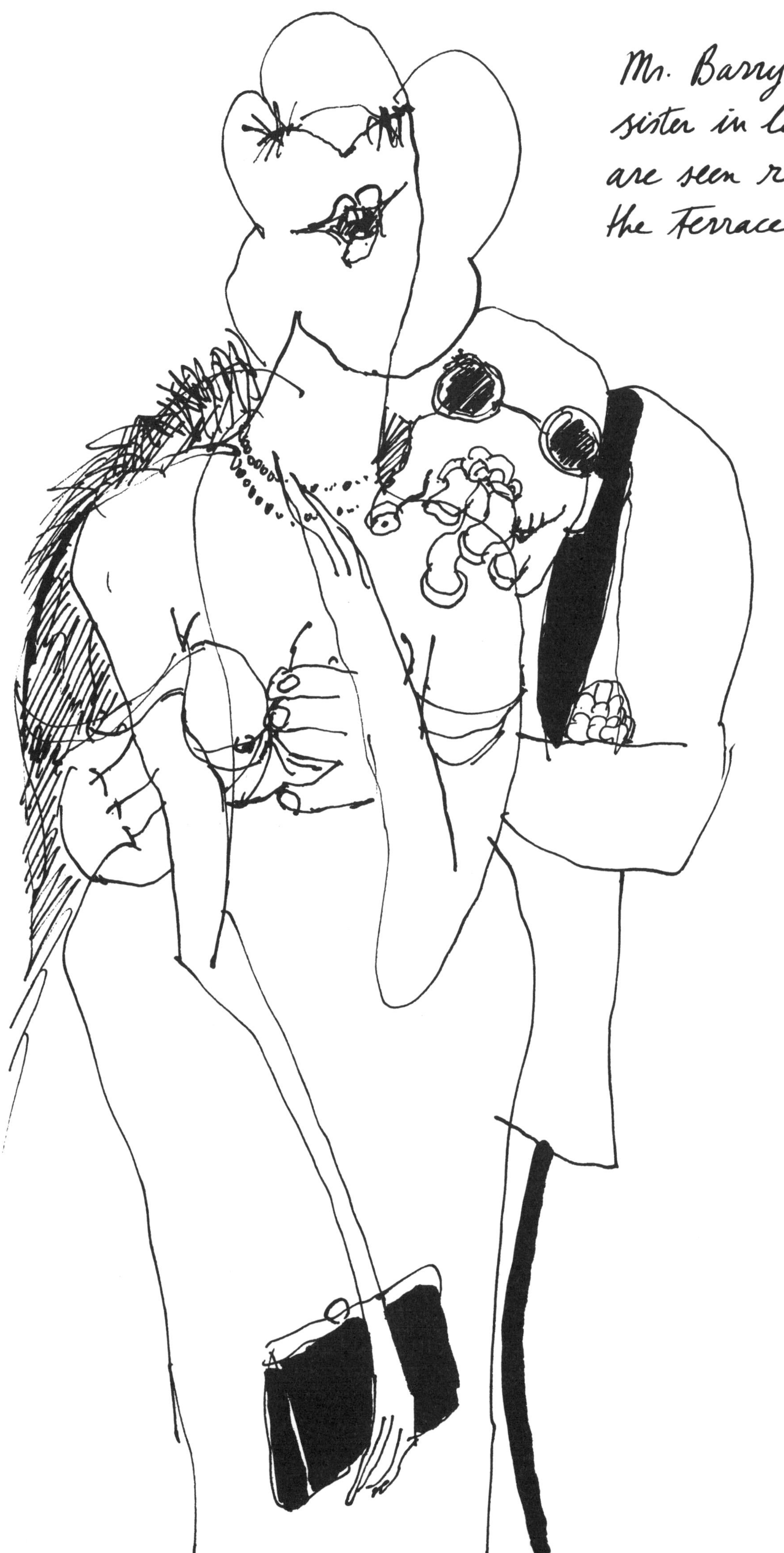

Mr. Barry Leech and his sister in law Lorna Leech are seen returning from the Terrace.

Broadway producer David Hitheimer talking shop with Mr. Aldrich Blisterford well known Broadway angel

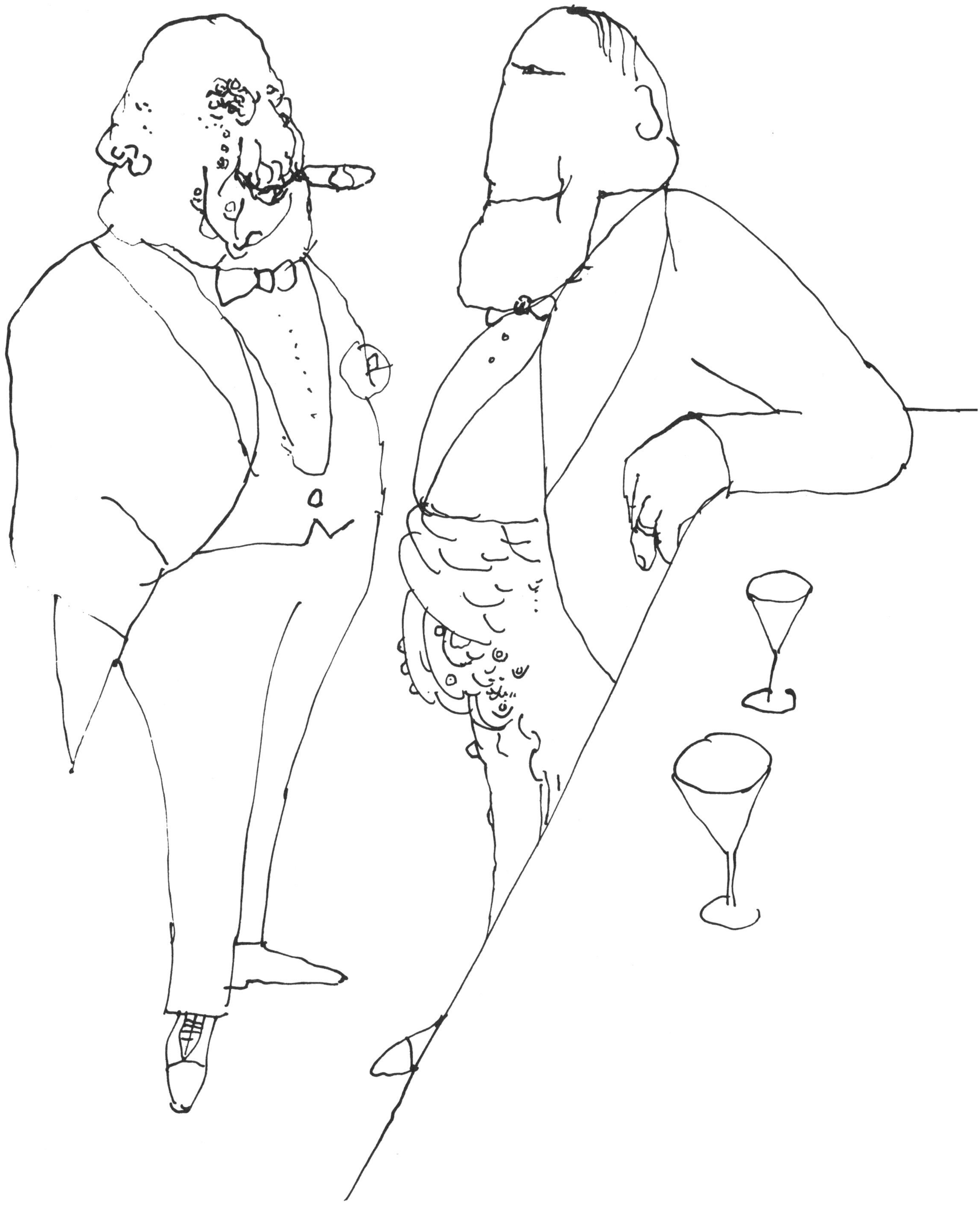

Old friends meet again.
Mr. Arthur Gopher and Miss Susan Osprey
both patrons of the Audubon society.

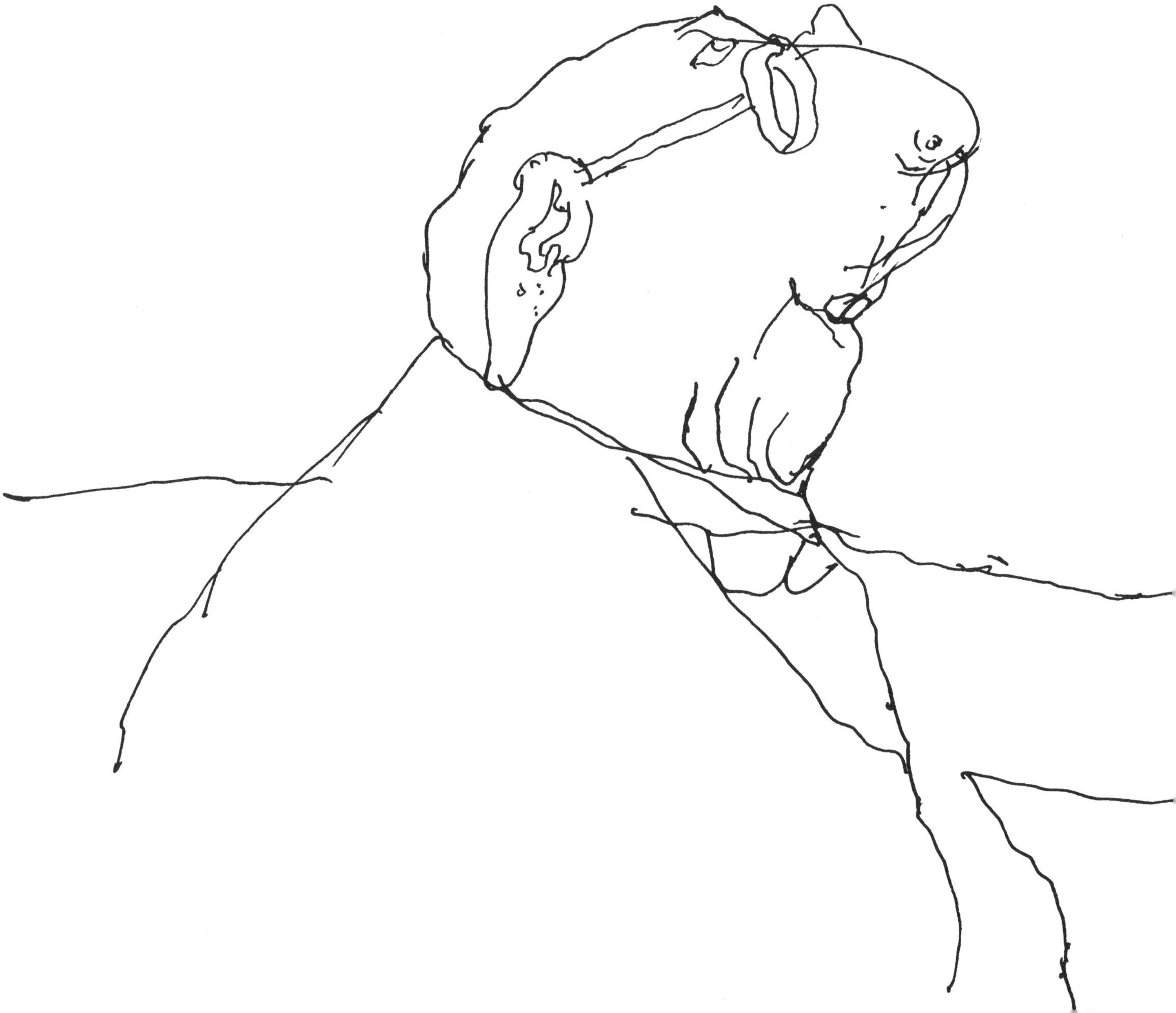

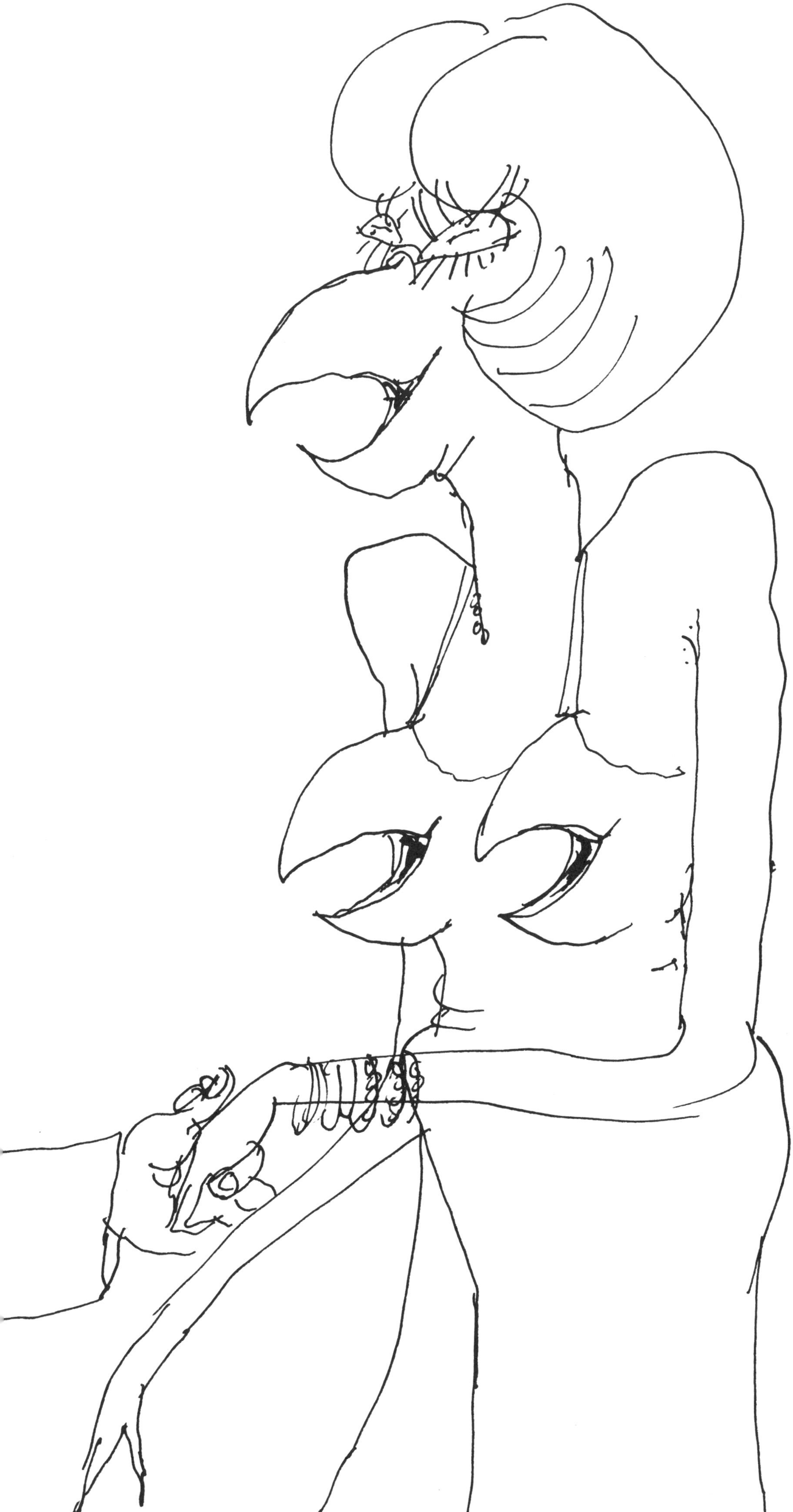

Inseperable Mr. & Mrs. Graham Fillingsworth have now been married eight years. they live in Manhattan when not cruising in their yacht "Selma" named after Mrs Fillingsworth.

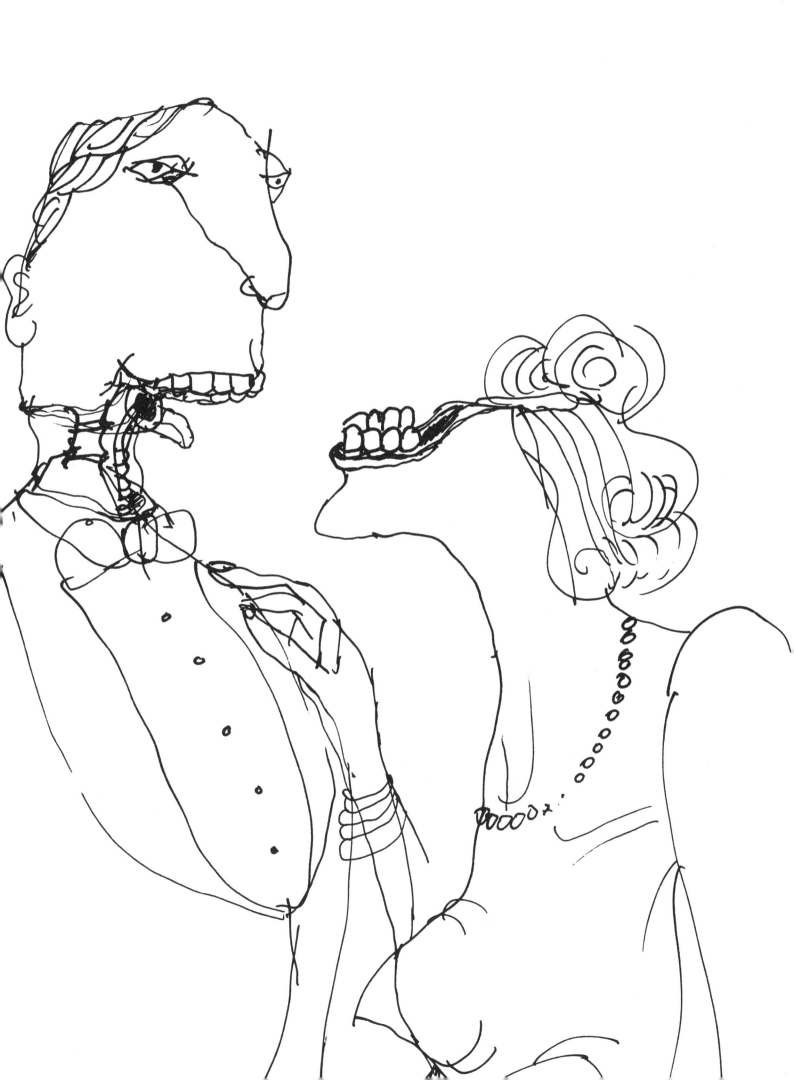

Miss. Ann Van Flooze the hostess' younger daughter
passing the cigars. She is here with
Mr. Gerald Letch from Miami and N.Y.

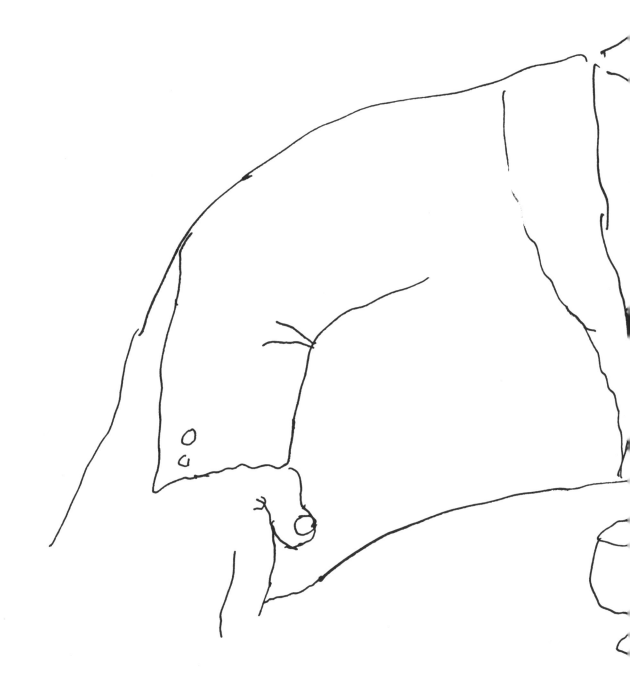

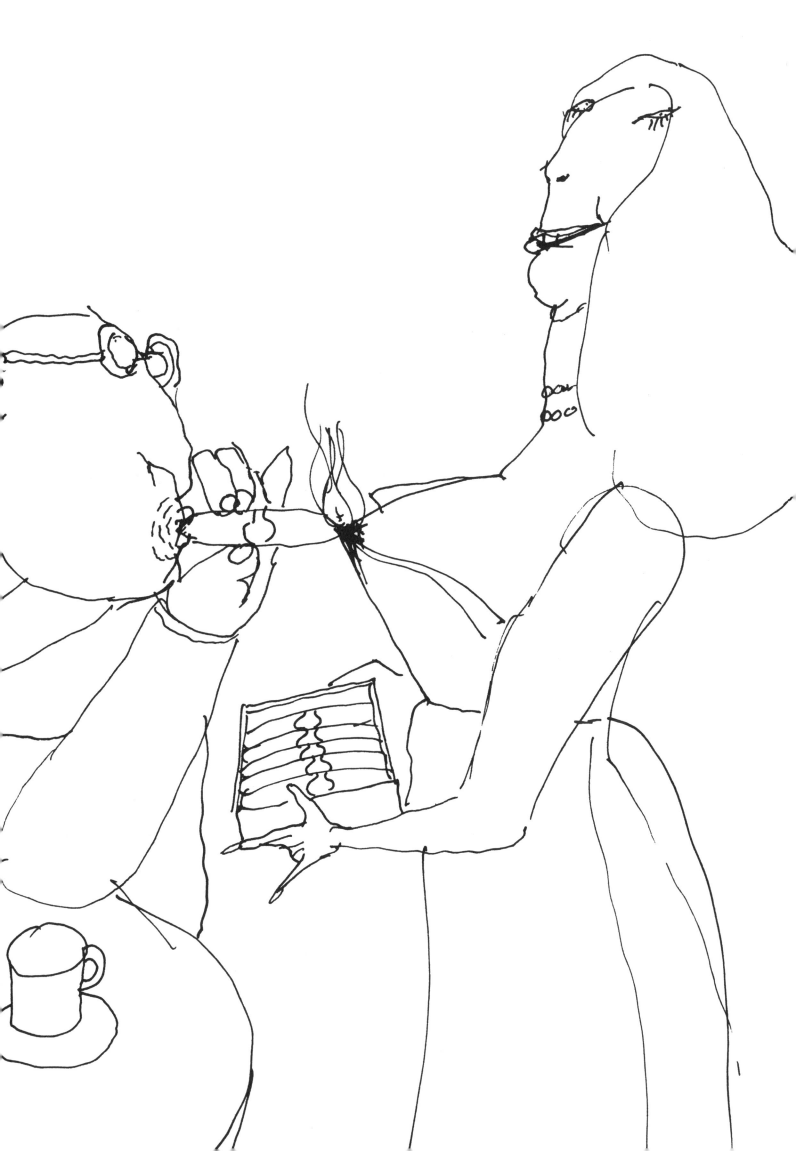

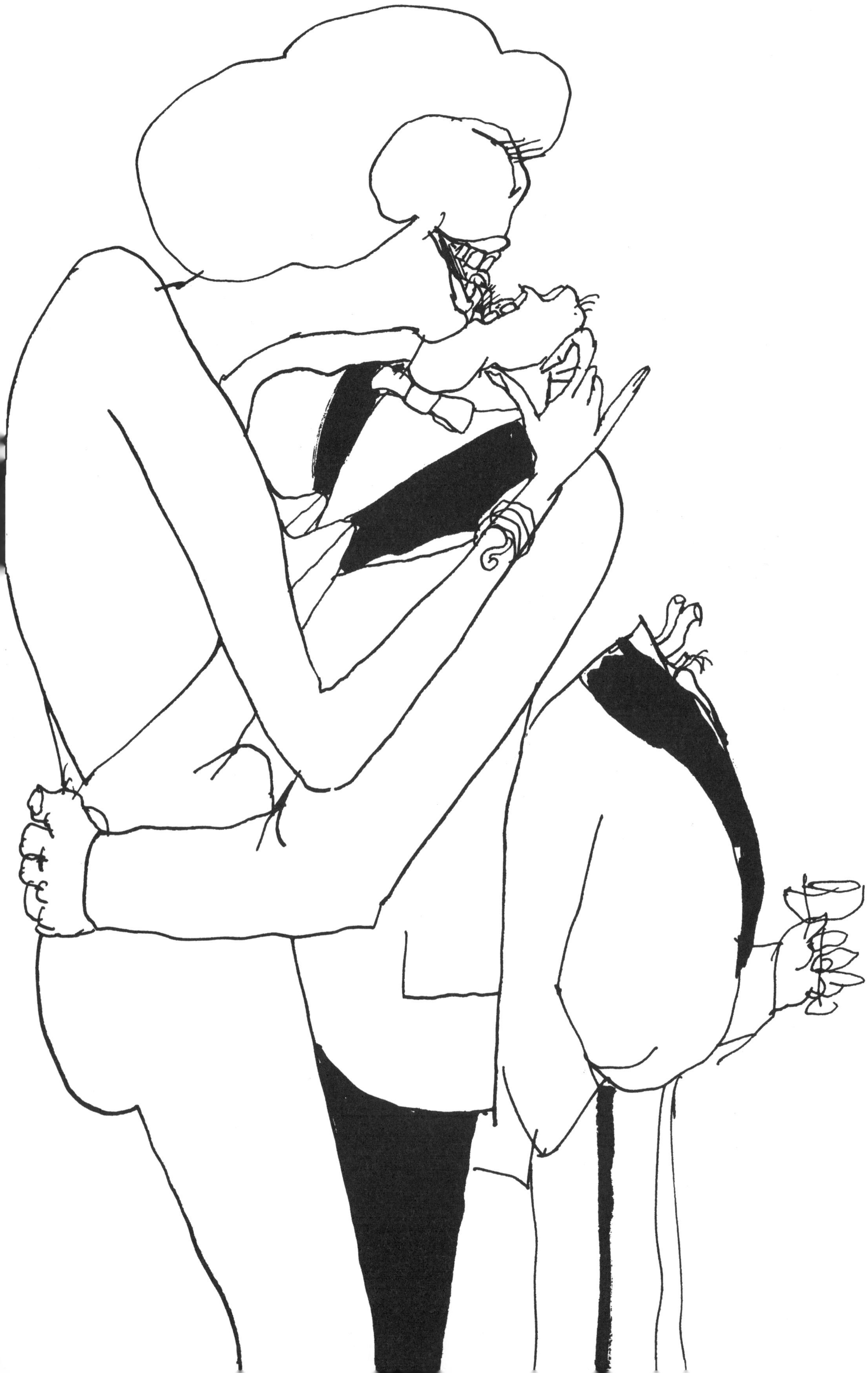

"Intimité".. in the library

Dynamic Daphné Clit. Lombart
the life of the party.—

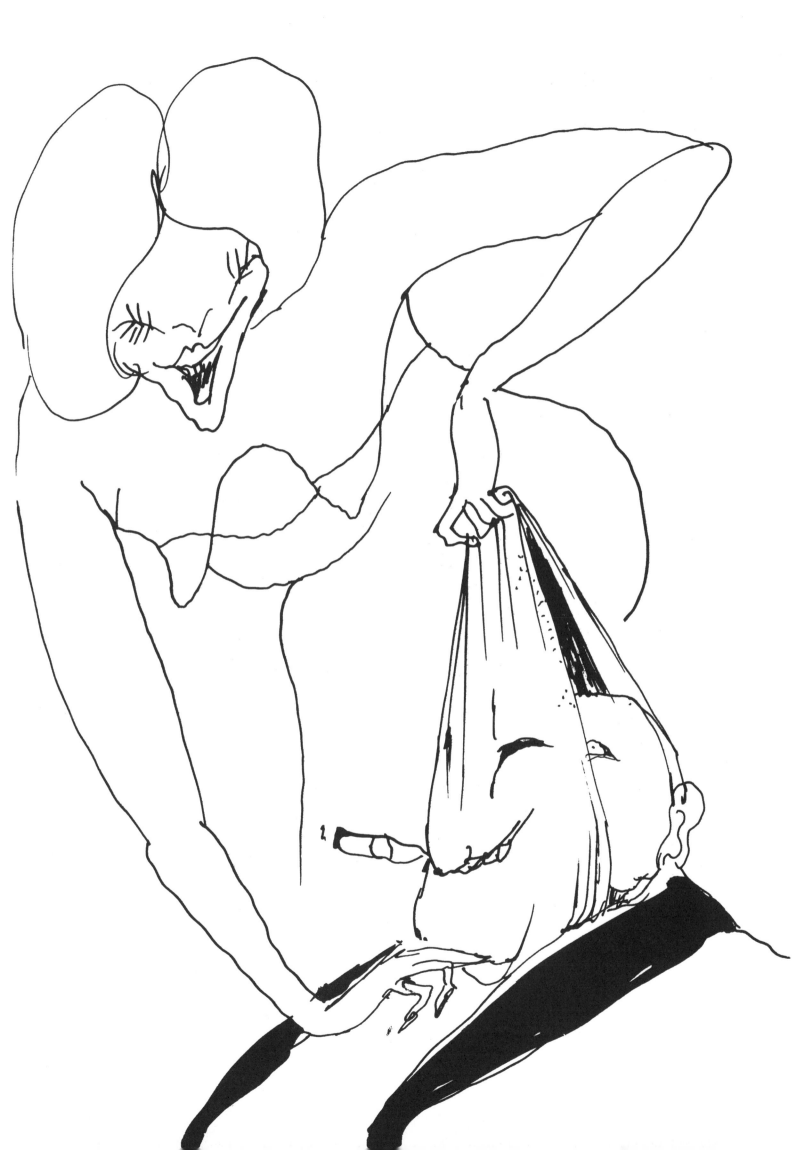

Count Grosso Modo Chilosa once ovipositor to his majesty Ferdinando IV.

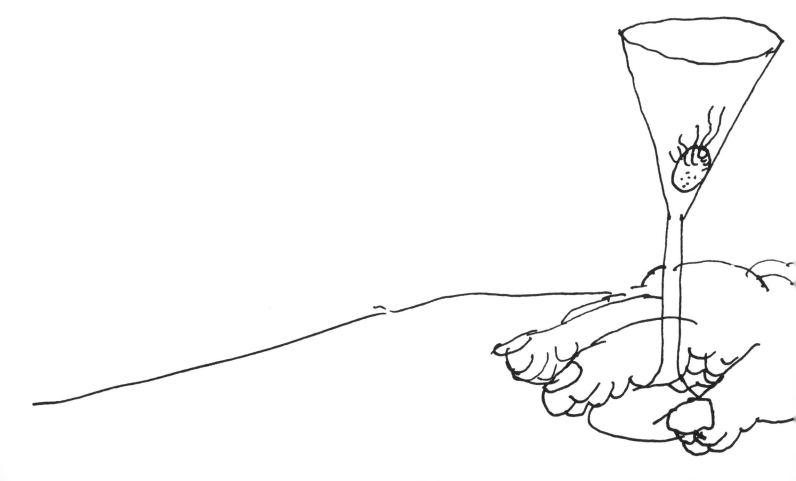

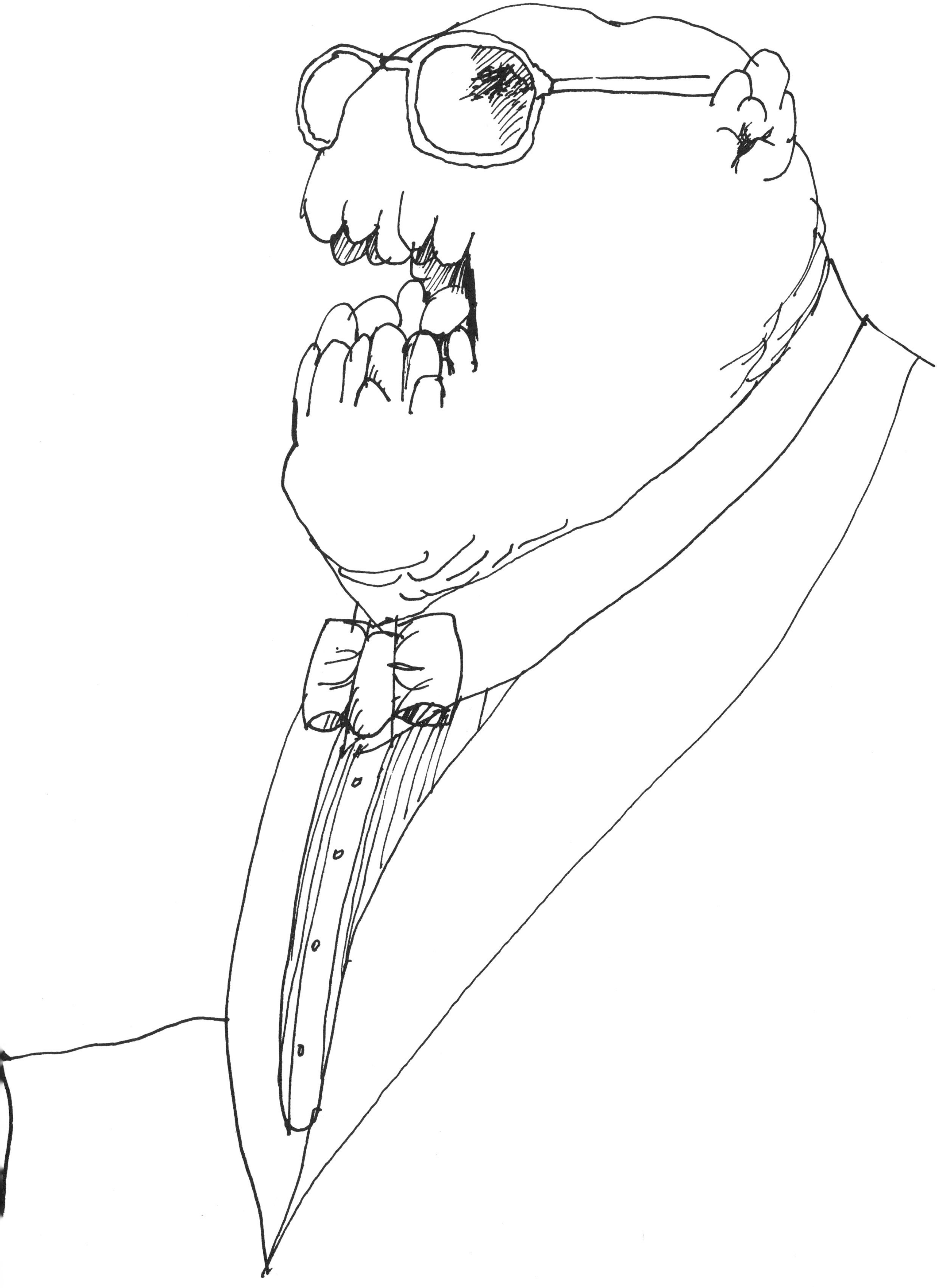

Everpopular Grace Fluke taking a rest

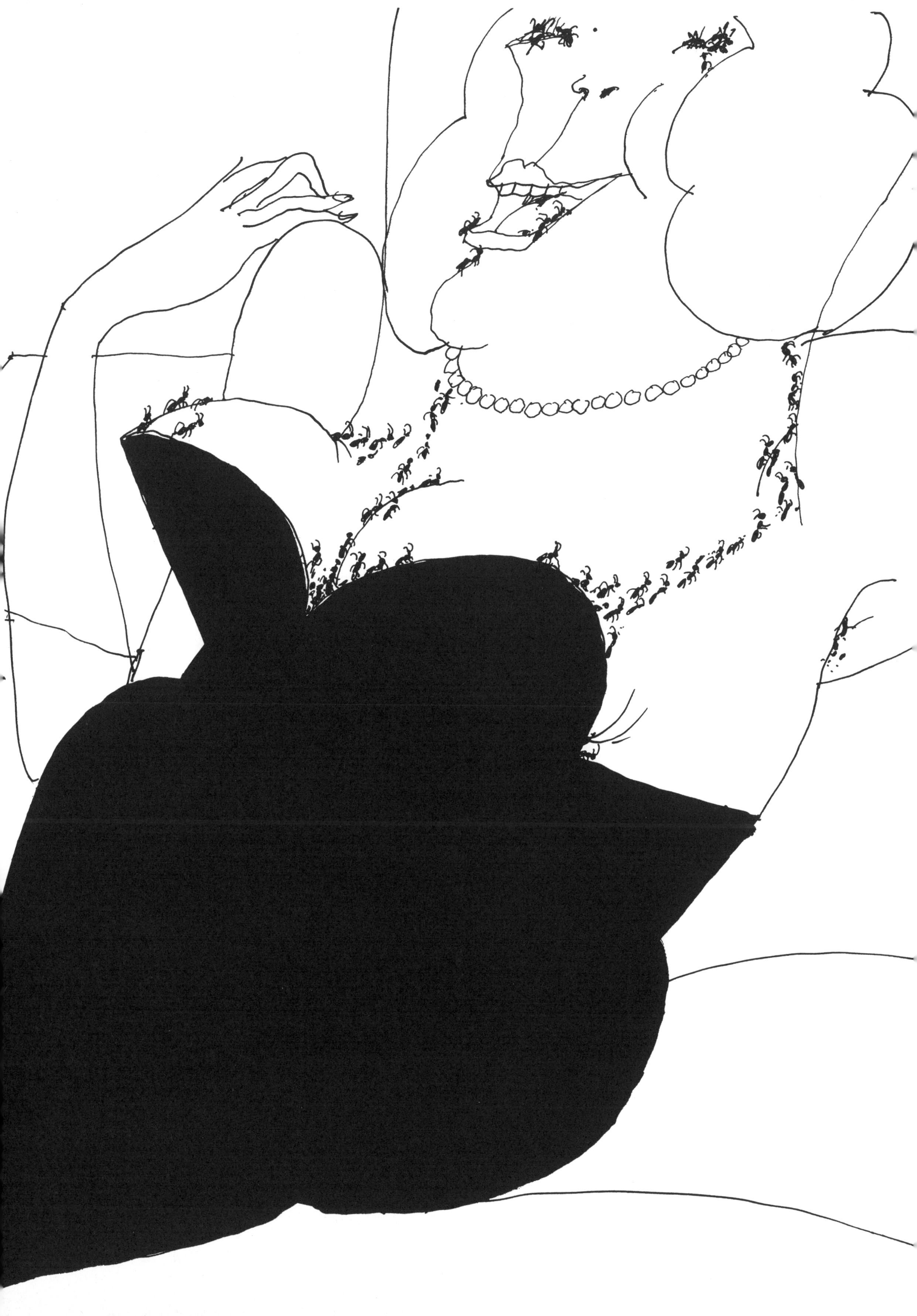

Mr. Floyd Colon and Mrs Dildo Canthus find themselves

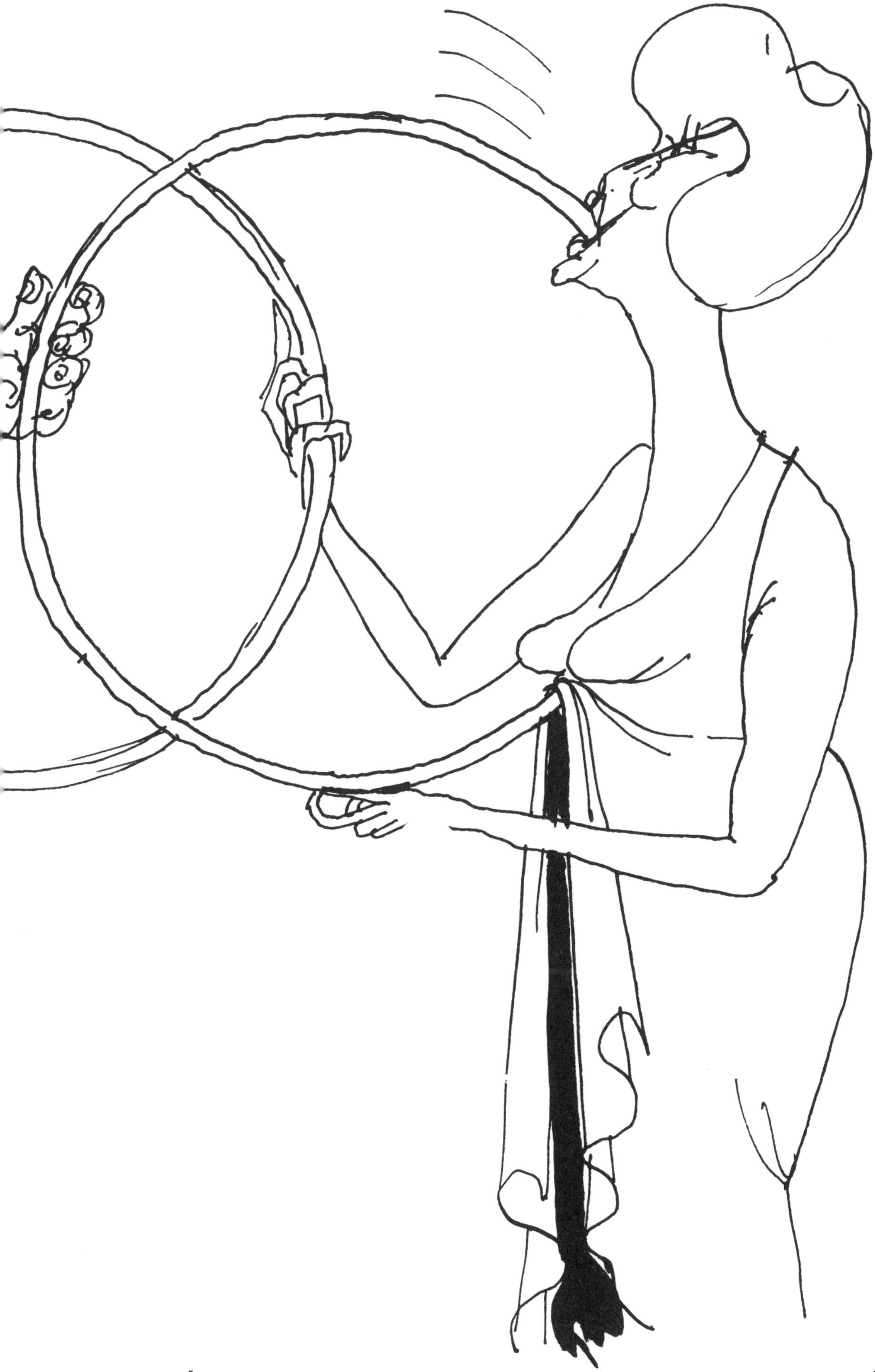

making the social circles from Palmbeach to the Hamptons

Rallying to one of the new fashionable party games are Mr & Mrs Brazen Saddle, Mr. Truman Tampon and Miss Nancy Tuckin his escort for the evening.

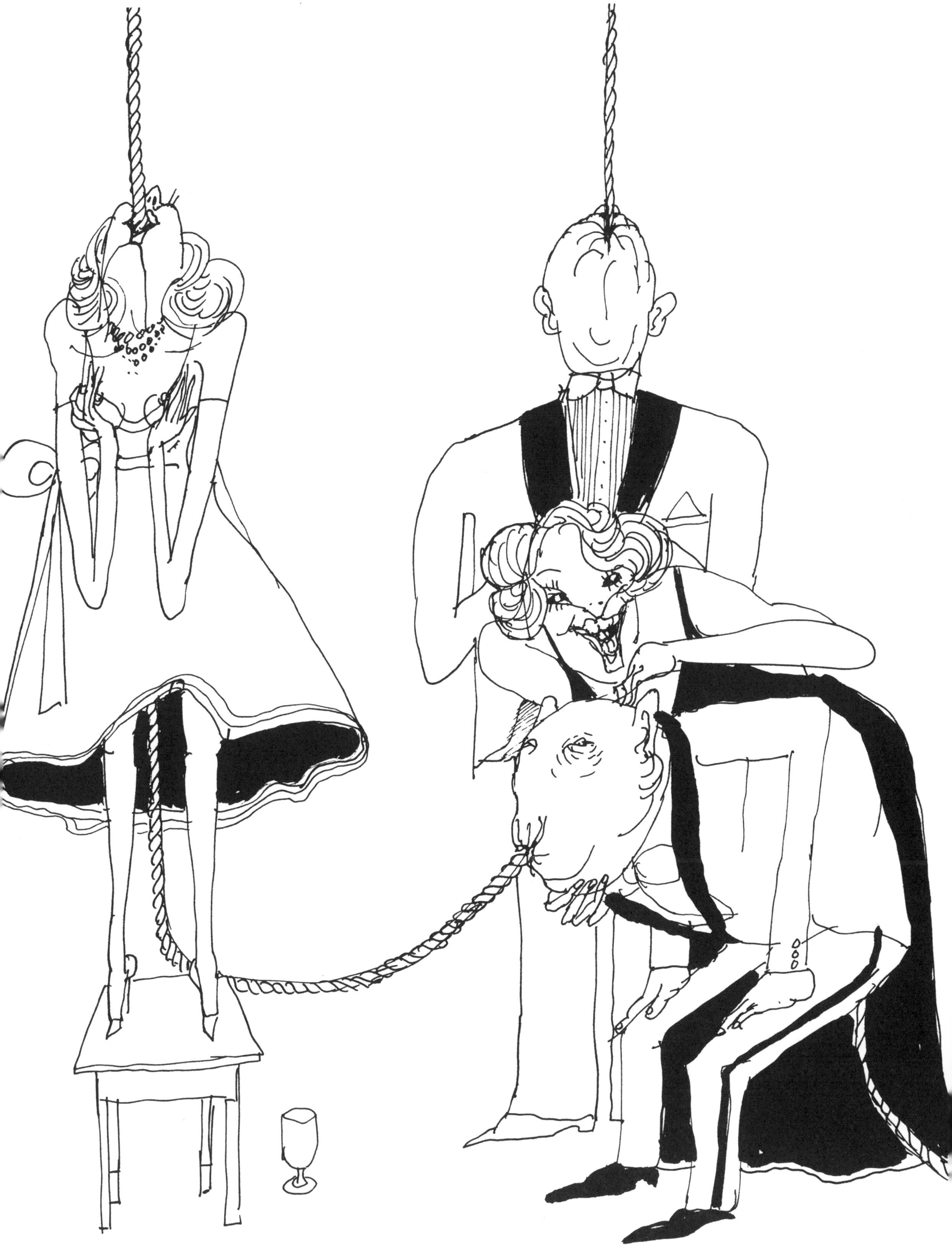

General Milton Mc Mollock accompanied by
his wife Mamie and his son in law
Kenyon Clamdrop — General Mc Mollock is.
remembered for his action in the battle of
the Bulge were he was critically wounded.

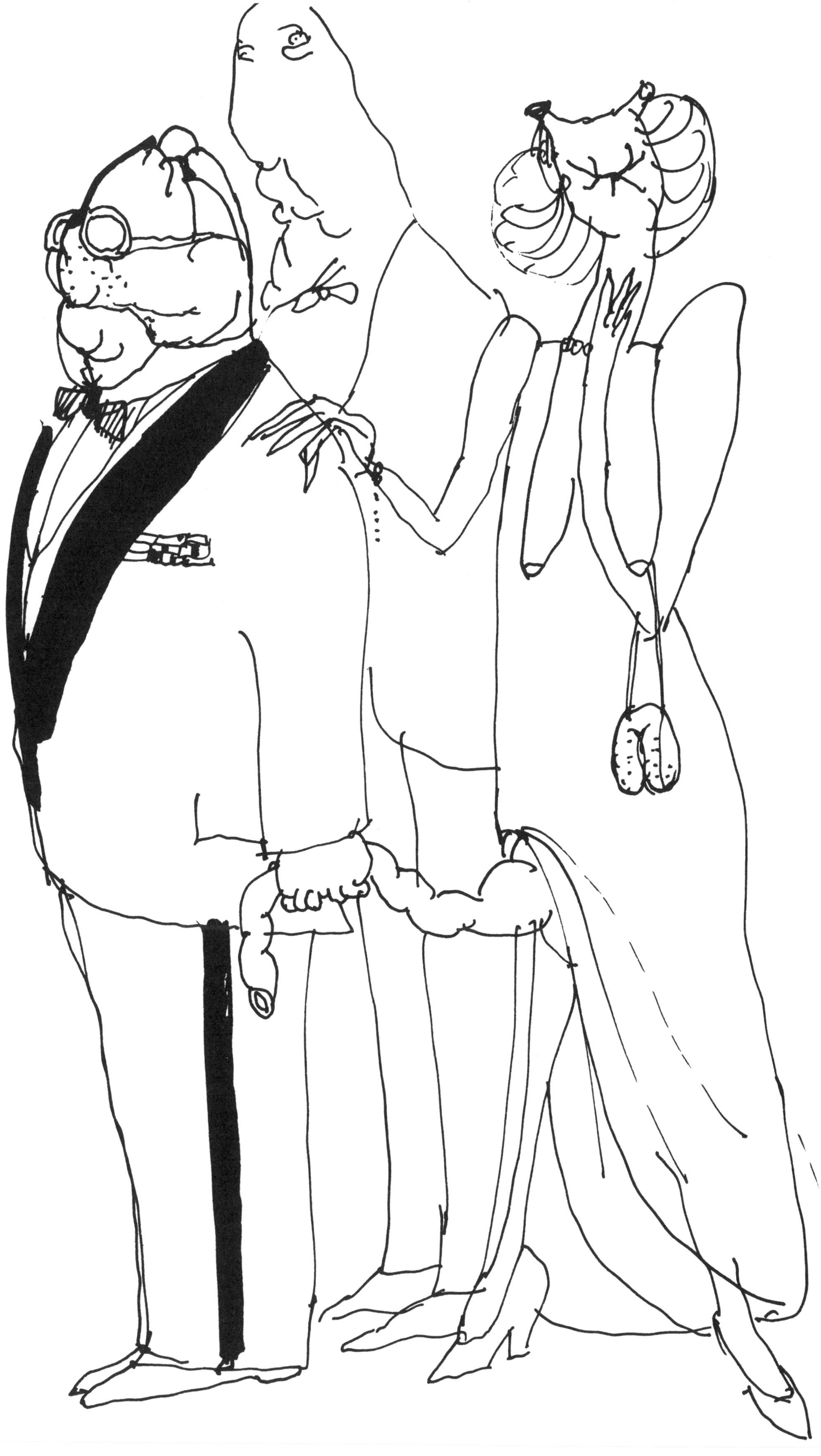

Mr. Melon Bladderhorn looking admiringly at Miss Amphora Upistart from Boston

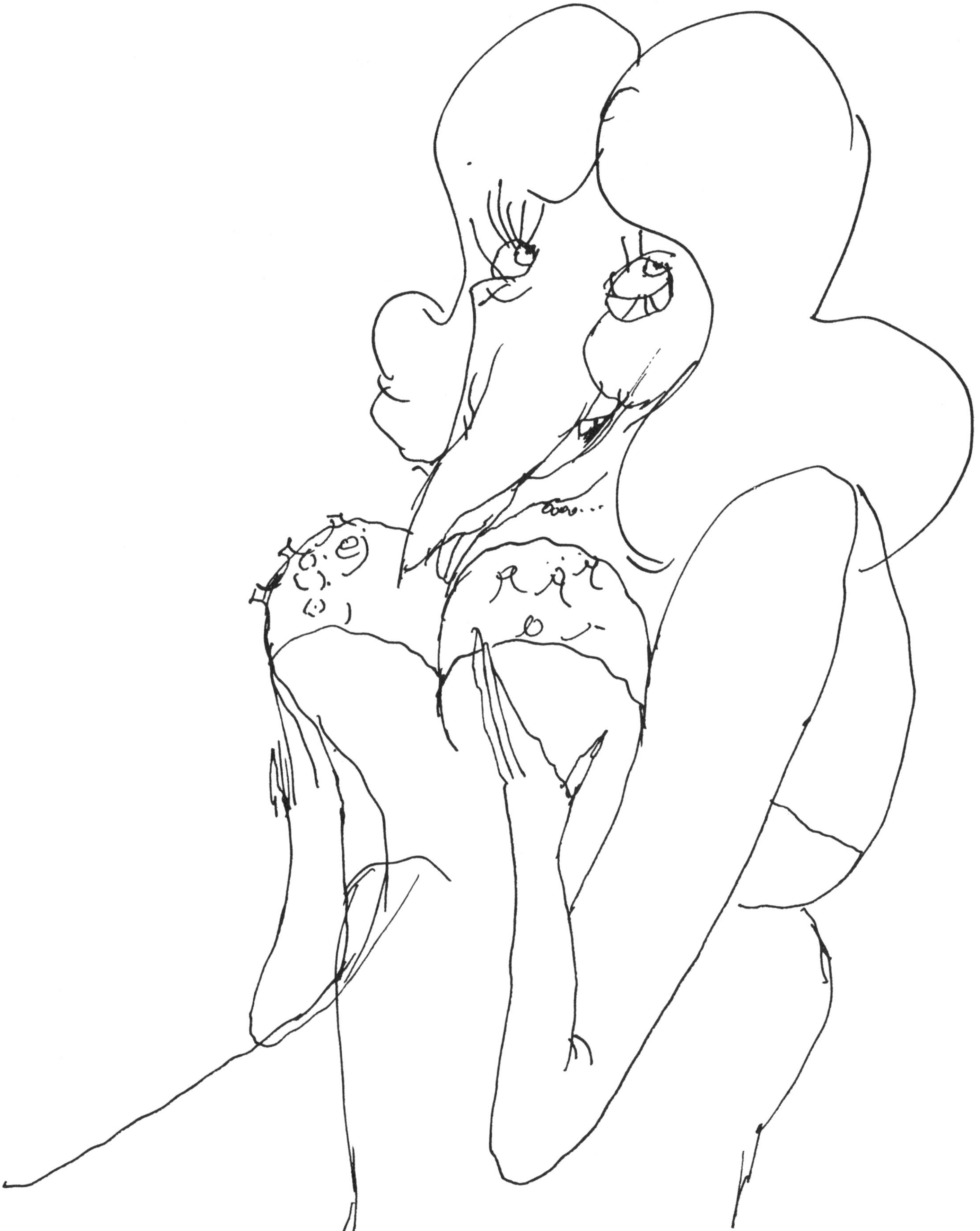

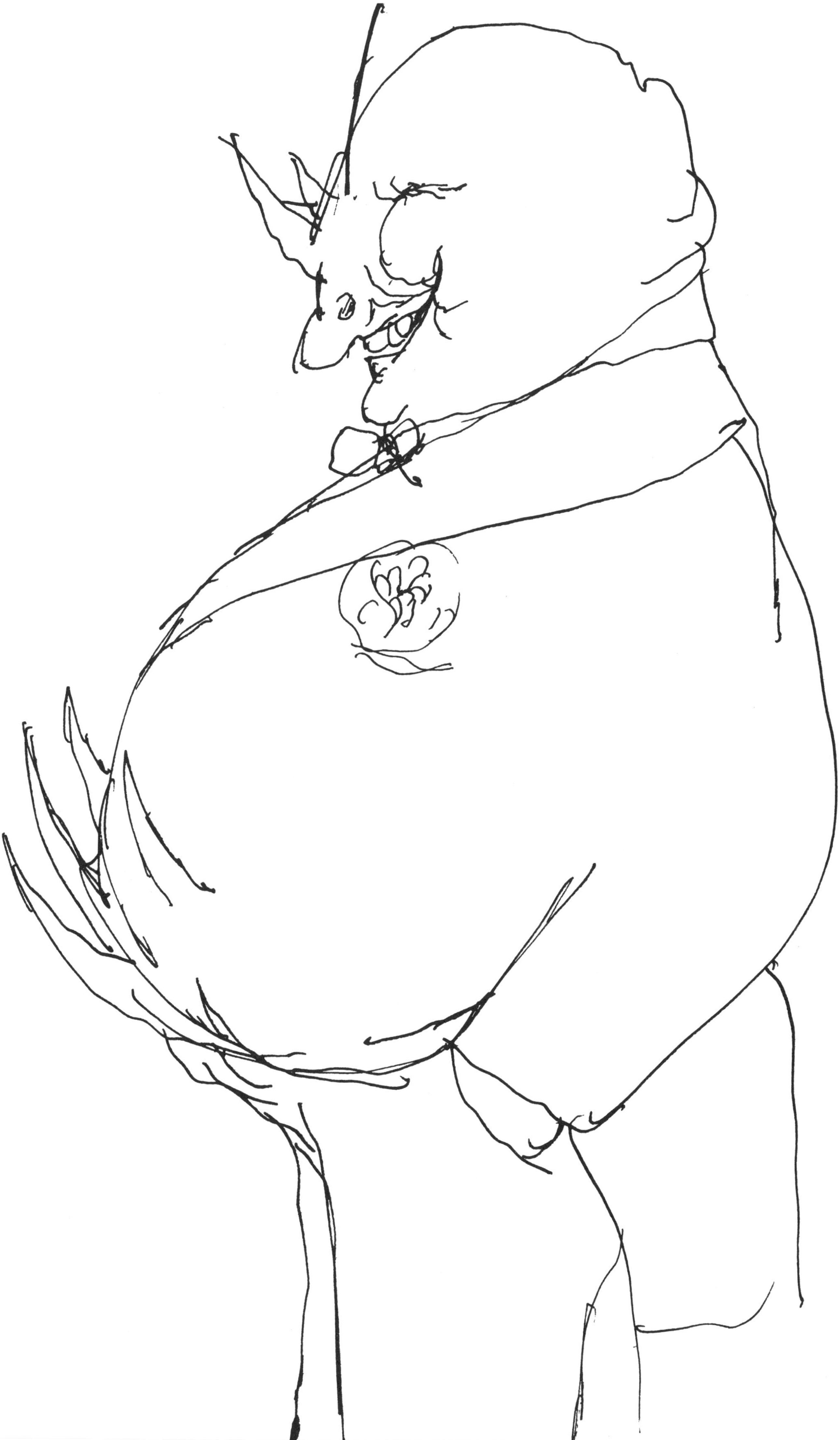

Retired Hollywood Star Pam Tax, all smiles and wit.

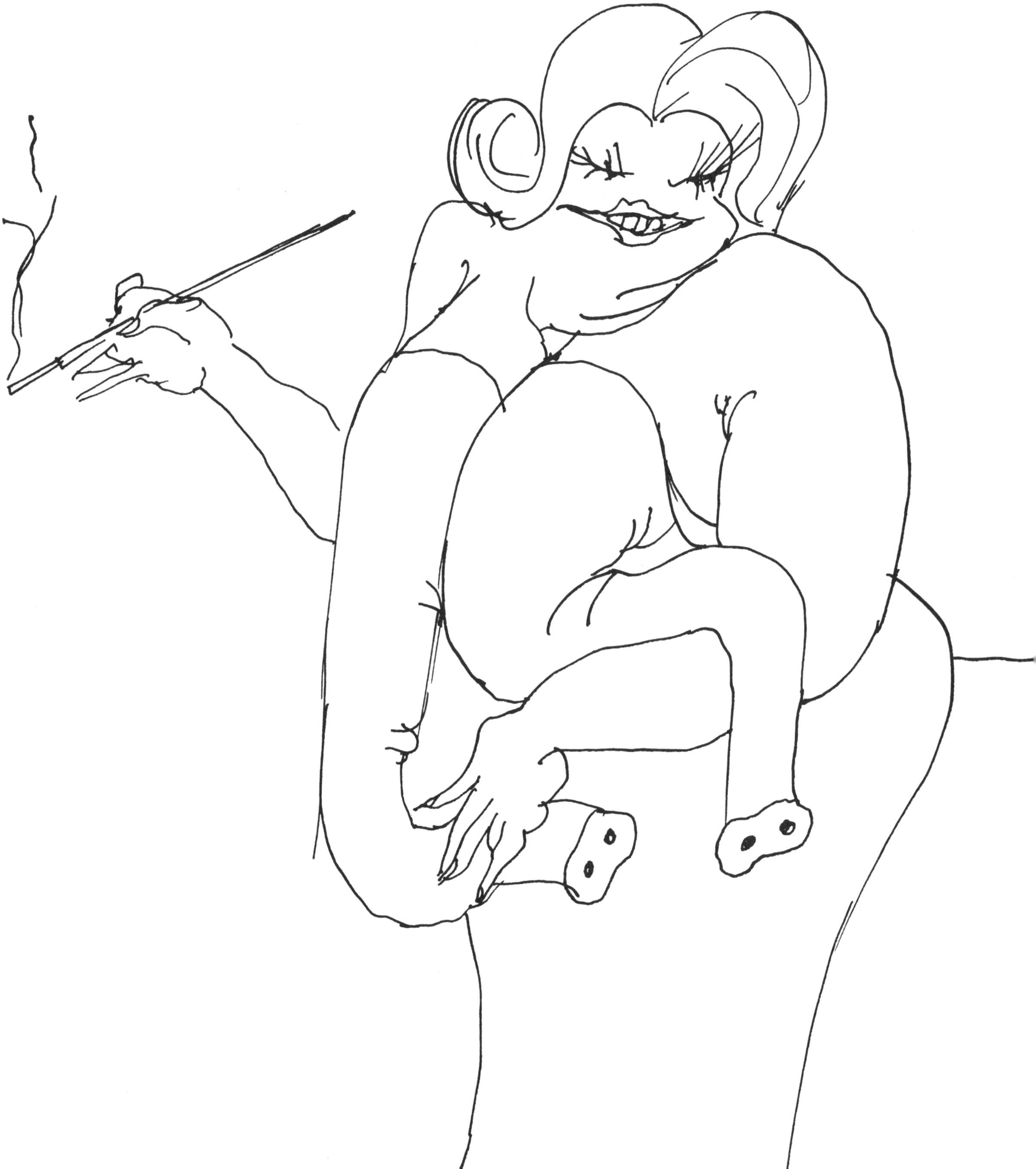

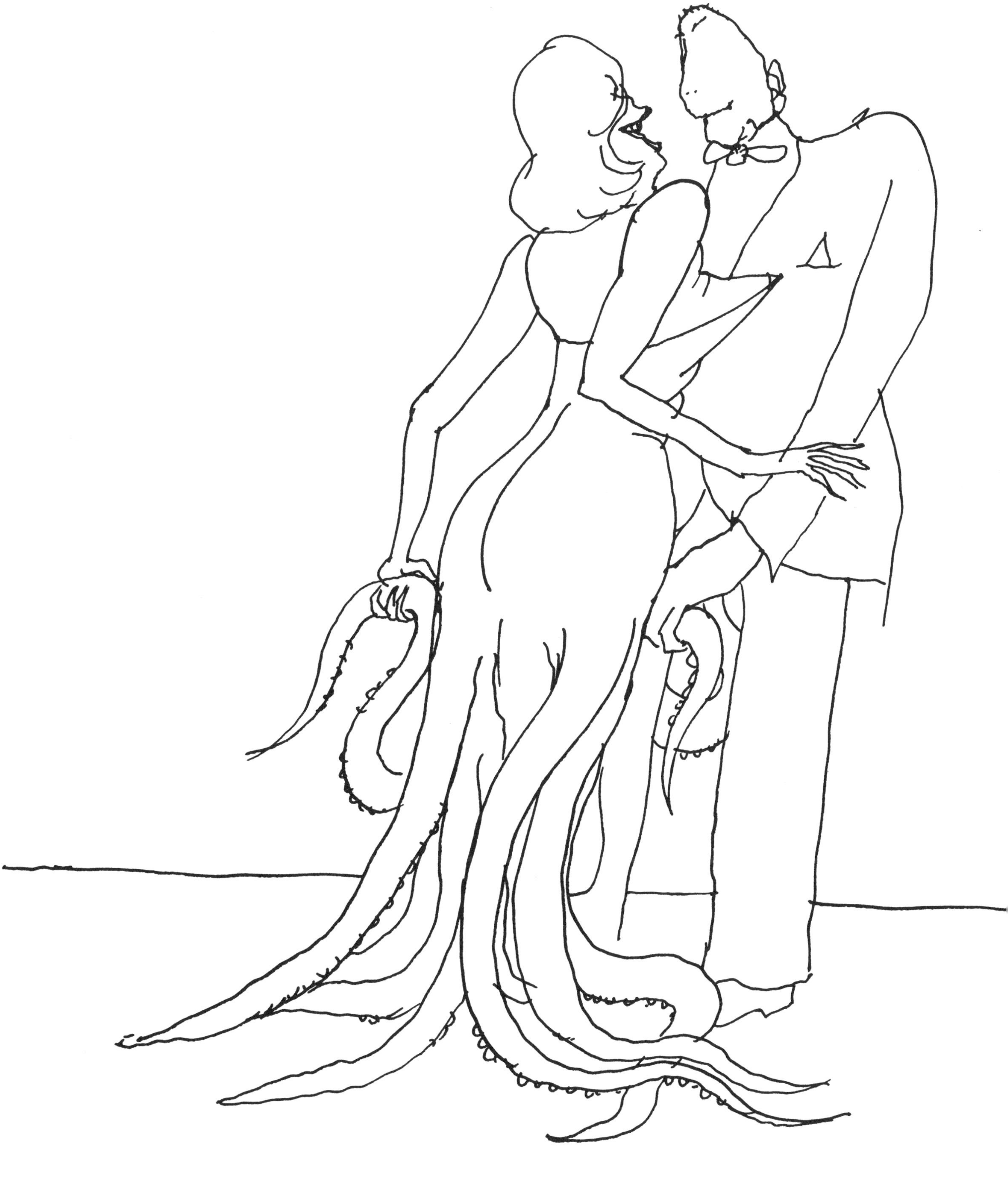

Mr. Mucus Plancton with Countess Zora de Lapissa-Laguli
whose mother was a Brothchild.

Mr. Rand Snout finding a lot in common with

Mr. Rand Snout finding a lot in common with

Mrs. Saliva Sowset whom he just met.

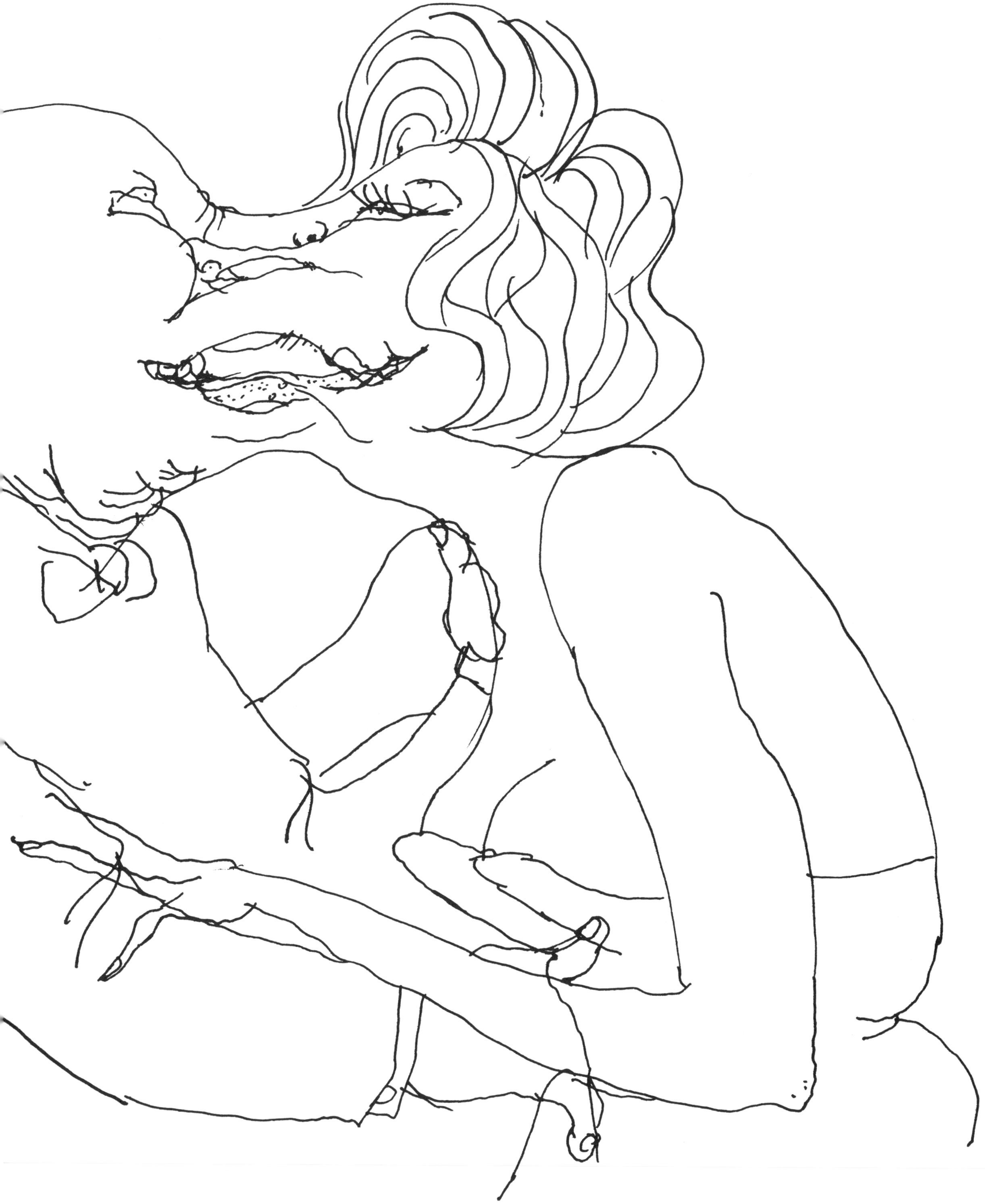

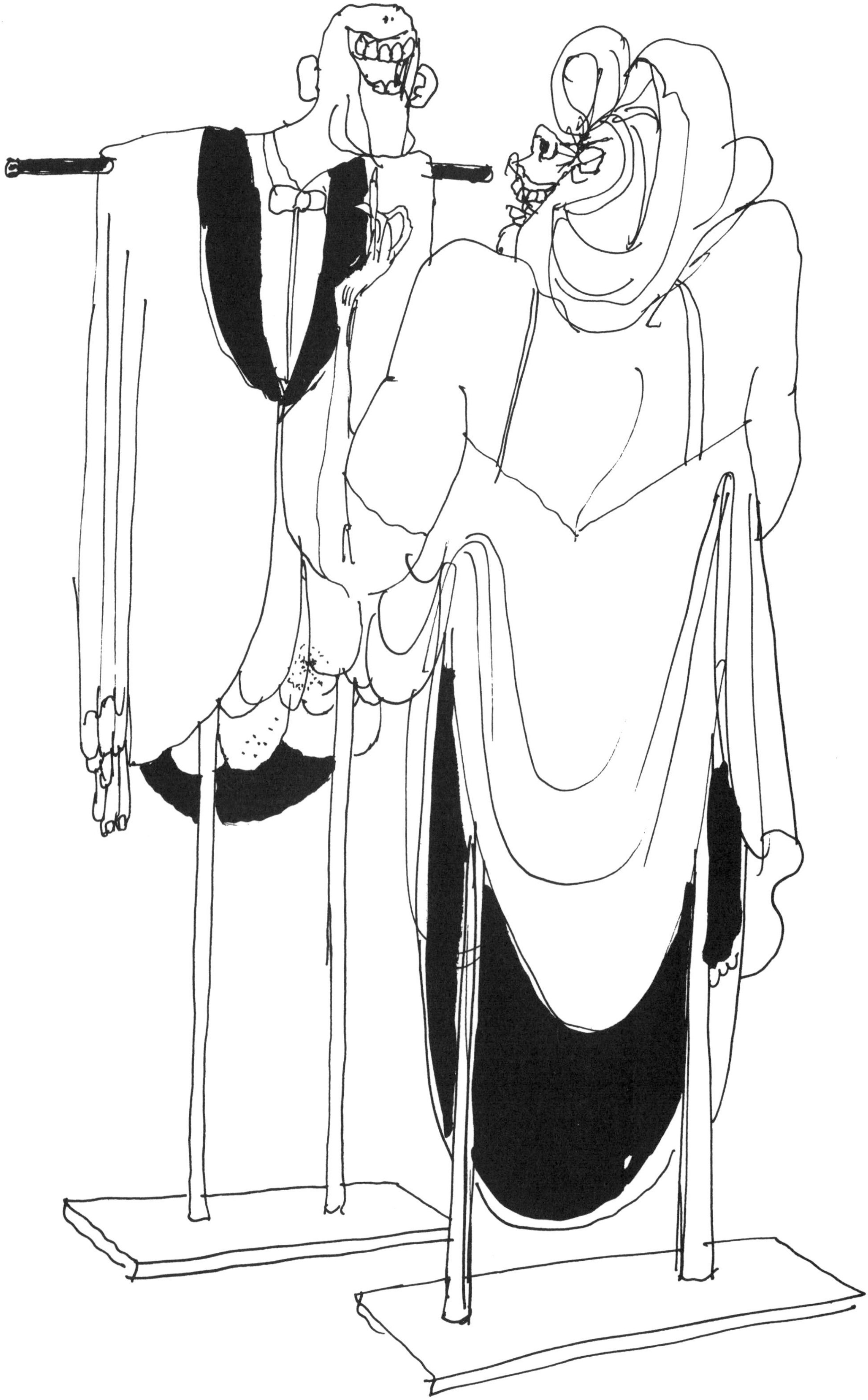

Back to the coat room as the evening draws to an end

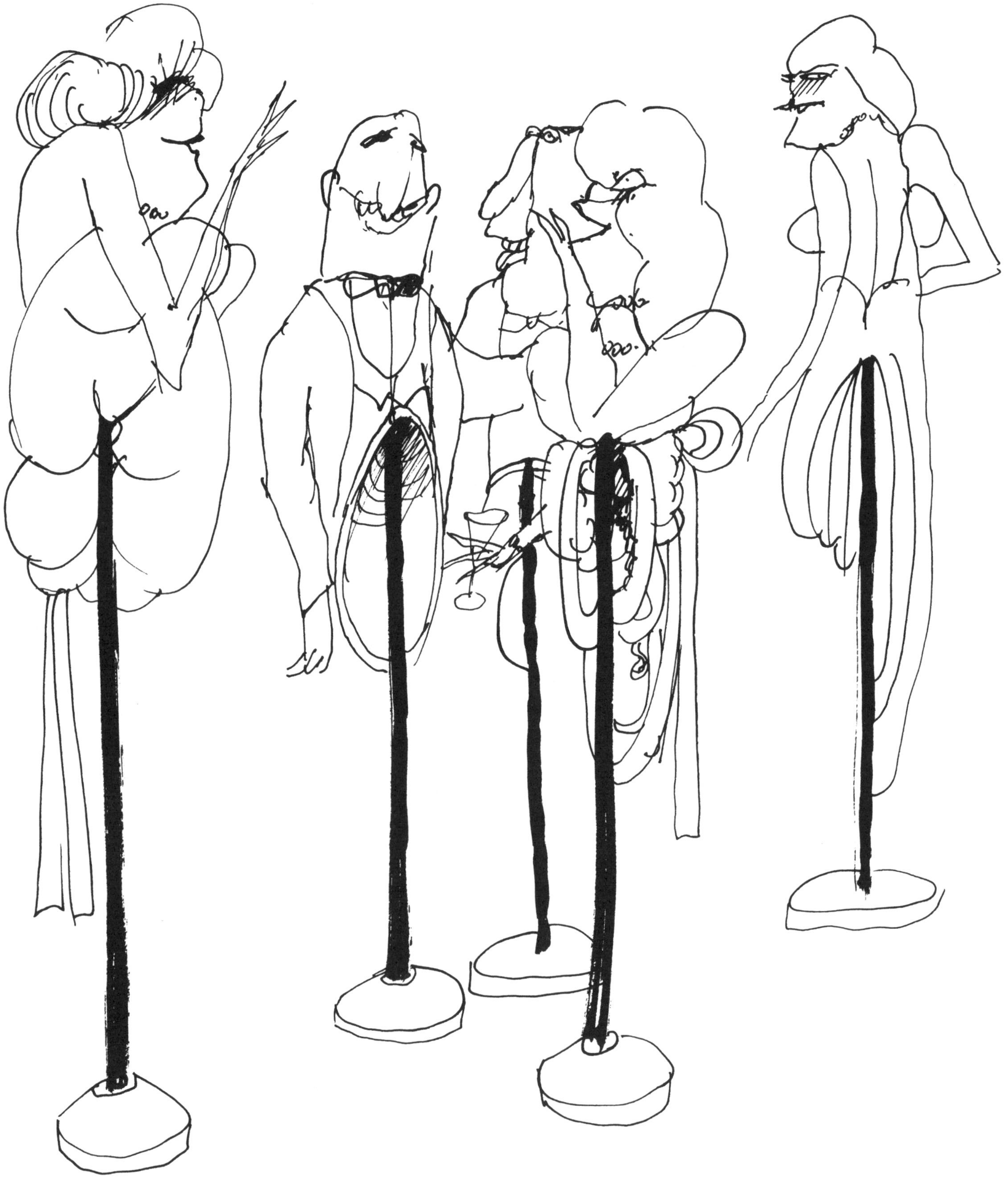

Pillars of society bidding each other adieu

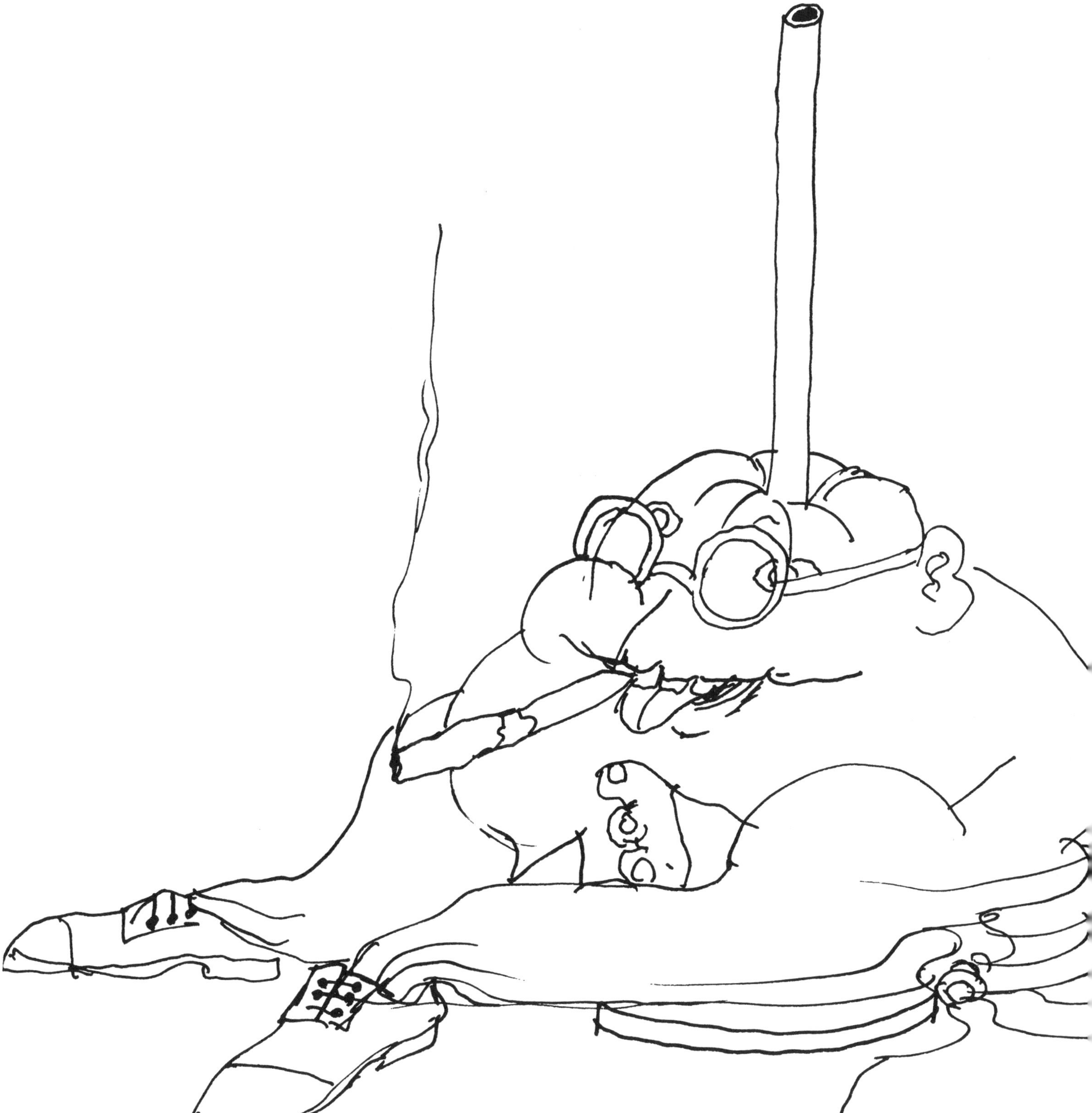

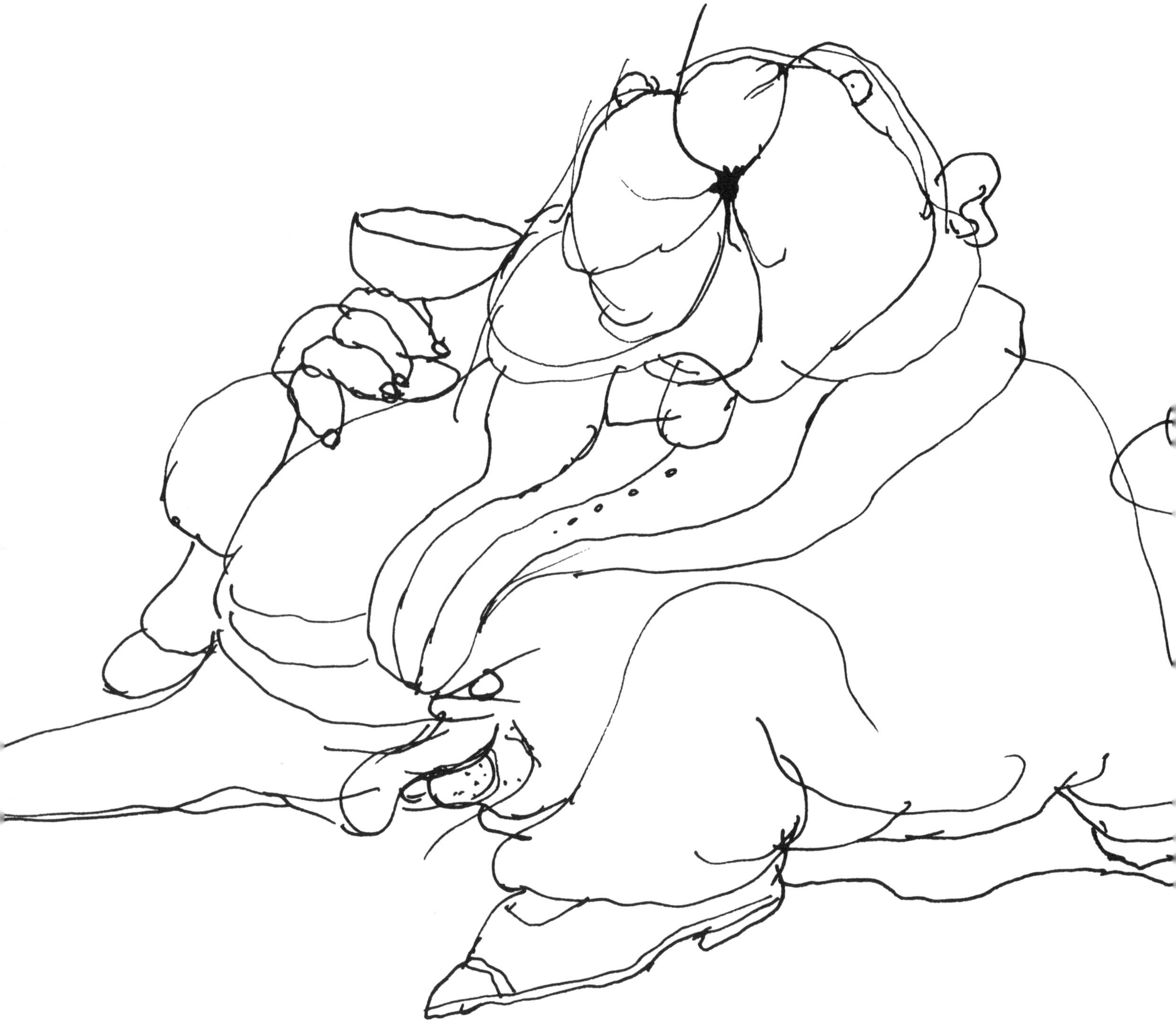

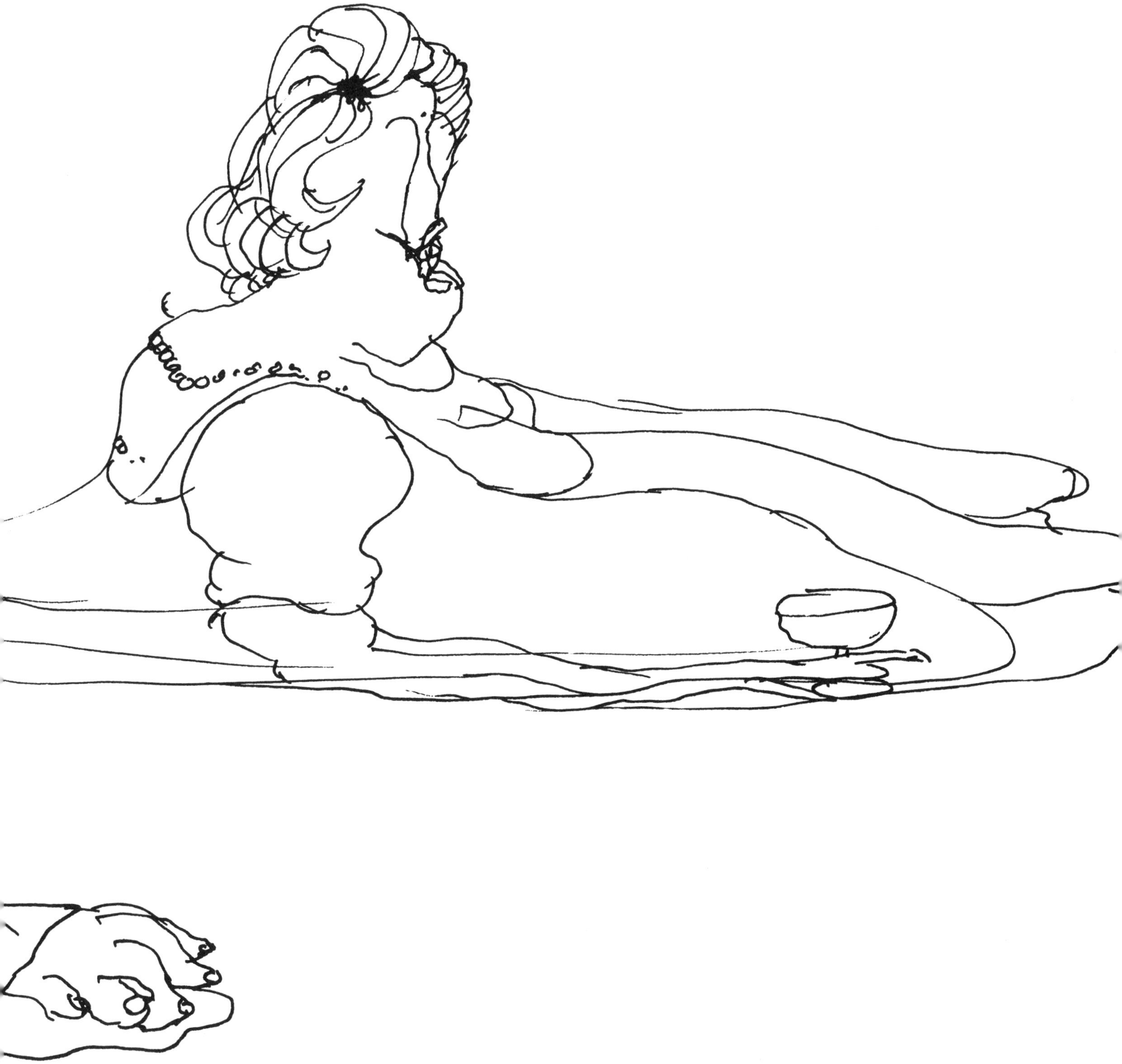

Mr. Harry Pocks and his sister Placenta Paps enjoying a last "coupe de champagne."

Mr. Jason Oystagum taking leave of Lady Myrtle Fluid -

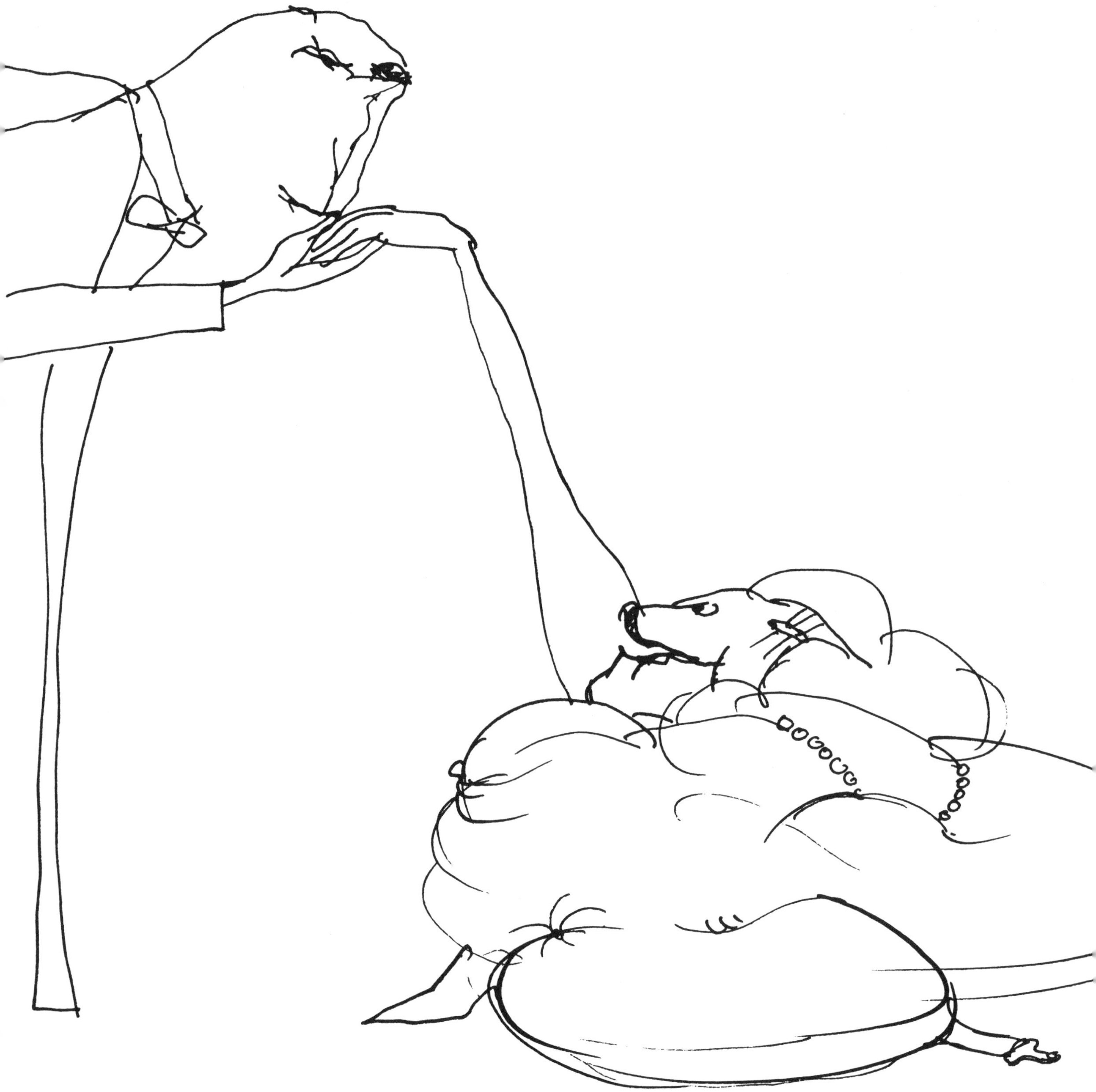

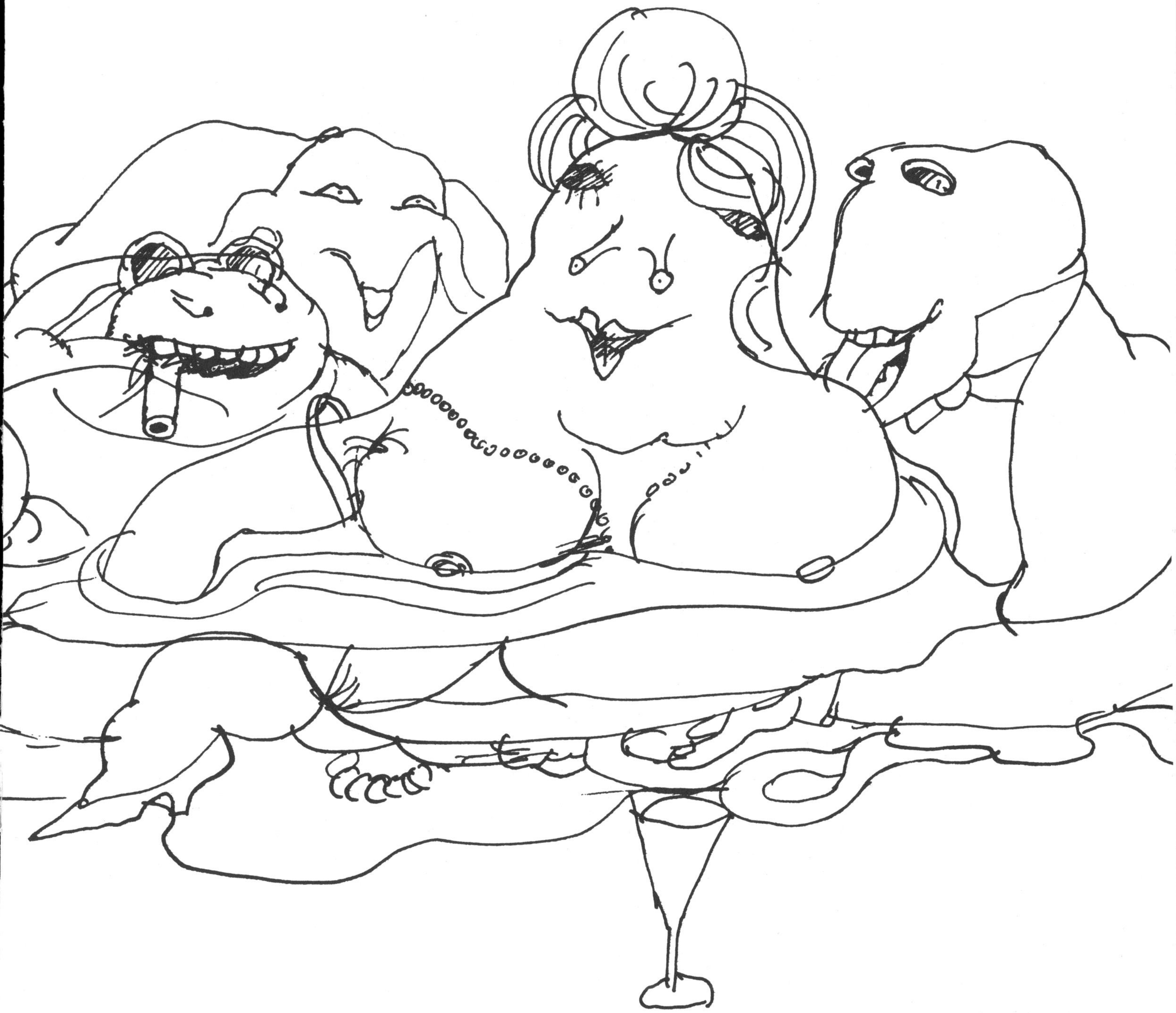

Warm Togetherness among the late stayers joining into a chorus of Broadway Melodies gave a final touch to the end of an unforgetable night.

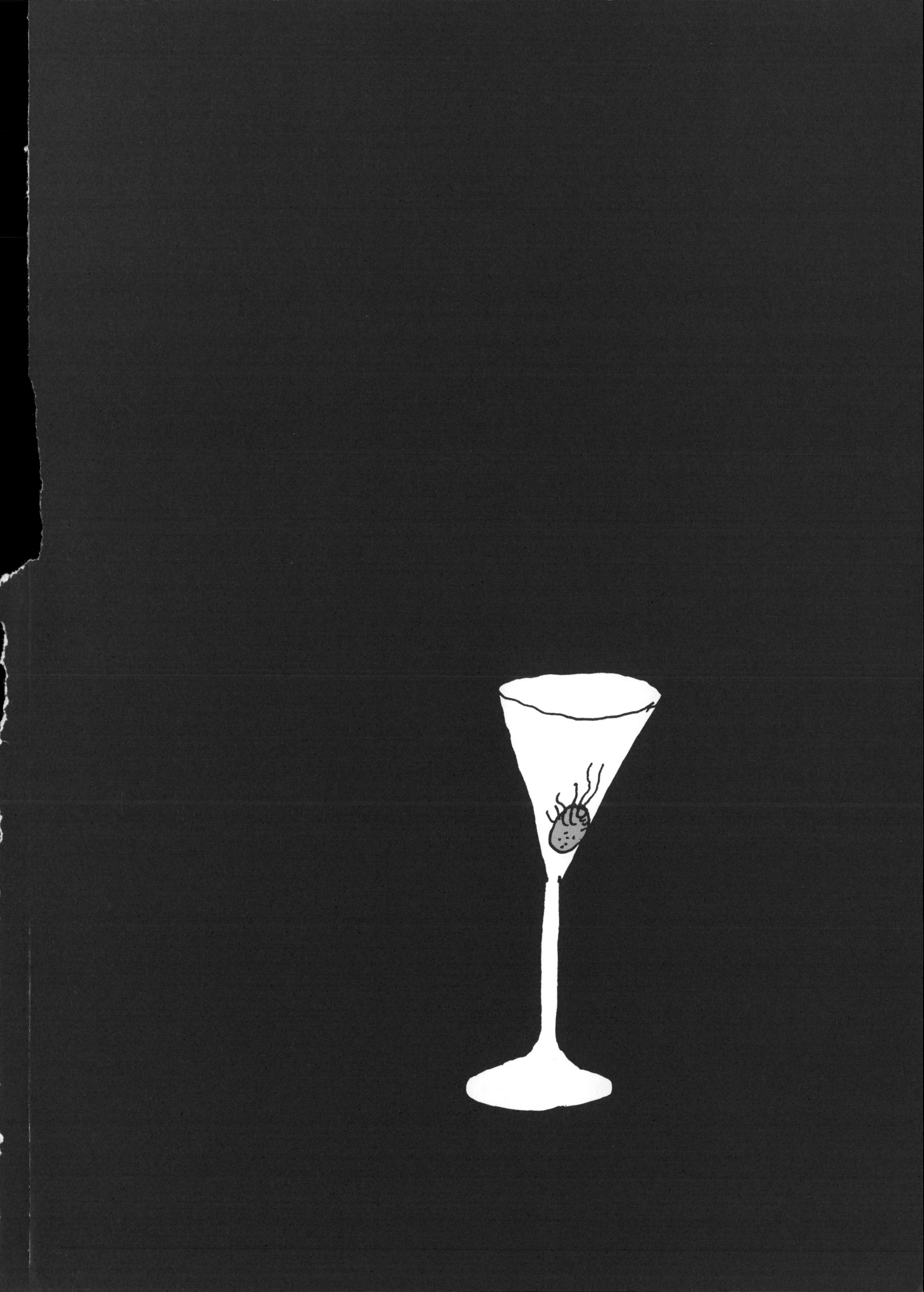

THE PARTY is the second volume in Fantagraphics' publishing program to reprint Tomi Ungerer's classic works and to introduce them to a new generation of readers. *The Underground Notebook* was published in 2020; future editions will include *Adam & Eve* and *Bablyon*.

TOMI UNGERER is an internationally renowned cartoonist of international repute: a best-selling children's book author, an illustrator, a collagist, a prose writer, a sculptor, an agent provocateur, a political dissident, and more. He was born in 1931 in Strasbourg, France. From 1941 to 1945, he lived under the Nazis, who took control of Alsace, and about which he wrote an autobiography, *Tomi: A Childhood Under the Nazis*. After a series of false starts — hitchhiking across Europe, working on cargo vessels, joining the French Camel Corps, briefly attending the *École des Arts Décoratifs* — he arrived in New York City in 1965 with 60 bucks in a pocket otherwise filled with dreams, which he fulfilled by becoming a hugely successful artist, illustrator, and writer. He wrote and drew a series of children's books, including *The Three Robbers*. He also published a series of books containing scathing, satirical, and id-fueled imagery, of which *The Underground Sketchbook*, in 1964, was the first. He was enormously prolific, going on to publish nearly 140 books, and receiving more awards than one can keep track of — including the Jacob Burckhardt Prize; *L'ordre national du Mérite*, France; *Commandeur de la Légion d'honneur*; and the Hans Christian Andersen Award. Ungerer died on February 8, 2019, at the age of 87.